MW00831405

She is his heart... he is her armor.

The open road and horsepower of a Harley is my
freedom. My escape. Looking forward, I forget the
past, forget my responsibilities, and lose myself to the
ecstasy.
It's a way of life. One I was born into and one I will die
a part of.
But with that freedom, comes a price.

PROLOGUE

NIX

"Keep pacing and you'll wear a hole in the floor."

Jake's heavy boots come to a stop. Pulling his black ball cap off, he scratches the back of his head.

"I'm losing my shit, Nix. What if I'm a terrible father? What if I fuck this kid's life up? My own father was a piece of shit. I want my son's life to be better than what I had."

Standing, I cross the few feet between us and place my hand on his shoulder, looking into his emotion-filled eyes.

"He will have a good life. He's not just your son, he's my nephew too. I'll have your back, always, brother. You're a better man than you give yourself credit for, and besides, I wouldn't let you fuck up his life. I'd beat sense into you first."

With a chuckle, his shoulders lose their tension, and I drop my hand.

"I wouldn't expect anything less. Goddamn, having a kid makes you crazy. When is a nurse going to come out? I can't take worrying like this much longer."

The man's mind is going a mile a minute, and I get it. Jake loves my sister with everything he has. She's everything to him, and now they're about to have a family. His level of protectiveness is about to skyrocket... who am I kidding? So, will mine.

Liz is my sister, but I'm the one who raised her. From the time our mother took off when we were kids to making sure Liz got into college, I was always there. I made an oath to my father to protect her and do right by her, and I've kept that promise. Now, I'll do the same for my nephew.

A pretty brunette nurse in pink scrubs enters the waiting room, and Jake's attention whips to her, his tone anxious.

"Is she all right? Is my son okay?"

"She's just fine. Your son is too. You can come and see them," she tells him with a genuine smile.

Following his steps, we enter the hospital room, and Jake goes to Liz's side. Eyes filled with love and wonder, he gazes at her first, then his newborn son. Arms crossed and leaning against the doorway, I watch my sister hand my nephew to his father. With a confident stance and solid arms, he gently takes him from her outstretched arms.

"Isn't he beautiful?" she asks, her voice revealing her fatigue.

Unable to pry his eyes away from the little man in the blue blanket, Jake's voice goes soft. "He's perfect, Peach. Our son is perfect."

CHAPTER ONE

NIX

FOUR WEEKS AGO, I became an uncle to a tiny version of Jake Castle, and I couldn't love him any more than I do. Tonight, is Liam's grand entrance into the Kings, and I've warned all my brothers to be careful. Jake was already protective of his woman—add in his son, and you have a wolf ready to tear into anything that threatens his pack. That is exactly why I haven't told him Tolito's cousin, Reed, has been released from jail, along with a few other members of the Wild Royals. He's got enough on his plate right now. He deserves this night to enjoy with his family. Club Business can wait... at least for one night.

The front door of the Kings' clubhouse swings open, and Liz enters, carrying Liam bundled in her arms. All eyes go to them, then Jake entering behind her. It's a very different look, seeing him carrying an infant car seat versus the cocky playboy smirk he wore two years ago. It took the right woman to settle him down, and although at times it was tough for her, my sister was that woman.

Setting the infant car seat down on a nearby table, Jake accepts the pats on the back and watches carefully as others approach Liz and Liam. Wearing an orange and black onesie, Liam's shirt reads, *My Daddy Rides A Harley*. The awws from the women are in vocal unison.

Nodding my head to Jeff, my longtime bartender, I point to the liquor bottles and shout, "Get a round of shots for everyone. Tonight, we celebrate!"

Liz is corralled to a table where the club member's girlfriends have gifts for her. Liam is taken in the arms of Jenna, my woman and Liz's best friend. Crooning in his ear, she holds him snuggled against her, whispering private words to him. Seeing this brings the frequent thoughts I've had lately to the surface. After two years together, it's time to put a ring on it and make her mine.

Drinks are passed around, and the celebration of Liam goes into full swing. Presents are opened, and Liz creates a pile of Harley Davidson themed clothes, toys, and baby supplies. Lifting a pool cue, I tap Jake on the shoulder, drawing his attention away from Liz.

"We're in the clubhouse. Nothing to worry about here. You can take it easy tonight."

Lifting a beer to his lips, Jake laughs. "It's not that. I can't stop watching them. I'm afraid if I do, I'll wake up from a dream, and it'll all be gone. They're my everything. I didn't think it was possible to love two people so much, the thought of losing them can keep me up at night. I'll sit outside his crib and watch him for hours, amazed at what Peach and I created." Setting his beer bottle on the nearest table, he reaches for a pool cue. "Fuck, they've turned me into a pansy. Listen to me."

"Who are you kidding?" With my lip curled into a humored smile, I laugh. "Liz turned you into a lovesick pansy long before Liam came."

"Fuck you. Make a bet, so I can win all your money."

Tossing a few twenties on the table, I top them with my beer.

"Let's make it double tonight. I'm feeling lucky."

Pool is a pastime Jake and I enjoy. We're equally good, making for challenging games and no guarantee of who will take home the cash at the end of the night. The thought of intentionally letting him win, so he and Liz can enjoy the extra cash crosses my mind, but fades just as quickly. Honest games are something the whole club takes pride in. We push each other to be better at everything—better men, better riders, better brothers, better spouses—you name it. A lot has changed for the Kings. We're closer than ever. The past has taught us, breaks in the chains that hold us together weaken our strength as a club. We've learned from our mistakes, and we're a stronger club because of it.

On Jake's break, the balls scatter across the felt, and he makes a legal break, sinking four balls into the pockets. He takes solids and moves around the table for his next shot.

"I heard Reed is out of the slammer."

Damn it.

"How'd you find out?"

"Trevor."

If only he'd kept that news to himself longer.

"Think we need to be worried?" Jake asks, ticking his jaw when he misses his shot.

Moving around the table, I calculate the angles for the striped balls.

"I wish I knew the answer to that. Either way, we need to be prepared. Reed and Tolito were close, and I hear he's the new Pres for the Royals. There's a chance he or his crew will want blood."

Tipping back a beer, Jake takes a long swallow. "A year and a half of peace and now we have to watch our backs because of these fucks again. They're a never-ending menace."

"What do you think about us offering a truce? I don't know Reed. He was always in the background. Maybe he isn't like Tolito."

"You're too good of a man, Nix. Even if Reed isn't as evil as Tolito was, he's still going to be a Royal. You know what they have to do to earn a patch."

"Fuck, I know. I can't help wanting to get ahead of this, though. The rivalry needs to end." I look over at Liz and Liam, watching my sister kiss my nephew's forehead. "For all of us."

∼

WITH MY HAND wound through Jenna's soft red curls, I pull her head back and thrust harder into her slick opening. With my cock buried deep, I cum inside my girl, my muscles going lax as my body gets its needed release.

Slapping her ass, I free her hair and pull out. Her body's still shuddering through the end of her orgasm. I kiss her shoulder, giving her affection for the pleasure she's given me. Dropping onto my back, she wiggles her body closer, lying over my chest. Twisting a ringlet of her hair around my finger, I show her more affection, bringing her pink lips to mine.

"I've been thinking."

"Uh oh."

"About us."

"Oh?" Perching her chin on her raised hand, brown eyes focus on me with interest. "What about us?"

"Seeing you hold Liam tonight had me thinking about our future. It had me thinking about diamond ring shopping."

"Really?"

I hope the higher pitch of her voice is indicative of her feeling the same way I do.

"Would you want that?"

Nerves jumble in my gut as I watch her eyes.

"Yes, I would. I love you, and there isn't anyone else I'd choose to be with. It's absolutely what I want."

9

Leaning forward, she claims my mouth, our kiss filled with heady emotion. Limbs tangling, my cock hardens. Taking her in my arms, I put her on top of me. Bending her knees, she straddles me, sliding my thick cock into her pussy.

Running my hands along her sides, I hold her steady as I look into her warm eyes.

"I want to make you happy. As happy as you've made me."

"You already do," she replies, moving her hips.

FEELING the warmth of Jenna's body tucked into mine as I rouse from sleep is the perfect way to wake up. Slipping my hand between her legs, I circle my fingers around her clit until they're covered in her desire for me.

"Will you suck me off? I'm craving your mouth around my cock." Teasing my lips across her ear, I suck her lobe into my mouth as I thrust my fingers inside her.

"Mm-hmm," she moans. "But it'll cost you a good tongue fucking."

A needy growl slips through my teeth. "You know I love it when you talk like that." Thrusting forward, I press into her ass. "It gets me hard."

The rumble of Harleys in the distance stops the motion of my fingers on her clit.

"Damn it. They're earlier than I expected."

A throaty whine escapes her as she rolls onto her back.

"Let someone else open the shop."

Stepping off the bed, I adjust my fading erection in my briefs and scour the bedroom for a pair of jeans.

"Can't, babe. William needs some repairs to his transmission. I told him I'd give him a hand. We'll finish what we started later."

"You better." With a wink, she turns and wiggles her ass in the air.

With a pair of jeans in hand, I come back to the bed and slap her ass.

"Quit teasing me. It's hard enough walking away from you."

Sliding a leg into my jeans, I kiss her as she leans over my shoulders.

"At least let me make you something quick to eat. I know how you get sucked into work and forget about eating."

"All right."

The scent of bacon and eggs drifts into the bathroom while I'm getting ready. Hunger pains draw me to the dining room, where Jenna has two plates of food served and ready.

"Thanks, babe. I appreciate it."

Kissing her on the head, I join her at the table. A couple of bites in, I set down my fork when I hear

Harley engines cut off in my driveway. Jenna rises from the table.

"I'll get some more food cooked."

Heavy steps stomp across my porch, unfamiliar voices snapping my attention to the door.

"Jenna, get down!"

Bullets tear through the wooden door. Diving for her, pain rips through my lower abdomen. The bullet grazes my side, but I can't worry about that now. With Jenna beneath me, I reach for the gun stashed under the sink. The front door bursts open, and I don't waste time getting acquainted with the intruders. With the pull of the trigger, I unleash several bullets at our attackers. Wild Royal patches come into my view as they run from the shots.

Dropping the gun, I check to see if Jenna is all right. Blood is soaked on my shirt and hers. With trembling hands, she's holding her stomach.

"Jenna, baby, hold on."

"Nix..."

"It's okay, baby. I'm calling 911."

My shaky hand manages to press the numbers. Rushing for something to compress against her wound, I give the dispatcher the details. Hanging up, I press a towel firmly to her stomach.

"Baby, look at me. You're going to be okay."

Heart hammering in my chest, I fear the worst. A red pool of liquid soaks the floor, our bodies, and our clothes. Face pale, she's lost too much blood.

"Nix..."

"Hang on, baby. They're coming."

"I... love... you."

Arms dropping to her sides, her beautiful brown eyes lose their shine. Staring blankly, her life fades, taking away the woman I love.

A roar bellows from my chest. Trembling, aching, my muscles constrict, my gut wrenches. Pain—physical, mental, and emotional—comes in crushing waves of agony. Holding her against my chest, I rock her as my grief destroys me, gutting me from the inside out.

The sound of footsteps and voices barely register. Men try to take her from me, and I swing my fist.

"Don't touch her!"

"She needs our help," I hear them say.

My heavy weighted arms fall as her body is lifted onto a stretcher. I'm inconsolable, unable to move.

"You've been shot. We need to get you to the hospital."

"Leave me the fuck alone. My life doesn't matter. She's gone."

CHAPTER TWO

NIX

I THOUGHT I'd buried enough people in my life, but I was wrong. I was wrong about everything. My decisions led to this day—the day I watched a coffin holding the body of the woman I love lower into the ground. Instead of taking her engagement ring shopping, I'm saying goodbye. The scars on my body and on my heart will forever remind me of my mistakes.

Next to me, Liz cries over the loss of her best friend. Reaching my arm out, I hold her against my chest and console her. Jenna's parents look at us—under their puffy red eyes, I see hatred. They blame me for her death, and they're not wrong. It was my fault. I brought her into my life—a life filled with bloodshed. Over a year and a half ago, I made the wrong choice of helping the TBI. It was Liz who paid for my mistake first, and now Jenna has paid with her life.

Rain droplets tap on my leather jacket. Black

umbrellas sporadically open around me. The damp breeze of an oncoming storm sweeps across my face. Inside, my emotions match the weather—a dark brewing rage.

Ahead of me, the road is empty, gray, desolate. I don't know where I'm going. I don't know how long I've been driving. The thought of finding a private gravel road and ending my misery with one bullet plagues me. It's the innocent face of my nephew that's keeping me from following through. I can't leave him and Liz behind with the Royals still out there, intent on destroying my family. They've taken enough from me, darkened my soul, and now, it's revenge I want.

TWO MONTHS LATER . . .

DISAPPOINTMENT TUGS at my lips and brow as I stare at the bottom of the bottle of Jack on my desk. It's not enough... never enough to drown out the memories of her. A bike bunny is sucking my cock like it's her favorite lollipop, and I'm too drunk and numb to tell her the effort is futile. The door of my office opens, and I'm saved by the unexpected guest. Whatever-her-name-is stops sucking and looks up.

"Sorry sweet stuff, you need to go," Jake tells her.

"Bu—" Blue eyes center on me with a pissed-off expression.

I carelessly shrug my shoulders.

"Fucking asshole." The words are cast in my direction as she tugs her panties back up her thighs and tucks them under her skintight dress.

A laugh escapes my chest, and I don't know why. Maybe because she's right.

"Thanks a lot, Jake," she snaps, storming past him.

The door closes, and I tuck my junk back in my jeans.

"What do you want?" My own voice sounds foreign, distant, angry. Trying to stand, I lose my balance and slam back into the chair. I'm past drunk and a few steps from passing out and waking up with drool all over me.

"You're a fucking mess. It's time to go home."

"I'm fine, and I'm sleeping here." Rubbing my eyes, I momentarily block out the blinding light of the room.

"You haven't slept in your own home in two months."

"Is this an inter... vent... ion?" My words slur, and Jake's mouth twists, matching the pity in his eyes. "If so, you can fuck off."

"Tomorrow, we're going for a long ride." Arms crossed, his back is against the door. "You need one, and we have specialty parts that need to be picked up."

"Where?"

"Ohio."

With the look on his face, he's not taking no for an answer even though that's what I want to tell him. I'd have to fight the stubborn prick to win this argument, and I don't have the energy.

"Fine," I say between clenched teeth. "I'll go."

"Get some sleep. You're gonna need it."

With the light flicked off, he closes the door of my office behind him. Sitting in my chair, my head falls back, and the memories of her beautiful face and red hair dance across my mind. But the same thing that happens every night reoccurs—the memories fade to darkness.

CHAPTER THREE

SYNNE

LEVI IS up to his usual games. I thought we'd moved past it, but as I can see by the way he's pawing the blonde's ass, he's still the same asshole I foolishly fell in love with. The attention of several club members follows my stride as I storm to the bar where Levi and the blonde are groping one another. I don't go after the woman as I would have in the past. It's not her fault he's a cheating son-of-a-bitch. It's him I'm after this time.

Picking up my pace, I put out both hands, shoving him into the bar. He briefly winces as his back hits the steel edge of the bar. Yeah, fucker, I did that on purpose. Not giving him time to react, I slam my palm across his cheek.

"We're done. For good this time." Glancing at the blonde, I smirk. "He's all yours, but I'm warning you, he sticks his dick in anything that moves and won't give a fuck how much that hurts you."

Hazel eyes narrow in on me. He's pissed I just embarrassed him like that. Gripping my wrist, he squeezes hard, sending pain up my arm. Waving off the blonde, he drags me away from watching eyes. We're about to enter into our usual fight the club members have gotten used to. It's always been a love-hate relationship between Levi and me. He'd cheat, we'd fight, he'd apologize and grovel for my forgiveness, then we'd fuck and make up—pathetic, I know.

I was young when I met him and became infatuated. I didn't want any other man and believed I could change him. I was wrong. The first year was good, then the cheating began. Four more years of his games, and I've finally come to my senses. It took Skip, a man I consider to be a father figure in my life and one of the oldest members of the Sinister Sons, to make me realize Levi's never going to change for me. He doesn't love me enough to want to be committed, and he's learned I accept his behavior because of how much I wanted to be with him.

Shoving me into one of the club rooms, Levi slams the door behind him. It's unheard with the loud beat of the music coming from the clubhouse. Eyes blazing with hatred, the back of his hand whips across my cheek. Stumbling back, I'm in as much shock as I am in pain. Levi's never hit me before. Our arguments were never more than a yelling match.

"You think you can embarrass me like that in front of my brothers, bitch?"

The fucker can think again if he believes I'll cower to his rage. Knee to his groin, he buckles, and I slam my fist into his face as hard as I can. Pain ripples through my hand and into my arm, feeling like my bones have exploded, but I'll deal. *No man* has the right to lay a hand on me.

"I've been loyal to you for five fucking years, and you think you can hit me? You've forgotten what *my* brothers taught me. Never *ever* let a man lay a hand on me." Slipping from my property jacket, I throw it at his stunned face. "You never loved me, and I finally realize that. I meant it when I said we're done. I don't want your filthy cock anywhere near me."

"You walk out that door, and I won't take you back, Synne. You won't have my protection anymore either. You really want that?"

Raising my chin, I meet his gaze. "I no longer have a reason to stay here. You should've treated me better. No one will ever be as loyal to you as I was."

"You knew what you got into when you met me." The asshole doesn't even look sorry, but his face will tomorrow.

Walking to the door, I look back over my shoulder. "It still doesn't make it okay. I loved you with everything I had."

Opening the door, I hear his boots beat the floor behind me.

"Synne, get back here!"

Not turning back, I curl my fists at my sides and

avoid the eyes of the people I've lived alongside and called family for years.

"Synne!"

Levi's voice bellows through the clubhouse, and my feet pick up the pace as I pull my keys from my pocket. Out the door, I rush to my Harley. A hand grabs my arm, and I prepare myself for Levi's assault. Skip looks down at me with a mixture of pride and concern in his eyes.

"Ride far away, Synne and never look back. Find a new home where the Sons can't find you."

"I will. I promise."

"I'll miss ya, you sassy girl."

"I'll miss you too."

With a thumb swiped across my cheek, he steps back and watches as I fire up my Harley and ride away.

CHAPTER FOUR

NIX

WITH MY BACK against the cool tile of the shower, the hot water runs down my body, giving my muscles a reprieve but not my mind. It's clouded, thick with tension, worry, anger. My mistakes haunt me, plaguing me each day, and nothing eases the pain. Hearing movement downstairs, I turn off the knob and step out. Towel around my waist, I grip the handle of my Glock.

"Nix!"

Lowering the gun, I set it on the sink counter. Liz's voice echoes through the house once more as I open the bathroom door.

"I'll be down in a minute."

Hair damp, I brush it away from my face. Looking in the steam-edged mirror, I don't recognize myself. My hair is long and tangled, my eyes sunken and dull. It's been a few months since Jenna's death, and I've done nothing but slip further into my misery. I know it's affecting the club, but I don't know what to do about it. All I want is to forget—forget her beautiful face, her laugh, the way her eyes lit up when she saw me enter a room.

Fist tight, I pound it against the counter. I'm ashamed of what I've become, that I've let her death go without vengeance. That I've fallen this far, let my pain swallow me whole. Sniffling, I fight back the overwhelming sensation washing over me. Wiping at my face, I startle when I hear the bathroom door open. Standing in the threshold, my sister's eyes soften with sympathy when she looks at me.

"I brought you dinner. I'd like to hang out tonight, just you and me."

Nodding, I accept her offer. I don't want to admit it, but I need her company. Stepping farther in, she brushes my messy hair away from my face.

"Can I give you a haircut?"

"Yeah. This shit's out of control."

With a giggle, she smiles. "It is."

"Do whatever you want with it."

"Come down to the kitchen. I'll cut it, then we can eat."

Leaving me in the bathroom alone, I take one last glimpse at myself in the mirror, wishing it was another man looking back.

A chair is set out on the tile floor. I've only been back in my house a couple weeks, and every time I walk into this kitchen, my gut wrenches. This is where I lost her. Seeing me standing there, completely still, Liz lifts the chair and brings it back to the dining room.

"We'll do it in here."

On the table, Liam's bouncer is lightly vibrating and playing soothing baby music. Attention drawn to him, I walk over, and with my index finger, I rub his soft cheek. Brown eyes look up at me, and he makes happy sounds, blowing slobbery bubbles from his lips.

"He's growing fast."

"I know it. And he has an appetite like his father."

Seeing the Harley Davidson hat tugs at the corner of my lips. Pretty sure Jake doesn't let Liam leave the house without something Harley on him.

Tucking my hands under his back and neck, I lift him, bringing his face to mine. Kissing his forehead, I feel a moment of peace. He's the string that ties me here, him and Liz both. They're my anchor, my reason for continuing each day. Knowing how much she worries about me stiffens my muscles. Guilt is like a constrictor tightening around my waist.

"You're worried about me, I know."

"I am. The whole club is worried. You're their president, and when you're hurting, we're all hurting."

"I'm trying. Everything reminds me of her."

"I can't fathom the pain you're feeling. If I lost Jake, I'd be broken, but I know you'd take care of me. So, let me take care of you."

The scent of baby is a soothing aroma reaching deep

within. Reluctantly setting him back in his bouncer, I look at her.

"Let's start with the haircut and dinner."

My stomach is growling. I can't remember the last meal I had. Maybe yesterday morning. Everything has been one long blur lately. Sitting in the chair, thick, dark strands fall to the floor. Finished with the scissors, she reaches for the trimmer. The buzzing stops a few minutes later, and she lifts her handheld mirror. Touching the top of my head is a foreign feeling. My hair is gone. It's short now, slightly longer on the top, but not much. With both hands, I rub my fingers over the new cut. It feels lighter, better.

"You like it?"

"Besides the fact I feel bald, yeah, I like it. You did good."

Lengthy strands of dark brown hair are strewn across the floor. Gathering her tools back in her bag, she moves to the closet for a broom.

"You going to recognize your uncle after what your mama just did to all my hair?" With my finger touching his soft cheek, Liam stares at me for a moment before cooing happily. "I guess so."

"Of course, he recognizes you. You're his family."

The closet closes behind her, and she pads across the kitchen to the bags on the counter.

"What are you making?"

"Pasta."

Another grumble from my stomach, and I smile appreciatively. "I'm glad you came over."

"Me too."

"Where's Jake?"

"At the clubhouse with the guys."

"I owe them an apology. I haven't been around much. They've been picking up my slack."

"It's what we do, and you'd do it for any one of us."

Taking groceries out of a bag, she sets out a box of noodles and a jar of sauce. Opening the fridge, I pull a pound of ground beef out and hand it to her.

"Thank you."

Unsealing the package, she preps the meat.

"William says we need to hire someone for the front desk of the bike shop. Brittany quit."

"Why?"

"She was sleeping with William. He started seeing another girl he met at a clubhouse party, and they got into a huge fight, so she split. Kicked his bike on the way out. He was pissed... about the bike. Didn't seem too concerned about Brittany."

"Fucking William, he's like Jake was."

"Hey!" Tossing a few dry noodles at me, she frowns.

"Sorry, but it's true. William's all about chasing tail right now. Go ahead and put a listing out for the job. The sooner we get it filled, the better."

"I'll do that. You know Full Throttle bike week is coming up?"

With a shrug, I tip my head. "I forgot about it."

Liam cries, and Liz responds, walking toward the table. Waving her off, I take the few steps back to the table.

"I got him."

"He's hungry. There's a bottle in the bag."

Spreading the bag open, I see the bottle in the right pocket and bring it to Liam. Tiny hands reach for it, but they're not strong enough to hold it yet. Keeping the bottle steady, I hold it for him, watching how quickly he becomes content.

"The guys will want you there. You gonna come?"

With my long pause, she continues.

"You should come. It's tradition we all go. We need you there."

Vengeance is something I've wanted since Jenna died, but I've been too much of a mess to plan any kind of retaliation against Reed and the Royals. If I go, I'm afraid I'll risk my freedom by shooting him straight between the eyes with hundreds of witnesses there to see it. But it was never Jenna they wanted. Jenna was collateral damage. Why risk more of my family when the bounty on my head is still steep?

"It's best I don't go."

Dropping the last of the noodles into the water, her attention centers on me. "Why don't I fast forward this conversation. You're going. If you don't want to be president anymore, then step down, but if you still care about this family, the whole family, then swallow your shame and be the president the Kings need."

Liam hiccups, as if saying, yeah, what she said. Lowering the bottle, I rub his tiny belly. She's right. I need to get my shit together and take care of business, or I might as well do the Royals a favor and put a bullet in my temple.

"I want my life back."

A small warm hand touches my shoulder. She looks at Liam, her gaze loving, then back at me, full of hope.

"We all need you."

CHAPTER FIVE

NIX

WRENCH IN HAND, I tighten the bolt on the Harley engine in front of me. Hearing the front door of the shop open, my head rises, and I peer through the shop doorway to see who's come in. Sun rays shine through the front window, preventing a clear view of the woman's face, but I can see her long red hair cascading down in loose waves over her shoulders. Mouth dry, the wrench falls to the floor.

Jenna.

Stepping forward, the sun's rays disappear, and the woman becomes visible. Grabbing a rag, I wipe my hands and swallow down the rush of pain that ripped up through my esophagus. Joining her in the front office, I look her over. The hair is similar to Jenna's, but the rest of her isn't. Striking hazel-green eyes look up at me from a curvy, muscular body. Her right arm is covered in a tatted sleeve, several beautiful colors intertwined with black ink. With a V-neck shirt on, I can see more tattoos peeking out from the fabric next to her right breast. Eyes drawn to the creamy skin etched with ink, I catch myself looking too long at her chest and fidget uncomfortably at the reaction my dick is having to her body.

"How can I help you?" I ask, tossing the rag on the counter.

"Here to apply." Throwing her thumb over her shoulder, she points to the *Now Hiring* sign in the front window.

Her voice is confident, sexy. I like the sound of it, but the last thing I want is to hear it again.

"Job's been filled."

With a frown pulling at her lips, the light in her eyes dull. A stinging sensation lingers in my chest watching the disappointment show on her face. The side door to the clubhouse bar opens to Liz entering the shop office. Stopping in her tracks, she stares at the woman.

"Need help with anything else? I could really use the work."

Attention drawn to me, Liz tilts her head and scowls.

"Unless the job was filled in the last hour, it's open," Liz tells her, looking sternly at me.

Grabbing the rag, I storm into the shop, slamming the door behind me.

—SYNNE—

"WHAT'S WITH HIM?"

The pretty dark-haired woman in front of me has sadness in her eyes but still smiles at me.

"That's a story for later. Come into the clubhouse. We'll do an interview."

Waving me around the counter, she invites me to follow her through the side door. Inside, the clubhouse is cleaner than the Son's was. The wood floor and bar look old, but the tables, chairs, and pool tables are newer and nice quality. Motioning to one of the chairs, the woman takes the one next to it.

"I'm Liz, but to my man, I'm Peach."

"Synne."

"Like s-i-n?"

"Yeah, but spelled s-y-n-n-e."

With a nod of her head, the corner of her mouth twists up. "I like it. It's pretty."

"Thanks. So, the job is still open?"

"Yeah, but we need someone reliable. We don't have the time to deal with someone who no-shows a lot. Everyone around here has their own job to do."

"I'm reliable. I promise you."

"How about your experience? You know how to run a register, balance a drawer, keep efficient reports, and organize invoices?"

"Yeah, I've managed a bar and the books."

"You got a resume?" She looks to the sheets of paper in my hand.

Handing them to her, Liz takes a minute or two to read them. When she's finished, she sets them down and looks me over, studying me closely. This girl's smart. I can tell.

"I'd like to offer you the job. You can start tomorrow as long as it's not too soon for you."

"It's not. Thank you, Liz. I appreciate this."

Hand on my forearm, she stops me from leaving.

"Stay clear of my brother, Nix, for a while. He's going through something. Lost someone he cared for deeply."

"That the guy I spoke to?"

"Yeah."

"The person he lost... I look like her?"

"No, just the red hair. It's similar."

"Did you know her well?"

"Since we were kids. She was my best friend."

"I'm sorry for your loss."

Head lowered, she holds her emotions in.

"Me too."

Seeing the pain in her eyes, I feel for her. I know that pain.

"You a... want to have a beer together? Technically, you're not my boss until tomorrow."

With a laugh, she rises from the chair and motions her head to the bar. "Yeah, come on."

Two beers in and I already like Liz. Talking with her

feels natural like we've been friends for a while. It's nice. I haven't had this in years. Most women I came across were desperate to become a biker's girl and screwed over any other woman to get to the dick they wanted.

"How old is Liam?"

"Six months. He's so damn cute. Wait until you see him."

"Where is he?"

"With my Aunt May. She'll be dropping him off soon. She watches him if Jake and I have to work. Today is my day off, but I needed to help Nix catch up on things around here."

"You two close?"

"Very. He pretty much raised me. Made sure I went to college. Now I'm an RN at Nashville Medical Center. I'm thankful for everything he did. He ran the bar and bike shop and sent me money every month."

"Sounds like a good man."

Tipping her beer back, she agrees.

"He is, he's just lost right now, but he'll find his way. I don't know anyone stronger than my brother."

It's good to know my new boss isn't a dick. It's not something I need right now. I can use all the friends I can get. I'm alone, no family, no protection, completely starting over, and it's scary as hell. If the rest of the Kings MC is anything like Liz and her brother, I might've found a new home. It's what I need. Three months of keeping on the move has taken its toll on me.

"I'll steer clear of him, give him his space. I won't cause trouble. I need this job."

Eyes roaming over my face, she studies me, clearly taking in every detail.

"What's your story?" she asks with a confident expectation. "Is there anything we should know?"

"I didn't bring any baggage with me if that's what you're worried about. I left it all behind."

Looking me in the eyes, she searches for signs of deceit. When she finds none, her lips turn up in a kind smile.

"Why don't you come back tonight? There's a party, and its fight night. The whole club will be here. It'll be good for you to meet everyone."

It feels good to be welcomed. Her friendship is what I need. Having been raised in an MC, I miss the feeling of family, of people having your back.

"Thanks. I'll be here."

Pulling her phone from her back pocket, she awaits me to do the same.

"I'll text you later."

We swap numbers, and I leave, feeling hopeful for the first time in months.

—NIX—

LEANING BACK in one of the clubhouse chairs, I tip the

shot glass and down my liquid cure. Beneath me, the chair scrapes the gritty wood floor as I rise to my feet. Each step is heavy as I enter the makeshift ring. A new prospect is going through his initiation, but I'm not worried about this one. Guaranteed, Dominic will be the last one standing after he fights all of us. Arms like boulders, he raises them, ready to lay me at his feet. I sure as hell won't make it easy for him.

Going in fast, I bury my fist in his ribs. He anticipates my next shot, blocks, and rocks me in the mouth. With my burning, busted lip, I gather the rage I've been carrying and unleash. Dominic's the perfect opponent, giving me back what I give him. I need this —to let go in the ring with someone who can handle it.

It's a dance of skill, rage, and blood. It spatters the floor when I spit and drips from the broken skin of his brow. I'm pretty damn sure he's enjoying this as much as I am. Stepping back, we each take a breath and analyze our next attack. Red hair catches the corner of my eye, and I turn my head to see the woman from earlier today strolling through the club. What the fuck is she doing here? With my thoughts distracted, Dominic's fist plows into my stomach, and I buckle. Fuck! His fist feels like a brick. Chasing the breath that's been knocked out of me, I tap out, and Max goes in next.

Pushing through the crowd, I see her approach Liz and Liam. Scooping him up in her arms, she stares at him with soft eyes. Agony rips its way through my heart. The memory of Jenna holding Liam flashes through my mind. Shaking the thought away, I redirect to the bar. I can't do this, not now. I need to keep it together. I can't fall apart every time I see a woman with red hair.

"What can I get ya?" Jeff looks at me concerned. I've been drowning my sorrows at the bottom of a bottle of Jack for five months now. I know he's worried that's where I'm headed again. Glancing over my shoulder, I see Red hand Liam back to Liz.

"Three bottles of beer."

With three cold bottles in hand, I walk over to my sister and Red. Handing them both a bottle, she looks up at me surprised.

"Thanks."

"Liz, can I talk to you alone?"

Red's expression changes, becoming worried, but she still nods and tells Liz she'll watch Liam.

Stepping a few feet away, my eyes narrow. "Tell me you didn't hire Red."

"Her name's Synne, and I did. She's qualified, seems reliable, and we need that position filled yesterday. Don't hold it against her that there are similarities to..."

Seeing the look on my face, she doesn't say her name. It'll hurt too damn much to hear it said out loud, and she knows that.

"She can't help she's a natural redhead." With sorrow in her eyes, I soften at the hint of her tears. "I miss her, Nix. I miss my best friend."

Pulling her to me, I hold her head against my chest,

soothing away her tears of pain. "I miss her too." With a kiss to her head, I let her go. "All right. Red stays, but you'll have to show her how things are done around here. I can't. You understand?"

Wiping a stray tear away, she nods. "I do."

CHAPTER SIX

NIX

WALKING INTO THE FRONT OFFICE, there's a fresh mug of coffee waiting for me. Scooping it up, I take a drink, but I can't completely relax from the refreshing liquid. Sitting on the stool behind the counter, I can see Red's black leather leggings tight around her ass, her red top cut low, revealing more of her creamy, full tits. My dick jerks, and I grimace. I'm going to need to blow this load I've been carrying around into a bike bunny's mouth for fuck's sake. I can't take this shit anymore.

"Liz get you up to speed on everything?"

"Yeah, I got last month's invoices filed, and current invoices in alphabetical order. Two are outstanding. I already called them this morning. And a guy called and asked if he could drop off his scooter. I didn't see anything on the calendar, so I booked him for eleven a.m."

Damn, she's good.

"Nice job, Red. Keep the coffee coming."

Pretty hazel-green eyes light up at my praise. Before her smile can get wider, I dart out of the office. In the garage, I pull my cell out of my pocket and adjust my junk.

"Lindsey, you wanna come by the club tonight? I could use the company."

With a little whining about what happened last time, she agrees. I know she'd like to be my ol' lady, but I can't do it. I'm an asshole for using her, but I need the touch of a woman.

Lunch rolls around, and I know it's that time by the sound of my grumbling stomach. I really need to make eating a priority—coffee and liquor aren't cutting it anymore. The garage door opens, and Red walks in with a leather jacket on. The cut fits her curves perfectly, and I look away before my cock gets a mind of its own again.

"You hungry?"

"Yeah."

"I'm going to drive over to Louie's and get a couple of sandwiches for us. That cool?"

"Yeah." Not looking at her, I lift the new tire onto the raised bike in front of me.

"All right. See you in a few."

Moments later, I hear the sound of a Harley take off. Stepping out of the garage, I see Red is the owner of the Harley. Watching her ride down the road, she disappears, and I realize how long

I've been watching. So, I might be a little impressed she can ride. With her out of sight, I get back to work.

When the rumble of her Harley returns, it's not long after the garage door opens.

"You didn't say what you wanted, so I got you turkey bacon. That work? If not, I can give you my ham and cheese."

She's thoughtful; that'll be nice to have at work.

"Turkey and bacon is fine."

"Great, I'll leave it here for you."

Glancing over at her, her leather jacket is off. Leaning over to set the sandwich on my tool counter, her shirt fabric falls forward. Fuck me, she doesn't have a bra on. A glimpse of her nipple has me staring like a horny ass teenager. Damn it, I need laid.

"Thanks."

Lingering, she watches me, licking her pretty pink lips.

"You have a nice ride," I tell her, breaking the awkward silence.

"Thank you. It's a smooth ride. It's picked up a hissing sound, though. I don't know what it is."

"An exhaust leak. I heard it when you left. Bring it in after lunch. I'll take a look at it."

"Thanks, but I don't have the money for that right now."

She seems embarrassed, and I feel guilty mentioning it.

"On the house. Payment for lunch. I can seal it. It'll only take me minutes."

"I appreciate that. Really."

"Don't mention it."

"Nix..."

Whatever she wants to know, it's territory I don't want to enter into.

"Thanks for picking up lunch. You better get back to work."

She seems to understand I want to be left alone and closes the office door behind her.

SOFT BLONDE HAIR fisted in my hand, I move Lindsey's head up and down my cock. I needed this. Needed to get my shit blown and get my head straight. Moaning, she swallows my cum, and I sit back, muscles lax. Light blue eyes look up at me, and I hiss from the sensitivity of her cleaning my head. Smile wide, she backs off, then straddles my lap, long legs touching the floor on each side of my office chair. Fingering the patch on my cut, she circles the word, *President*.

"Maybe we should make this a thing. You and me?"

Hand on her hip, I scoot her off my lap. "Too soon, Linds. I'm not looking for that kind of commitment."

Standing, I tuck my dick back in my jeans and head toward the door. The party is active in the clubhouse, and with her talk, I'm motivated to join it.

"I like you, Nix. I want to see you more."

"Fuck, Linds. I just want to keep this simple."

"Simple as in I blow you when you want it, and I get nothing in return?"

Getting my cock sucked wasn't worth this kind of nagging.

"It's too damn soon for any woman, don't you get that?" My bark comes out strong, and she straightens her shoulders.

"I'm sorry. I…"

"Forget it. We're done. I'm not going to use you. Thanks for tonight, but don't expect my call again."

Walking out of my office, leaving her there, I feel like a complete asshole, but it's best I end it. She wants more, I don't. No need to lead her on. A woman doesn't deserve that. Standing outside the door, I hear her cuss me out and knock shit off my desk. I'm pissed she's disrespecting me, but really, I don't blame her.

Entering the clubhouse, I grab a beer on the way past the bar before joining my VP, Max and old Wesley at the pool table. Glancing around the clubhouse, I see Liz on Jake's lap, him whispering in her ear. Won't be long and they'll be in a room fucking. The clubhouse door opens, and Dominic and his girl, Erika, enter. Those two are never apart. I respect that about him. Watching him greeted by my brothers, I think about his final initiation and the vote to make him a full patch member. I already know what everyone will vote. He'll fit right in.

Walking tall and with tense shoulders, Dominic approaches Jake. A few words are spoken, and Jake's expression changes. Searching for me, Jake finds me and tips his head for me to join them.

With a whistle to Wesley and Max, they follow behind me. Entering the courtroom, we stand facing one another.

"What's going on?" I ask Dominic.

"Royals. Ran into one at the Harley shop. Erika was shopping, and one of the dumb fucks approached her and grabbed her ass, calling her a Kings' whore. I dragged him outside and broke his face."

"Any witnesses?" Jake asks.

"Only the cashier."

"Daisy won't say anything," Max assures him. "Daisy and the manager favor the Kings."

Dominic's shoulders relax. "Good, I don't need any heat on my back."

Jake pats his shoulder. "We got your back. Max and I will visit Daisy and make sure there won't be any statements made if the police show up asking questions." Jake looks at Max. "You know if they got any cameras outside in the parking lot?"

"Pretty sure they do."

"We'll get it erased," Jake replies confidently.

"Thanks, brothers."

"Head on out, Dominic. I need to speak with the board."

Dominic leaves, and I look at each of them.

"We need to vote on him becoming a full patch. If it's unanimous, I think we should give him his patch at Full Throttle."

"That'd be a hell of a patch ceremony," Jake grins.

"What about Ink?" Max asks, "He's been prospecting longer than Dom."

"We'll vote on both. Patch them both."

"That mean you're joining us?" Thumbs tucked into his cut, Wesley awaits my answer with hope in his eyes.

"Yeah, my ass will be there."

A few pats on my back etch a smile on my face.

"It's good to have you back, brother." Max's smile is large and genuine.

"Thanks for taking care of shit while I was down and out."

"Of course, we all got your back."

"The Royals—" Jake presses.

"Not tonight. I just got my head clear."

"We'll talk later. Let's get you a beer and some pussy."

Arm around my shoulders, Jake leads me back out to the clubhouse and bar. It's a busy place tonight. Every club member is here, including our newest prospect, Ink. He and William are talking to Red, hanging on her every word. By the looks of it, William's new girl, Maci, isn't digging it. I see a catfight in the near future. That, I wouldn't mind watching. My money's on Red.

Jake waves his beer-filled hand around the room.

"There's a lot of bike bunnies here tonight. Who's it gonna be?"

"Let's start with a beer."

"You telling me you're gonna pass up on the new girl?" Jake points the top of his beer bottle at Red. "She's got a hell of an ass on her."

"Don't let Liz hear you say that. She'll kick yours to the next state over."

"You know hers is the only pussy I want, but I'm not blind, brother."

Red turns to talk to someone else, and that ass comes into view. Jake's right. It's full, round, and would take a good pounding. Ink and William seem to think so too. Ink grabs a cheek and squeezes. Elbow to his chest, Red turns on him and throws a punch, knocking his ass back a step.

"Damn, she's got an arm on her," Jake laughs.

Whatever Red said to him has Ink raising both hands for mercy.

"She's a spitfire. That's for damn sure."

Liz approaches us, taking Jake's hand and pulls him toward the stairs.

"Sorry, Nix. I need my man. We're off parenting duty tonight."

Jake shrugs his shoulders and winks at me, a mischievous grin splitting his lips.

"See ya in a while, brother."

Still watching Red, my curiosity grows. I don't know anything about the woman—where she's from, her family, if she's got any. It's my job to protect this club and the members in it. It's time I do some digging.

Getting two fresh beers, I step up behind Red. Ink and William make space for me, respecting the patch.

"That's going to be a hell of a shiner, Ink."

Red turns at the sound of my voice, expression softening when she looks at me. I tilt my head, surprised to see the change in her body language.

"I brought you a beer. We should talk."

Body stiffening, she accepts the beer and follows me to the back porch behind my office. Sitting down, I pop the top of my beer and bring my legs up, resting them on the railing. Taking the seat next to me, she looks nervous.

"I'm sorry for hitting your prospect. That won't happen again."

"That's not what this is about, Red. And you're free to defend yourself from unwanted groping from those fools."

Relief washes over her face, and she leans back into the chair, taking a swig.

"Thanks."

"So, what's your story? Why are you here? And don't give me a spin on it. I want the truth."

Her brow rises, and she drifts off in thought for a moment.

"All right. The truth is, I fell for a scumbag when I was young. The next five years I fell deeper in love, and he spent that time fucking every pussy that showed him attention. I broke it off and left."

"What MC was he in?"

"Chicago, Sinister Sons."

She looks far more nervous having given up that detail.

"Don't worry. I don't know them. Only heard the name. You running from him?"

Looking off into the distance, she avoids eye contact with me.

"Not just him. The Sons too."

"They outlaw?"

She tugs on her beer a moment, clearly needing the liquid courage.

"They're headed that way. A patchover was scheduled."

"What did you do to warrant the animosity?"

"Kicked his ass before I left. Walked out on him. Disrespected him in front of the club. If I stuck around, they would've punished me for it."

"What kind of punishment?"

"Maybe rape, maybe a beating. Can't say for sure. I wasn't willing to stick around and find out."

"Jesus, you made the right decision leaving."

Emptying her beer, she sets it on the porch floorboards below her chair.

"I know club business is private, but the Kings don't seem like outlaws."

"We're not, our shit's legal. The most we'll do is an

escort for a business that needs protection from gangs or a one-percenter MC. It's how we became rivals with another MC called the Wild Royals. Our clubs have a long, bloody history."

"Is that what happened to—"

"I could use another beer. You mind?" Holding up my empty bottle, I give it a wave, disrupting where her conversation was headed.

With her lips pinched, she nods, accepting the hint.

"Yeah, I'll get us a couple more."

As she walks away, I stare at her ass. Shaking my head, I laugh. I'm no better than Ink or William. While she's gone, I look out at the dark sky dappled with stars. Closing my eyes, I take a breath, breathing in the cool night air. There were nights like this when the parties got wild, Jenna and I would sneak away, ravage each other in my office, then come out here. She'd sit on my lap, and we'd watch, waiting for a shooting star. It was something she loved, and I was happy making her happy.

A warm hand touches my shoulder, and my heart skips a beat. Opening my eyes, I look up at Red. Glossy hazel-green eyes stare down at me, her expression affectionate.

"You miss her, don't you?"

Taking her hand, I hold it in mine, running my hand over her soft skin.

"Every day."

With her movement forward, I lower my legs off the

railing, letting her step between my knees. Leaning against the railing, she hands me one of the two beers in her left hand. Setting the beer down on the wood floor, I move my hand to her hip, pulling her to me. Setting her beer on the railing, she runs her fingers through my short hair. The sensation is comforting and something I didn't realize I needed. Forehead against her stomach, I breathe her in, the aroma of cinnamon drawing me in deeper.

The sound of heels pounding wood disrupts us. Lindsey turns the corner, her expression quickly turning to rage.

"Fuck you, Nix. I suck your cock earlier, you tell me to get lost, and now you're trying to get into her too tight leather pants. You're an asshole."

Stepping back, Red drops her hands. She seems pissed. I'm sure the sucking cock earlier bit initiated that. Tension rolls across my shoulders, bringing back every emotion that had momentarily ceased to exist.

Rising to my feet, I head toward Lindsey. She's clearly drunk and looks close to crying.

"Calm the fuck down. What I do and who I do it with is my business. Now, come on. I'll take you home. You're drunk and making a scene."

Glancing over my shoulder, I nod to Red. "I'll see you at work."

CHAPTER SEVEN

SYNNE

POURING COFFEE INTO TWO MUGS, I set one on the edge of the counter and bring the other with me. I haven't seen Nix yet this morning, but I'm hoping when I do, it won't be awkward. We had a moment at the party. What kind of moment, I don't know. Maybe we're both lonely. Maybe there's a mutual understanding of having a broken heart. Maybe it's both. Either way, what I do know is, there's something that keeps pulling me toward him, wanting to know more. Beneath his striking green eyes is a man who's broken but doing everything he can to mend himself for the people around him. It says a lot about his character.

Even after the fender fluff, Lindsey, bitched at him he made sure the woman got home safely. Levi never would've done that. He would've shoved her, told her not to disrespect him and his ol' lady, then dragged me out behind him, saying she's a liar and nothing happened. What the fuck was wrong with me? I put up with that shit for years. Looking back, I'd like to slap sense into my younger self and tell me to stay as far away from Levi as I could. If he hadn't been such a rockstar in bed, I doubt I would've stuck around as long as I did. Fuck that man for being so skilled.

The garage door opens, and moments later, Nix walks in the office, running his hand through his short hair. Under his eyes, the skin is darker, sunken. He clearly didn't sleep well. Gathering the mug, he walks behind me through the door to the clubhouse.

"Thanks, Red."

Disappearing on the other side, he doesn't say another word. William walks through the door behind him, grinning like a fool.

"I'll be in the garage today. Let me know if you need anything."

"What's Nix doing?"

"Club business, honey. Going on a ride with Jake and Max. I work with Nix in the garage, so you'll be seeing a lot of me." With a wink, he saunters over to the coffee machine and pours himself a mug full. "That was an impressive right hook the other night."

Looking up from the files in front of me, I notice the glimmer in William's blue eyes. It's evident he likes what he sees. He's not bad to look at—tall, blond hair lengthier on the top, shorter on the sides, broad-shouldered with artistic ink curling around both arms—

only he's a little too pretty for my liking. I prefer dark-haired and rough around the edges.

Lingering with his mug in hand, his attention is drawn toward the sound of Harleys. Nix and the other two Kings pass the front windows and disappear down the road.

"So, where you from?" Placing an elbow on the counter, he leans forward, making it clear he's here to stay awhile.

"Chicago."

"Never been, but I'd be up for going. You like road trips?"

Pointing the pen in my hand at my Harley outside, I raise a brow. "The green one out there. That's mine."

"No shit, well damn, baby, you just got a hell of a lot hotter. We should take a ride together sometime. I promise it'll be enjoyable." With another wink, he ensures I catch his sexual innuendo.

"What about your girl? How would she feel about you riding another chick?"

Lowering his mug, he shrugs his shoulder.

"Maci's cool. We're just hanging out. She's not my ol' lady if that's what you're asking."

This William is a real lady's man, and I don't mean that as a compliment.

"Right."

Looking William in the eyes, I lean forward and his eyes drop to my cleavage before returning to my face.

Curling my finger, I bring him closer. Licking his lips, his smile stretches into a lascivious smirk.

"This"—I point between him and me—"isn't going to—"

The rumble of Harleys speeding toward the shop cuts off my words. Shattering glass jerks me off my seat. Throwing myself against the wall, my eyes go wide as I look over the counter at the smoking, broken bottle on the floor.

"Get down!"

Mug gone from his hand, William jumps at me, taking us both down to the floor. Heart pounding rapidly in my chest, we both await bullets, but thankfully, none come. Easing me out of his arms, we peer over the counter. The sound of Harleys become distant as they quickly make their escape. I catch a glimpse of a back patch—Wild Royals.

Darting to the burning rag on the floor, William snuffs it out, stomping on the flames with his heavy boot.

"Fucking Royals! I need to call Nix."

"What the hell was that about?"

Ignoring me, he dials and puts the phone to his ear.

"Royals just paid a visit. Put a burning bottle taped to a brick through the front window." William's attention turns to me. "Yeah, she's good. Pissed off and confused, but fine... All right, see ya when you get here."

Pocketing his phone, he tilts his head toward the garage.

"Let's get this shit cleaned up. We have duct tape and plastic sheets in the garage."

"Why did they do this?"

"Retaliation."

"For what?"

"Club business." With a stern look, he indicates that's all the information I'm going to get.

With the floor clean and the last corner of plastic taped to the frame of the window, I hear motorcycles entering the parking lot. Looking through the glass door, I see Nix and the other two Kings. Red-faced and jaw tense, Nix's expression reveals his rage. Stopping a few feet away from the entrance, he stares at the window, then says a few cuss words before coming inside. Right away, he looks at me.

"You okay?" Unexpectedly, he rubs his hand over my hair as his eyes roam my face, inspecting me. "If you want to quit, I understand."

His anger is hidden behind something else—worry. Vibrant green eyes lock on mine, and my composure softens. Every damn time he's near me, my body reacts to him, tingling in all the right places. Taking his hand from my hair, I link my fingers with his, momentarily enjoying the feel of his strong hand before I release it.

"I'm okay, and a bottle through a window isn't going to scare me off."

"Good. I was just starting to get used to you."

Hand grazing my shoulder, his smile is brief. Attention turning to William, he dips his chin.

"Come into the clubhouse. We need to talk."

All four men slip through the side door to the clubhouse. Nix stops in front of the door.

"Can you call and see how much a window replacement is going to cost us?"

"Yeah, I'll take care of it."

"Thanks."

The door closes behind him, and I get back to work.

$\approx$

—NIX—

AFTER CALLING in all the members, concern etches their brows as they take their seats around the courtroom table.

"Tell them the details, William."

With a recap of the morning event, I sense the anger growing throughout the room.

"Synne okay?" Ink asks.

"Yeah, she's all right. Didn't shake her. She's tough," I assure him.

I'm glad to see the guys are taking to her. It's a good sign she'll fit in with us.

"They're taking the opportunity to send a message. They think the Kings are weak."

I know Dominic is right. Rubbing my fingers over the scruff on my face, I take a moment to think about my words.

"After five months, I'm sure Reed thinks I don't plan on retaliating for what he did to me. He probably thinks I'm afraid, but the truth is the opposite." Leaning forward, I put my hands together, rubbing my thumb over the other. "I didn't plan a retaliation because I was a drunken mess. Jenna's death tore me up bad, brothers. It's taken me a while to get my shit together, but now that I have, it's time we remind the Royals who the Kings are."

A few fists pound on the table, letting me know they agree.

"We're behind you on this," Jake tells me.

"We've been waiting for you to be ready." Max taps me on the shoulder.

"All of you on board?"

In unison, Trevor, Max, Wesley, William, Ink, Axel, Dominic, and Jake give their signal of approval.

"We are," William confirms.

"What I'm about to ask of you is a lot. It's a dangerous risk."

"Let's hear it," Jake presses.

"We're going to need to get our hands on some explosives."

CHAPTER EIGHT

NIX

STANDING in the doorway of the front office, I wipe my hands on a rag and watch Red bent over, fussing with files. Ass in the air, I shamelessly enjoy the view. When she stands, she catches a glimpse of me in her peripheral.

"Admiring the landscape?" she laughs.

"Just walked in."

"Uh-huh." Her brow lifts, and she smirks. "I believe that."

Stepping up to where she's standing, I lean over her, coming in close as I reach for the newest work orders. Tongue slipping between her lips, she nibbles the bottom one, and my dick jerks.

"I'm going to leave these in the garage for William to work on. I need to work in my office today. I have things to do for the bar." Swallowing, she raises her chin, and I see the pink flush coming to her cheeks.

Lips full and slightly parted, I find myself lingering, staring at them. "I'll see you tonight if you're coming to the clubhouse."

"As busy as we've been this week, I'm definitely in need of a beer... or three."

Swiping my finger under her chin, I let a genuine smile slip from my lips.

"I'll see you later tonight, then."

As I put space between us, she releases a breath. She's not the only one feeling the heat between us. Every damn time she's near me, my cock lets me know how much it'd like to feel her pussy around it. Too bad my head and heart aren't in agreement.

WITH FULL THROTTLE COMING UP, we're all ready to let loose in the clubhouse tonight. This week, we've had customers coming from hundreds of miles away to get the best parts available or to ensure their bike is repaired and ready for the week of partying, concerts, races, and motorcycle contests. Each of the Kings is entered in one or more of the contests. It's what we all look forward to each year. Full Throttle is a biker's paradise—day after day of pussy, liquor, food, Harleys, and music. They do have one rule, though. No outside rivalry during the field meet. It's the only time all motorcycle clubs have to remain neutral, at least while inside the grounds. Outside of it, there are no rules.

Thumping music pumps out of the speakers in the corner as I stand at the edge of the bar, monitoring my club and the customers. There are non-MC customers here tonight, but most are regulars, along with the usual biker hang-arounds. They've seen enough of our parties to not get spooked. They come *for* the atmosphere and entertainment. My boys do good to share the bar, keeping mostly to one side, letting the customers have the other. It also keeps club members from tearing into customers if they do something out of ignorance or something as bold as getting handsy with one of their ol' ladies.

With the assistance of William and Ink, Maci and another bike bunny climb atop one of the tables. Hoots and hollers echo around the room as the girls begin to dance. With their short dresses, little strips of fabric peek out between their bare cheeks, giving the men a show of what they're workin' with. To ensure they've aroused every man in the bar, Maci and the other girl end their dance with a tongue-on-tongue kiss. Falling backward, Maci lands in William's waiting arms. Applause breaks out around the room—there's no denying every man enjoyed the show and are probably sporting a semi as proof.

With the liquor glasses and beer bottles flying off the shelves, Jeff looks tired. Thankfully, I've hired some help with Jeff's approval. He chose his sidekick, and so far, the young guy is doing well. No doubt, the women will like him with his messy brown hair, pierced lip, and ink-covered muscled arms, but the way he's been eyeballing my brothers, I'm pretty sure he swings the other way.

Stepping behind the bar, I grab myself a fresh beer while Jeff and Andrew serve the customers. Beyond the bar, I watch the poker game going on at the center table, a mix of club members and customers. That's one thing they all take serious in here—their gambling.

At the table where the girls were dancing, they've taken to grinding on William and Ink. William's hand is beneath Maci's dress, finger fucking her for the whole club to see. They need to get a room before it becomes a full-on porn show with him bending her over the table. Eh, fuck it, I wouldn't mind seeing it. With a swig, I watch the two of them, and sure enough, her dress slips farther up her hips, revealing more of her ass. It's obvious where this is headed, and I'm not surprised. Maci wants to stake her claim on William, and what better way than to ride his dick in front of every chick in here? Only that doesn't mean shit to William. If he wants another pussy, he'll ditch her in a heartbeat. I was wrong when I told Liz that William is like Jake— William is far worse than Jake was back in the day.

With her dress hiked up enough, William drops into a chair. Pulling her onto his lap, he adjusts his jeans, letting his dick out. With her straddling his lap, he hugs her hips tight and pounds her down on him. Those around them, not into their pool, poker, or conversation, have taken notice. At the poker table,

Trevor taps Wesley's arm, and they pause the game to watch Maci ride William.

Pulling Maci's dress off her shoulder, her left breast pops free, and I know that move is for his brothers. He wants to show off what he's got just as much as he wants to give them a peek. Pulling her hair back, William tilts her head as she rides him hard. With a tight grip on her hip, he keeps her rhythm going.

Scarlet hair stands out among the crowd, and my gaze switches to Red. She's walking through the bar within view of William and Maci. Taking a drink of her beer, she stops and watches. She seems to be enjoying the show as much as I am. Gaze dancing past them, her eyes catch mine. Slipping her tongue between her lips, she winks at me, a playful smirk briefly sweeping across her face. My already hardening dick thickens.

William and Maci's bobbing comes to an end, and the clubhouse whistles and cheers. Maci grins like she was just crowned the Queen of Fucktown. With his junk back in his jeans, William stands proudly and slaps her ass. The two lip-lock, and I stop watching as a gut-wrenching ache hits me. I haven't been laid in months, and the relief of Lindsey's blow job has worn off. Part of me regrets telling her to get lost, but I shouldn't. I only wanted her for sex. Dodging the scene, I grab another two beers and head to the back porch to wallow in my sexual self-pity.

Sitting back, I finish my half beer and look out at the horizon, thinking about the one thing that's been frequently on my mind—revenge. Hearing footsteps approaching, I glance up to see who my visitor is. Red is a sight for sore eyes as she comes into my line of vision. With a sexy smile, she takes the seat next to me and doesn't say anything, just joins my quiet contemplation.

Putting a hand on her bare leg, I rub my fingers across her soft skin.

"Coming to check on me?"

"I am. I saw you leave the bar and knew you'd be back here."

"Yeah, got a lot on my mind."

"Want to lessen the burden?"

With a chuckle, I raise my hand and rub along her cheek, showing my appreciation for the offer.

"Can't. Club business."

"I see. Maybe I could lessen it another way."

My hand rests on her thigh, my dick becoming far more alert. I know what she's insinuating. As much as I want to feel her pussy, I can't do that to her. I'd only end up hurting her, and she deserves better. Removing my hand from her leg, I tip my beer back, finishing it off.

"You should go back to the party."

If she's angry, she doesn't show any sign of it. She quietly stands, and I expect her to leave but she doesn't. Stepping in front of me, she removes the empty beer from my hand and places it on the railing. Taking the next one, she pops the top and hands it to me.

"What do you want, Nix? To spend the rest of your life wanting, needing but never having happiness?"

Chugging my beer, I stare up at her beautiful hazel-green eyes. Expression bold and challenging, she fuels my desire for her. In the tight, dark red skirt, her creamy thighs taunt me, antagonizing me even more than her words.

"Happiness is a luxury I can't have. Because of who I am, anyone I care for gets hurt."

Straddling my legs, she sits on my lap. My hand goes to her ass, cupping her against me.

"I'm not asking you to love me. I'm offering to satisfy our needs. I'm a big girl. I don't need you to protect my heart."

Gaze matching hers, my wall breaks down, diminishing into a pile of rubbish. I want this woman—want to feel her clench around me as I fuck her hard and hear her beg for me to make her come—but I know if I do, I'd be setting myself up for disaster.

"Don't think, Nix. Just live."

Soft lips demand me to give in. Tongue slipping between my lips, I taste her, and at that moment, I lose all self-control. A thud sounds as my beer drops to the floor. I don't care if it's pouring all over the place, I need her lips on mine. Fingers tucked under her skirt, I raise the fabric, revealing the part of her my cock aches to be inside of. Rising to my feet, I drop her legs and spin her. Hand on her back, I bend her over and tug her lacy thong down her thighs. With her hands gripping the railing, I unzip my jeans and fold them down, releasing my erection.

Wet, slick heat surrounds me as I thrust into her pussy. Instantly, my body buzzes to life. Thrusting hard and fast, I find my rhythm and sink into ecstasy. Slamming her hips against me, she begs for it harder. Hands tight on her hips, I repeatedly pound into her, forgetting all the pain, feeling nothing but pleasure.

She feels too damn good. I'm about to cum, too soon, but I can't hold back. I need the release. Pulling out, I raise her shirt and cum across her lower back. Looking over her shoulder, the corner of her mouth is raised in a lascivious grin. Squeezing her ass, I grin back. Removing my cut, I lift my black tank off and wipe her back clean before tossing the shirt next to the spilled beer.

Sliding the lace fabric back up her thighs, she lowers her skirt, then turns to face me. With a glance down at my cock, she looks back up at me with a wickedly sexy smile. Hand wrapped in her hair, I lean down and kiss her. The scent of sex and cinnamon fills my nostrils, making the sensation of guilt in my chest tighten. Head to hers, I release a weighted sigh.

"You felt amazing, Synne but we can't do this again."

Zipping my jeans, I grab my leather and walk away, leaving her and the moment of joy I felt with her.

CHAPTER NINE

NIX

WALKING INTO THE FRONT OFFICE, I expected her to have called in sick or at least be angry. I tilt my head at the mug of coffee waiting for me. Lifting it, I watch her type into the computer.

"Morning." Voice low and sexy, the word slips easily from her lips. She doesn't seem pissed off at me, and I'm relieved as much as I'm confused.

"Morning, Red. What do we have today?"

"Three new parts need installed and one repair."

Swiveling on the stool, she turns to face me, and guilt drops into my gut like a heavy anchor. Hazel-green eyes shine bright with no sign of animosity. With the way I left her last night, I was sure there'd be repercussions.

"If you're waiting for me to burst into tears or tell you that you're an asshole, it's not going to happen. Last night was what I expected. I don't need you to cuddle me or whisper sweet nothings into my ear. We're good, Nix. You can relax."

Lowering the mug, I take a moment to absorb her words. Mixed with a combination of guilt and relief, my lip twitches, and I bob my head, accepting what she said.

"All right. I'll take the work orders."

Handing them to me, she winks and gives me a reassuring look.

"I'll be leaving for lunch today. I'm meeting up with Liz."

Papers in hand, I remain still. "You are?"

"Yeah, we wanted to hang out together, and she's filling me in on what to expect at Full Throttle. If I'm not too late, I might enter a race or contest."

Surprise isn't something I should be feeling because I admit, she's a total badass, yet she still manages to surprise me. I like it... too much.

"Need me to give your scoot a lookover?"

The corner of her mouth tilts upward, and I know the answer is yes before she says it.

"You don't mind?"

"Nah, if you're going to Full Throttle representing the Kings, I want to see you succeed. Park it outside the garage when you get back from lunch, and I'll take a look at it."

"You're all right, Nix."

With a wink shot my direction, I chuckle at how easy it is to like her.

"Later, Red."

—SYNNE—

It's perfect timing when Liz pulls up in her Camaro. My stomach started growling a couple of minutes ago. Putting away the invoice in front of me, I greet her when she walks in the door.

"You ready?" Dark brown hair pulled up in some kind of fancy twist bun, her smile is wide, brightening those same green eyes as Nix's.

"Yeah, let me tell Nix we're heading out."

With a wave of her hand, she heads toward the garage. "I'll tell him." She disappears through the door, leaving it slightly ajar, their voices a murmur through the opening. When I hear my name, I move closer.

"I'm glad you invited her to Full Throttle. She staying with you in the camper?"

"I was gonna ask her to."

"That'll be good. It'll make me feel better to know you're both sleeping there."

"Do you like her?"

"She does a good job. I'm glad you hired her."

"You know what I mean."

"She's a gorgeous redhead, Liz. What do you think the Royals will assume? Just being around me makes her a target. Short of telling her to get lost, the best thing I can do is keep my distance."

I can hear the anger in his tone. Not at Liz, but at something far deeper I'm beginning to understand.

"I'm sorry." Emotion breaks through her voice.

Tone softening, Nix's voice lowers. "You have nothing to be sorry for. It was my decisions, my fault we lost her."

"You shouldn't believe that. The blood war with the Royals started long before us."

"Yeah. Get going. Don't waste your lunch talking to me about this shit."

"I love you, Nix. You know how much, right?"

"As much as I love you. Now, get out of here. I have work to do."

Liz pops back through the door, a somber expression on her face. When she looks at me, her expression morphs with her thoughts.

"Let's get some food."

Parking along the street, she brings me to a Mexican restaurant, stuffed between several shops attached together in one long brick building. Hole-in-the-wall restaurants are something we both love. You can't beat the service and food in these small businesses. Finding an empty booth, we slide in and give the waiter our drink orders. When they arrive, we rattle off our food orders.

"When the Kings go to Full Throttle, I drive Nix's truck and take the camper. The guys stay in tents around the camper, but you don't have to do that. You can stay in the camper with me."

"I'm good with that."

"Great! You'll be glad you did. If you stay in a tent, you'll hear nothing but grunting and fucking all night."

Laughter escapes my chest, and Liz laughs along with me.

"You think I'm joking. Seriously, it's as much a fuck fest as it is anything else at bike week."

"I believe it and appreciate the bed of comfort. What else do I need to know?"

"It's a giant outdoor motorcycle and music festival. There's cool stuff to buy, food vendors, concerts, contests, stunts, races, and long roads for motorcycle rides. There are a few options, depending on how long a ride you want. If you go online, they have the maps and distance of each ride. I'll text you the link to sign up for the events."

"Thanks. Do you know what rides or events Nix is joining?"

Our conversation pauses as our food is delivered, the cast-iron dish sizzling with heat, filling the air with the aroma of fajita meat and vegetables. Liz continues as she preps her fajita shell with rice.

"Yeah, he and several other Kings are doing a couple of the rides. He'll be putting his motorcycle in the badass bike contest. He also sets up a tent at the event for the shop, and I help run it. He gets a lot of his custom business that way. I'm sure Nix hasn't asked because it's your first time going, but would you mind helping me work the tent during some of the event? I don't want you to miss out on any activities, but it would be good for you to learn what needs to be done."

"Of course. I'm in. It'll be nice to hang with you."

After a few bites in, I pull her attention from the food.

"I want to be honest with you about something. You've been a great friend, and I want to continue our friendship, so I feel like I need to come clean about something. You asked me to stay clear of Nix, but I didn't. We fucked."

The expression I expected forms her face with shock.

"What? When?"

"Friday night. Party at the clubhouse. Are you pissed?"

"No, just surprised. Do you like him?"

"I care about him, yeah. I think we're both coming from a broken place and get that about each other. I'm not trying to become Nix's ol' lady, just to be clear. The sexual tension between us was out of control, so I... you know... released it."

Liz's head falls back as she laughs.

"No, I get it. I'm not mad. Just... there's something about Nix you need to know. He's a badass biker on the outside, but inside, his emotions run deep. He's a one-woman kind of guy, and once he has feelings, he's loyal. So be careful. Don't dip in that pool if you're not looking for something serious."

"Maybe serious is exactly what Nix doesn't need."

The fajita stops on the way to her mouth.

"Maybe you're right, but as his one and only sister, it's my job to tell you, don't fuck with my brother's emotions, or I'll kick your ass."

Her mouth quirks into a smile. She's being playful, but beneath that, I know she's dead serious, and I wouldn't put it past her to try.

"I won't."

Liz accepts my honest statement, and we get back to our food. I finish another taco smothering it with more pico de gallo.

"Can I ask you something?"

"Yeah," Liz nods.

Lowering my voice, I ask, "Nix's ex, your best friend... was she killed by the Royals?"

Sorrow fills Liz's eyes. "She was. They came to Nix's house to hurt him, maybe kill him. She took one of the bullets and died in Nix's arms."

"Shit, Liz, that's horrible. It's why he's worried about me being around him, isn't it?"

"You heard us, huh?"

"Yeah, I overheard. It makes sense why he told me the job was filled."

"He lives with a lot of guilt and doesn't want anyone else he cares about getting hurt."

I know there's so much more she isn't sharing, but I get it. I'm new to the Kings. Trust is earned, and I've already told her I didn't respect her request to stay away from Nix. With the conversation getting tense, it's obvious Liz needs to escape it. With a subject change, she vents about work, and we make arrangements to go shopping before bike week.

Back at the shop, I wave goodbye to her and pull my Harley keys out of my pocket. Nix's attention is drawn to me as I drive it up to the garage.

Wiping his hands on a rag, he tosses it on a toolbox, and approaches my Harley. Taking the handlebars in his grip, he pushes it into the garage. The tightening of his back and shoulder muscles steal my gaze, and I quickly look away as my body reacts.

"I'll do a full maintenance check, make sure everything is running the way it should. You have a good lunch?"

"We did. Full Throttle sounds like a shit ton of fun. I'm glad y'all are letting me tag along."

"You'll have a good time. Just avoid back patches that say Wild Royals. Can you do that for me?"

"I can, and I will."

"Thanks." Tilting his head, he gestures to the office. "A call came in earlier, so I need to get to work. Come by the clubhouse tonight at seven. We're gonna make plans for Full Throttle."

"Okay, will do. I told Liz I'd help her with your vendor tent. Are you good with that?"

"I am." Full lips turn up in a smile, lightening his green eyes. "I appreciate the help."

Nix's gaze lingers on me as I walk to the office door. When I look over my shoulder, he's returned to work.

My legs still and I watch him. With a black tank on, the hard muscles of his back, shoulders, and arms stand out, flexing with his movements. A side profile of his face shows off his square jaw and the scruff that lines it. The memory of how good his thick cock felt heats between my legs. My body tingles, hungry for more of him. As I watch him, the ache between my legs strengthens. Before I give in and do something I shouldn't, I peel my gaze from him and hurry back to the office.

CHAPTER TEN

NIX

LIZ AND TREVOR'S GIRL, Audrey enter the clubhouse
with several boxes of wings and pizza. The guys lick
their lips and watch the food get set out on the empty
table next to us. Making two lines on each side of the
table, the Kings and their ol' ladies fill their plates. Jeff
sets six buckets of beer on the table, and I hand him the
plate I just prepared.

"Join us."

The wrinkles around the old man's eyes crease, and
he looks at me with appreciation before taking the
plate.

"Thank you, Nix."

Walking to one of the tables, he fills an empty seat.
Ink puts his plate in front of me.

"Here, Pres, take mine."

Trevor, Ink's sponsor, nods his head at him proudly.

"Thanks, brother." Patting him on the shoulder, I

take the plate with my free hand and settle at the table. My family fills the seats around me, and the room quickly hums with the sound of their voices. Listening, I enjoy the talk about the good things going on in their lives and their enthusiasm for bike week. Times like this are the next best thing to riding my Harley and burying my cock in pussy.

Gaze rising at the sight of scarlet hair, I watch Red enter and observe the way she's welcomed by everyone. Filling a plate, she takes a seat next to Audrey. Looking up, she smiles at me, and I wink before returning the gesture. Her attention returns to her food and the women around her. Jake catches me staring at her and studies me. I know that will lead to a conversation later —a conversation I don't want to have.

Sitting back in the chair, I drop the chicken wing and wipe the sauce from my fingers. Max sees my intent and lowers his food.

"Listen up! Pres has something to say."

The room quiets.

"We leave for Full Throttle on Thursday. By now, your Harleys damn well better be road ready and all your event applications in. We're staying at camp lot thirty-three. The journey rides have been coordinated by Axel. If you got any questions, he'll take care of it. Liz will be managing the Custom Ride tent with the help of William and Synne. My reaper will be set up at the tent except when it's in the badass bike show. Ladies"—my attention centers on Maci—"if you enter any bikini or dance contests, keep it classy for your ol' man. We don't want any fights breaking out."

Maci snickers and adds an eye roll for effect. A couple of brothers chuckle and a smirk tugs at my lips before my gaze sweeps my members.

"Kings, respect our patch and the patches of other clubs. Never leave a brother alone. If a brother gets piss-ass drunk, help him back to camp and make sure he doesn't start any fights on the way there. If you get arrested, call Jake, and we'll get you bailed out as soon as we can. And the most important, brothers... ride hard or stay the fuck home."

Hoots, cheers, and fists pounding the table tell me they're ready for shit to get wild. The chatter of their voices rise, and we get back to enjoying each other's company and our food. I'm busy talking to Dom about the events I want him to see when Jake calls my name, his tone anxious.

My attention turns to him, and he tilts his head toward the front door of the clubhouse. As quickly as I see my ex, Angela, standing in front of the door, I see Liz charging toward her.

"What the hell do you think you're doing coming in here?"

Jake is out of his seat, rushing to Liz's side.

Angela throws up her hands. "I don't want any trouble, Liz."

"Get the fuck out! You're not welcome!"

"What the fuck does she want now?" I growl. The

wooden chair scrapes the floor beneath me as I rise from my seat.

"Handle it, brother," I hear Max say behind me. "Before Liz gouges her eyes out."

"Baby, leave her in one piece, at least until Nix hears what she has to say."

"I don't give a shit what she has to say. Take your skank ass back out the door before I shove you out!"

"She's right. You're not welcome in the Kings clubhouse." Standing next to Liz, I brush my hand over her shoulder, calming her. Jake already has a hand around her waist, in case he has to hold her back from clawing at Angela's face. "I don't care what you have to say or what trouble you're in. You need to leave, *now*."

"Fine, I'll go," she drags out with frustration. Turning away from us, she stretches her arm out for the door. Before opening it, she looks back. "I'm not with Rex anymore. I want you to know that."

Liz steps forward. "Out!"

Angela jumps at Liz's bark, her reaction taking me by surprise. Angela was always confident, tough, one to give back what she got. Seeing her cower is an indication Rex beat it out of her.

Liz seems to sense the same thing I do, and her shoulders lower. The caring nurse in her switches on. She steps toward Angela to stop her, but Angela slips out, and Liz's hand drops.

"Maybe I should go after her."

Jake pulls her to him. "No, you shouldn't. I don't want you anywhere near her."

"He's right." I stare down at my baby sister, meeting her gaze of mixed emotions. "She brings nothing but trouble. The kind I don't want you or any Kings near."

With his arms around Liz, Jake kisses her cheek. "Let it go, Peach. We have Liam to think about."

Hearing that settles her. Returning to the table, Synne reaches out and touches Liz's arm.

"You okay?"

Liz shakes her head and takes the seat next to Synne. Audrey scoots Liz's plate over to her, and she puts up her hand, shaking her head no. She's lost her appetite, and I understand why. Angela brings back a lot of bad memories for all of us.

Stepping closer, Jake lowers his voice. "What do you think she wanted?"

"Who the hell knows? She either had information to share or wanted a hideout. Either way, we're not getting involved. She'll only bring us problems and fuck up the plans we have."

"She probably knows the answer we need."

"Probably, but we're not getting it from her."

"No, we're not," Jake agrees.

Patting him on the back, I gesture toward the table. "Let's get back to dinner. We'll talk more after the women leave."

The club members know not to ask questions yet.

Once the women clean up and head home, we enter the privacy of the courtroom.

Wesley lights a cigar and leans back in his chair. Looking at me, he speaks up first. "Any idea why Angela came to visit?"

"I don't, and every reason I come up with isn't good for the club. She says she's not with Rex anymore. She likely wanted a safe place to stay or had information she thought she could give in exchange for something. I have no doubt Rex put a tail on her. We can't be seen associating with her. Her coming here tonight puts us at risk if they're watching her."

Tipping his beer back, Trevor is deep in thought. "You think we should continue with our plans?"

"I do."

Axel, my road captain, sets his phone on the table and points to it. "My resource came through. He's waiting on my call for pickup. Guns, explosives, all of it."

"Call him. We move forward." My gaze lands on each club member. "I need all of you tonight. Dom, Ink, you too."

Dom raps the table. "I'm in."

Ink nods in agreement. "I'm in too, brother."

THE SOUND of seven Harleys and a pickup truck rumble down the dark, desolate road. It's two in the morning, and all the nine-to-fivers are sound asleep in their beds. Leaving town, we cruise down the freeway into the commercial district, warehouses and parking lots taking the place of cozy homes. Given directions by the seller, we turn onto an unlit road, then another before reaching a fenced parking lot. On the other side is a black van. Two men in dark work uniforms open the gate for us.

Entering the parking lot, I take notice of the moving trucks. It seems like an obvious way to transport illegal items. I guess obvious isn't that obvious. Axel steps off his Harley and approaches a man in black slacks and a black button-up shirt, a firearm attached to his hip, visible for us to see.

"Axel?"

"Mr. Galloni?"

Both men nod and shake hands. Axel points to me.

"My president, Nix."

Shaking the man's hand, I take note of his confident stature and strong grip. Brown intelligent eyes look me over.

"Thank you for your business, Nix." Pointing to the van behind him, he gestures for me to follow. "I have the goods you requested if you'd like to examine them."

"I would. Thank you."

Following him, Axel and Max flank each side of me, and the rest of my crew watch the other men and our surroundings.

Two of Galloni's men open the van doors and step

inside, using a crowbar to open one of the boxes. As I step into the van, Axel and Max place their hands on their guns and watch Galloni's men closely. Looking inside, I examine the firearms and explosives. Taking a Glock out, I inspect the weapon, insert a magazine, and rack the gun. With operations intact, I drop the magazine and lower it back into the box. With everything we ordered accounted for, I step down from the van. The two men close up the box behind me.

"If your men are ready, we can transport the goods from our vehicle to yours," Galloni tells me.

"I appreciate your business and your confidentiality." Pointing behind him, Max holds out a bag. One of Galloni's men takes the bag, places it on the ground, checking the contents.

"There's more than requested," the man tells his boss.

Galloni looks to me for an explanation.

"There's extra compensation to forget this transaction ever happened."

Galloni's lip curls into a satisfied smile. "Pleasure doing business with you, Nix. If you're ever in need of my services again, I'll do my best to accommodate you."

"I'll keep your number."

Behind us, his men load the large box into our truck trailer. With my Custom Ride trailer, it won't look unusual to have seven riders alongside it. To the law, we're a bunch of bikers traveling to an event. Back at the clubhouse, we're quick to unload the equipment and reload it into our gear for bike week. Once we're finished, I approach Dominic, who's sitting atop his bike finishing a text. He pockets the phone and gives me his attention.

"You good with your role in this?"

Leaning back on the seat, he relaxes his arms over his chest.

"It isn't a secret anymore in the club that I come with a certain set of skills. You chose the right man for the job."

Reaching out, I tap his shoulder.

"We've already voted. You're in. By the end of the week, you'll have a member patch to replace this prospect one."

The corner of his mouth pulls back.

"I'll wear it with honor."

"I know you will. It's good to have you and Erika here with us."

Dominic dips his chin.

"I appreciate you welcoming us in."

"It's where you both belong. Now, get your ass home to that sweet woman."

Dominic fires up the engine of his ride, taking off into the dark, quiet night while I climb atop mine. Behind me, my club officers follow me home, ensuring my back is covered before they travel home.

CHAPTER ELEVEN

NIX

ROLLING into the outskirts of Full Throttle, we find and set up our camp. There's an excited buzz in the air from the sounds of revving engines, music, and the scent of fried food, luring us to the main drag. Not wasting any time, Liz hops into my truck, and we lead the Custom Ride trailer through the back entrance, waving our blue vendor badge in the air as we pass the staff security. We stop at our location, the grass painted in yellow with our corresponding vendor number. My crew is quick to help me get the tent, banner, table, gear, and brochures set up while Jake and Max help me roll out the Reaper.

She's my bike baby—hours of meticulous labor installing specialty parts and a killer paint job. Along the sleek curves of chrome is a black background beneath smoke gray art, depicting a death reaper with its sharp, steel scythe. Every other part that's not sparkling chrome is stacked skulls with chains interconnecting their hollow eyes and mouths.

She's a looker and draws the attention of many fellow bikers and has won me a good amount of money in past contests, which I hope she will again this week. Running a microfiber rag over her curves, ensuring there are no fingerprints or smudges, I stand back, admiring her beauty.

Synne approaches and draws my eyes. In tiny leather shorts, black chaps, a little black T-shirt with frayed shoulders, and her wild red hair flowing down over the sides of her full tits, I forget about my Reaper—because the only thing doing any thinking is my cock. It's getting thick as my eyes drink her in and follow the lines of her lower abdomen down to the V-shape between her thighs. Without a property jacket, she's going to draw attention—there's no fucking doubt—and that irritates me, whether I like it or not.

"She's smokin' hot," she purrs, her eyes coveting my ride. "You definitely have a chance of winning the badass bike competition."

"That she is." I'm staring at her and the curve of her back as she bends over to admire the details of the paint job... and fuck me, I'm not talking about the bike.

She stands and catches me staring. With the curve of her full lips, she dips her chin and follows it with a flirtatious wink. Chuckling, I tuck the rag into the back pocket of my jeans.

"I'm getting a beer. You want one?"

"Of course."

"Walk with me. I'll show ya around."

Tipping my head at Liz and Jake, I let them know I'll be back soon. The rest of my crew is pairing up to walk around and enjoy the activities. My prospect, Ink and old Wesley join me and Synne, ensuring my back's protected. Putting my hand on the lower part of her back, I lead her to the beer tent where they're tossing out koozies. We take a couple and slide them onto our beers. Leaving the tent, we pass a station where biker bunnies are in bikinis, offering free bike washes. Ignoring the jiggling tits headed my direction, I glance back at Ink, who's enjoying the view, telling them he'll be back around later.

We walk to the main drag, lined with hundreds of Harleys in all shapes, sizes, and colors—a biker's paradise. Walking the stretch, we meander slowly, checking out the chrome lineup. Synne's eyes expand, and I get a kick out of her hot ass showing so much enthusiasm. The woman's a biker's dream—gorgeous wrapped in leather and lace, badass, sassy, sweet, and has a passionate love for chrome.

Across the motorcycle row, I catch the familiar patch of the Wild Royals. Two of them, toting beers, with biker bunnies hanging on their arms in their lingerie outfits and overconfident expressions. My thoughts of Synne are swept away in an instant, the reminder of why I can't be happy digging its claws into that coffin of longing I have buried deep. Shoving her into Ink's arms, I nod my head toward the Wild Royals. Ink picks up my message and shoves his tongue into her mouth just as the Wild Royal members look our direction.

Swigging back my beer, I keep my gaze deadlocked on them. The shorter guy raises his hand and flicks me off. Inside, my rage boils, that song of vengeance a melody in my head and heart. Synne shoves Ink off her.

"What the fuck? I thought I'd made myself clear?"

She wipes her mouth, and I move in behind her, leaning into her ear.

"It was for show. Sorry."

Walking away from her, I feel the guilt swelling in my gut, but I'd rather her be upset than dead.

Back at our vendor tent, I bury all my aggravating emotions with a couple more beers and get a comfortable buzz going as the sun warms the air. Sticking around the tent, I answer questions from potential clients and smile proudly at Liz and William as they help talk up the shop and my work. Synne arrives back at the tent with food for all of us. Pulling Ink aside, I put my hand on his shoulder and speak privately.

"I want you to keep an eye on Red when she's not with us."

"Done. Who's gonna watch your back?"

I tilt my head to Max.

"He's got me covered. Thanks, brother."

"No worries."

Ink, who got his name from the intricate black art covering most of his skin, turns on his heel and sits back in a chair, casually drinking a beer as he waits for Synne to pass around the hotdogs and sandwiches.

Jake takes up post next to me, keeping a protective eye on Liz and the group.

"Ran into the Royals already," I tell him.

"Any altercations?"

"Nah, they were on the other side of bike row. I had to shove Red into Ink's arms. The last thing I want is for them to think she's with me."

Jake angles his head, passing an empathetic expression my direction.

"I get it." Tipping his beer back, he finishes it. "Soon, brother, soon."

Later in the afternoon are the women's motorcycle races. My crew helps me put Reaper in the trailer and prep the tent for our absence. None of us want to miss Synne performing in this race as she's the first female to represent the Kings. We gather in a group on the wooden bleachers, leaning back with beers in our hands and our boots resting on the benches in front of us as the races start up. The first two women line up, one red bike, one white. One chick is covered in all red leather while the other is in white and light jeans. Surely, the race staff set it up that way. Some sort of angel verse devil concept. The bikes take off, and the red devil takes the lead and flies through the finish. As the crowd goes wild, I can't help thinking the first race was set up for dramatic flair.

Two more races are completed before the recognizable green motorcycle and red hair rolls out. Our crew hoots and hollers their support. Revving her engine, Synne acknowledges it. A moment later, the flag drops, and she and her competitor leave dust in the wind. She finishes first, and several of us stand, shouting our praise.

All the winners move onto the next phase. Synne keeps taking the win until it gets down to four riders. She wins again, and it's down to her and the red devil. The Kings are wild with excitement, eager to see her take the final win. My fist tightens around my beer bottle as I watch intently. She glances our direction, dips her chin, then focuses on the raceway. The flag drops, and she and the red devil take off. They're neck-to-neck for most of it, and I'm worried the red devil is holding back, about to take the lead, except it's the opposite. Synne speeds forward and rides over the finish line, her fist in the air.

"Fuck, yes." I stand and whistle, and my crew are just as thrilled. Leaving the bleachers, we work our way down to the raceway. When we reach her, she's getting photos taken and given an award. With the photos finished, she moves into our circle, receiving pats on the back.

Stepping up to me, she places her hands on either side of my face and kisses me, the energy of the race coming through her kiss like electricity. Between those lust-filled currents and my buzz, everything's a blur around me. Squeezing her ass, I tug her against my body, my cock thickening as she pushes against the length of it.

The Kings catcall, their energy a circle around us, provoking us, feeding the electricity between the two of us. Pulling back, my lids feel hooded, my cock stretched and craving the feel of her. She turns around, pushing her barely covered ass into my dick, and wraps my arm around her. Leaving it there, I take a swig and lead my crew back to the festival, looking down at her with newfound pride.

Among the crowds of leather cuts and patches, my mind finds its way back to the cage it lives in. Removing my arm from her shoulder, I put distance between us. She notices but doesn't make a fuss. Joining up with Liz, Audrey, Erika, and Maci, the five of them veer off in the direction of the women's vendor tents. Jake and I glance at each other and lead the crew in the same direction, keeping a close eye on our women. We keep a comfortable distance, bullshitting and talking chrome as they shop.

A few patchless riders pass by the women, their eyes glued to their asses. One stops, puts an arm around Erika, and gets way too damn close. Dominic expands several inches, making his already massive frame look like the hulk. He moves in, bloodshed shining in his eyes. Jake puts an arm up, stopping him.

"Nah, brother. I got this."

Jake, Trevor, and William clear a path right to our women. Pulling the biker off Erika, Jake gets in his face. The guy glances at the patch and puts his hands up.

"I'm sorry, man. We didn't see property jackets."

Jake motions his head, indicating the bikers need to get moving. Erika comes over to Dominic, and it's only after she's back in his arms, he calms down.

"The rest of the time we're here, I want you in either a property shirt or jacket," he tells her. She caresses his face, and he stares down at her, his eyes transitioning from the darkness I witnessed to a softness he only has for her.

"Not a problem," she coos, kissing him with unabashed desire.

Watching the two creates envy in me. She looks at Dominic the way Jenna looked at me, with unconditional love, and it causes my chest to ache.

"That goes for all of you," Jake orders the women. "As the party goes on, the men will be looking for available pussy. You need to make it clear you're not available."

Synne glances at me. She's the only woman in our group without a jacket, and I'm irritatingly aware. I pull my gaze from hers and take a swig of my beer as the group moves on.

Music draws us to the concert stadium, and we

create a space for our crew to drink and dance. Maci gets it going, pulling William into the middle of our circle and grinds her body against his. Pulling her ass against his dick, he practically dry fucks her there in front of all of us, without a care. Jake and Liz join in, Liz's arms around his neck, moving with the music as she sways her hips for him. The other two couples join them, and I'm standing on the outside of the circle enjoying the music and my nearly empty beer. That is until a couple of patch members from another MC put their hands on Synne. My muscles tense and I move their direction, but she already has it handled. She's turned them down and is motioning toward our group. Moving into our circle, she flashes me an upturned salacious grin as she sways her hips. Her body calls to me, and my feet respond, moving into her space. With her back to my chest, I put an arm around her waist, squeezing her hip as she lifts her hands, placing them around my neck and rubs her ass against me.

"You keep teasing me." I feather along her ear, biting it, and she pushes her ass harder into my cock, and the traitor reacts, hardening against her cheeks. "You need to stop."

"Do you really want me to?"

She turns to face me, her gaze enticing, her lips parting, teasing mine. Squeezing her ass hard, I watch her eyes widen as she bites into her lip. She likes it. Fuck me.

"What I want doesn't matter. You're not safe around me."

Brows dipping in thought, she studies me, questions written all over her face.

"Why do you think that?"

Dropping my hand, I put space between us as the memories strike at me, tearing open old wounds.

"Keep your distance from me while we're here."

Frustration burrows into my chest as I walk away from her. Looking down at my empty beer, I chuck it into a trashcan on the way back to camp. Wesley, Max, and Axel follow behind while the rest stay and dance.

Dropping my fourth empty bottle on the ground next to the others, I stare into the campfire, its orange flames performing a dance. As the sun goes down, I imagine Synne swaying her hips to the music, tantalizing every single biker in her proximity. Kicking my boot at a log, I chuck it farther into the flames and grab another beer to continue my descent into emotionless oblivion.

In the distance, I see several figures enter camp. The rest of the crew has returned, drunk and boisterous. Jake palms Liz's ass and ushers her into the camper. Synne glances at me, disguises a frown by looking away, and follows them in. Ink has his arm around a giggling, busty brunette and leads her into his tent. With everyone entering their tents to sleep or fuck, Axel and I are the only ones left sitting around the fire.

"You look tense, Pres. What's on your mind?"

Rubbing a hand over my stubble, I glance at his questioning gaze, then back to the fire.

"It's late. Let's do a walk around camp, then call it a night."

"All right."

Standing, my knees are wobblier than expected, but I shake it off, joining Axel to make our rounds. With the whole crew accounted for, I crawl into my tent and collapse onto my sleeping bag, the weight of sleep tickling the edges of my eyelids. Closing them, I listen to the crackling of the dying fire and imagine red hair falling around me. Drifting off, I give in to the relief the alcohol has given me from my hurricane of emotions and slip into that blissful oblivion.

The sound of my tent zipper snaps me awake. Grabbing my Glock, I aim it at the zipper and wait. Red hair is the first thing I see, and I immediately lower my gun, switch the safety on, and tuck it under the edge of the sleeping bag. Synne crawls in and zips the tent closed.

"What are you doing here?"

"I can't sleep with Jake and Liz grunting and moaning so damn much."

With a chuckle, I move over, giving her room to lie down. Lying on her side, her cleavage is plump and visible in her tiny, silky nightshirt. My gaze drops to her creamy skin, and I turn onto my back, trying to avoid the reaction my dick will have if I don't stop looking at her body.

"You shouldn't be in here." It comes out as more of a growl than I meant it to. Rubbing my thumb on my temple, I work at the headache forming.

"All right. I'll sleep in the truck."

There's disappointment in her tone, and I hate that it's because of me. She sits up, and my hand reaches out and takes hold of her forearm. She lies back down, slowly putting her hand on my chest between the opening of my cut. Lifting my tank, she caresses my abs, and I lie there, eyes closed, indulging in it. Her finger toys with the edge of my jeans, and I look at her, seeing desire flash in her eyes.

Sitting up, I put my hand through her hair and bring her lips to mine, craving that electricity that burned away the memories and pain earlier today. As she moans into my mouth, I take the kiss deeper and palm one of her luscious tits. Thumbing the nipple, I flick my thumb back-and-forth, feeling it harden beneath my finger. Moving down her stomach, I find the waist of her shorts and slip my hand down under them. My finger slides into her wet opening, and with a couple strokes of my finger, I'm adding another, pushing deeper, working that sensitive swell that turns her from moaning to tearing at my clothes. Helping her, I remove my cut, boots, tank, jeans, and briefs as she wiggles out of her shorts and tank. With my cock hard and pointing toward the sky, she lowers herself, wrapping her mouth around it. Looking down at her, I fist her hair, pumping my cock farther into her mouth.

Not wanting to cum without feeling her pussy, I pull her off and lean forward, grabbing her body to bring her on top of me. With her hand wrapped around my length, she raises her hips and slides onto my dick, her tight pussy a vise grip, working to squeeze the cum right out of my hard, fucking shaft.

Her hips rock forward as I grip them, slamming my dick into her, over and over, the sensation giving me the reprieve my mind and heart desperately need. Flipping her over, I push her back down with her ass up, spread her cheeks and slide into her soaking wet pussy. With my hands wrapped around her hips, I use them as leverage and fuck her hard, her ass slapping against my pelvis as she cries out in sync with each of my thrusts.

She reaches her climax, and her pussy gets slicker, clenching around my dick. With each thrust, she brings me closer to mine. Pulling out, I cum all over her ass and take a moment to admire her naked body, my cum marking her creamy skin, and her sexy satisfied smile looking over her shoulder at me.

Grabbing my tank, I clean her off, then toss it in the corner. Lying on my back, I open my arm for her, and she lies on it, her half-tilted smile sleepy and sexy.

"Why are you afraid of something happening to me?" she asks quietly, so low, I almost miss the words.

"It's complicated."

Sitting up, she stares down at me, her pretty red hair falling over her shoulder. Twirling it around my finger, I follow the strands, caressing her soft skin.

"I'm pretty sure I've put most of the pieces together, but I'd rather hear it from you."

My finger traces the curve of her breast, and I like seeing the spark in her eyes as she reacts to my touch.

"I've made a lot of mistakes, and those mistakes have caused the people I love to get hurt. I don't want anyone else I care about to get hurt."

She reads my eyes, and there's a subtle twitch around hers as if she can sense my pain.

"What happened?"

Lowering my hand, there's a long silence between us as I struggle to say the words.

"The woman I loved was shot by my enemies, the bullet meant for me. She died in my arms."

She takes my hand, raising it to her lips, and kisses it. The gesture surprises me, the subtle affection causing something in my chest to split, a crack of light pouring out through my dark depths of despair.

My thumb caresses her bottom lip, and she sucks it into her mouth, letting it slide out with a quiet pop. Sitting up, I comb my fingers through her hair before gripping her neck, bringing her close to me, her hazel eyes barely visible from the campfire light, yet I can still see the fierce desire in them. She's too damn brave, too beautiful, too tempting.

"I don't want to see you get hurt." There's an ache swelling in my chest, a massive wave of despair crashing into that foolish shell of hope. "The only way that can happen is if you stay away from me."

Gently, I turn her gaze away from me—I can't bear to see her disappointment, can't bear to see my pain reflecting in her eyes. She doesn't leave, and I grit my teeth.

"Synne—"

She cuts off my words with her finger to my lips.

"I lost my brothers. One to prison, the other to a bullet. I understand the damage caused by rivalries and revenge." A deep sadness takes over her body, her shoulders slumping slightly, the memories casting shadows in her eyes.

"What happened to them?"

"I'd been a part of the Sinister Sons my whole life. The club and my brothers raised me. If not for them, I don't know where I'd be or if I'd still be alive." Taking her arm, I lower us back down and pull the sleeping bag over her as she continues. "When I was seventeen, I was at a party, just being a stupid teenager, you know. There was a guy in my class I had a crush on. He was the attractive bad boy type with a muscle car and a cigarette hanging out of his mouth. Only I was too naïve to realize how much of an asshole he was. At the party, he and his two friends made sure I got good and drunk, then lured me into a room alone with them. They tried to rape me, but my older brother, Jay was at the party and thankfully, came looking for me. He got me out of there and came back with our older brother, Seth, and a few Sinister Son members. They beat the shit out of those guys so badly they put them in the hospital. My brothers weren't even charged with anything. It was all handled by the club.

"Seth was a patch member at twenty-three, and at eighteen, Jay was a hang-around and already hooked. I fell in right along with them but could never be a patch member because I was a chick. They were still my family though, and one of the members, Skip, my father's best friend, took to looking out for us after our father ended up in prison. But even before that, the three of us looked out for one another fiercely.

"Unfortunately, Brandon and his friends never forgot about that night, especially since Brandon was left with an ugly scar from his lip halfway up his cheek. At a senior graduation party, I was getting drunk and high around a bonfire with the rest of my classmates while Brandon was planning his revenge. He waited for the right opportunity to get me alone, then he and his two friends dragged me farther into the woods and beat me, breaking my wrist and a couple of ribs, then left me there, spitting up my own blood. Through my tears, I called my brother Jay and he and Seth came to my rescue. They lost their shit after that. Both being patch members, they gathered a few more club members and hunted down Brandon and his friends at a house party in town. I wish they hadn't. Everything changed after that night.

"While I was in the hospital, my brothers raided the house, and all hell broke loose. My brother Jay was shot by one of Brandon's friends who was high and didn't know what the hell he was doing with a loaded gun. Seth fired back and shot the guy. My brother died that night."

Tears pool in her eyes before one escapes, trickling slowly down her cheek. She wipes it away and takes a long, deep breath.

"Seth went to jail for assault with a deadly weapon. Got out three years later, only to go back two years later for illegal possession of a weapon and drugs. He's never been the same since Jay's death, and jail has become a revolving door for him. The sad truth is, I lost both my brothers that night."

Leaning toward her, I caress her cheek, following the smooth line of her jaw, and lift her chin to me so I can kiss away the sorrow. When I pull back, she stares up at me, her eyes a little less tearful, the curve of her mouth tugging at her lip before it falters.

"I still carry the guilt of what happened that night. I spent years obsessing over how if I'd done things differently, if I hadn't been at the senior party, Jay would still be alive, and Seth wouldn't be so messed up, but it was Skip who set me straight. He told me if I'm not dead, then I'm living, and I need to make it mean something. So, I did. I made the decision to stop feeling guilty about being alive, about wanting things for myself, and I started living."

Pulling my arm from around her, I sit up, my jaw tight as my guilt, anger, and frustration descend on me like a sudden downpour of rain on a sunny day.

"It's not that simple for me. For me to live, to have any kind of happiness, means putting others in danger. Being around me puts *you* in danger."

"Because I'm a redhead like she was?"

Avoiding those intense hazel eyes, I stare at the scuffs and dirt on my boots instead.

"Yes. The Wild Royals would hurt you to get to me." Turning to her, I fist her hair in my hand, tilting her head back, putting her lips inches from mine. "Because of this gorgeous red hair, this beautiful face, they'll assume you mean something to me. They'll think you're a tool to tear me apart."

Brows curving down, she stares at me, confusion filling her eyes.

"Why does it matter that I have red hair like hers?"

Opening my fist, I break contact. Reaching for my briefs, anger surges through my chest like lightning clawing through clouds in a darkened sky.

"Her name was Jenna. And before that, Angela. Both red hair. You're a walking target, and *you need to stay away from me*."

Grabbing her tank and shorts, I toss them in her lap.

"Jake and Liz should be asleep by now. Go back to the camper."

As disappointment fills her eyes, she crumples up the clothes in her fist and unzips the tent, walking out butt-ass naked. The colorful ink of her tattoos wrap around her right shoulder, arm, and down her ribs with the tail feathers of a phoenix touching the top of her ass. If I wasn't so angry, so disappointed in myself, I'd be enjoying that view far more, but I can't. I was weak, giving in to what my cock wanted and not thinking enough of what a mistake it was. I can't let her get close, can't have feelings for someone as incredible as Synne. I couldn't survive losing her too.

CHAPTER TWELVE

SYNNE

"So, your brother has a thing for redheads?"

Liz's brow creases as she hands me another stack of brochures. Pulling off the rubber band, I fan them out on the table in front of us. Liz glances over her shoulder, and we both look at Nix, who is trying to cure his hangover with another beer. All morning, he's been withdrawn, his posture slack.

Glancing our direction, he gives us a brooding glare, tips his beer back, then walks off with Max and Axel. With that attitude, it's better he's not at the tent. He's liable to scare off customers.

"Yeah, he does. I know you left the camper last night, and now he's walking around like a wounded animal. Care to explain?"

Liz is working a mom-pose with her hand on her hip, her brow raised, and a distinct air of expectation.

"We fucked, talked, and it got emotional."

"How emotional?"

"Emotional enough, he kicked me out of his tent and told me to stay away from him."

Liz runs a hand over her forehead and into her hair, letting out a puff of air.

"Jesus, he's got it bad for you. How do you feel about him?"

"I thought we needed the company and to get the sexual tension between us out of our system." I grab another stack of brochures and yank the rubber band off. "Now, I can't get your brother out of *my* system."

Liz laughs, squats down, closes the cardboard box between us, and shoves it under the table.

"You're hooked."

"Doesn't matter. He's right. It's best I steer clear of him. He told me I'm a target with the Wild Royals and why." Twisting a strand of red hair around my finger, I flick it into the air.

Liz's mouth turns down, sadness etching into the frown lines of her face.

"He has a legitimate reason to be worried about you. He's attracted to redheads, and the Royals know because of the last two women he was with. The Royals could easily think you're his girl and go after you to get to him."

Setting my hands on the table, I put my weight forward and let out a breath. Being with the Kings has brought back that feeling of family. I believed I found a place to start over with people who would care about me as much as I care about them. The thought of having to pack up and begin my search for another place, another job, another home creates a gut-wrenching ache in my stomach.

"Maybe it's best I leave Nashville."

Liz bites at her lip, sorrow blossoming in her eyes.

"I don't want you to leave. I don't think Nix wants you to leave either. He just wants to keep you safe by keeping his distance from you."

Facing her, I can't help smiling at the way she stares at me with hope in her eyes.

"I don't want to leave either, so I'll try to make it work and avoid Nix."

Saying the words creates an unexpected knot in my chest. I've come to respect Nix and care about him, and there's no denying he gets my body hot and bothered every time he's near. There was potential there for something more than great sex, but I need to let those thoughts go, for my own safety.

Taking a break, I venture out of the tent to go watch the bike tricks. Maci leaves William's side long enough to join me. She's wearing a new property tank top, and I'm glad to see William has stepped up, unless he's only doing it to mark her as his while we're at Full Throttle. I hope the guy isn't that much of a dick. Maci flicks a strand of her long, light brown hair off her shoulder and fusses with the bottom of her shirt, pulling it out of her cutoff jean shorts, and dips her chin at me.

"Can I borrow your pocketknife?"

Pulling it out of my jean pocket, I hand it to her, my brow raised. She cuts a slit down the side of her tank, then the other side, and hands the pocketknife back to me. Taking the split fabric, she ties a knot on one side, then the other, tucking them both under as she rolls up the bottom of her tank, revealing her lower abdomen.

"Now, that's better," she says aloud, winking at me.

Laughing at her cocky smirk, I push through the crowd and buy a cold beer before we find seats on the bleachers. A few rows down, I see the backs of Kings' jackets and vests. Maci taps my shoulder and points to them.

"Let's join them."

"Let's not," I say, sitting back. Nix is sitting in the center of the other guys, and this is the perfect opportunity for me to keep my distance. Maci makes a face at me, her blue eyes questioning, but she doesn't push it. She sits back too, and we watch the show. Men come out doing wheelies, burnout spins, then show off more advanced tricks—standing on the motorcycle while it's driving forward, sitting on it as it goes in reverse, then even crazier stunts with one guy doing a leg stand with another dude doing a leg stand on top of his back. The shit I'm seeing is astounding, and the crowd feels the same, cheering and shouting as the stunts get more and more death-defying.

A chick joins the stunts, coming out to the arena on the back of one of the stunt guys' motorcycles. Another motorcycle flies out, and they do spins around her, drive away, then one comes back toward her, raises up on the front wheel, and kisses her as the bike stops in front of her, its back wheel in the air. The crowd goes nuts, cheering, their beer bottles and liquor cups fisted in the air. The stunt guys line up and rev their bikes, then take in all the applause. The show ends, and Maci and I slip out with the crowd. The Kings are somewhere behind us, and I'm fine with that. Taking Maci's arm, I lead her toward the women's tent shops.

As we pass food vendors, she turns her attention toward those instead. With the aroma of meat and french fries, my stomach grumbles, and I follow her, looking for something appealing. Up ahead, there's a face that stands out among the bikers—his dark hair cut short, his broad shoulders, and the familiar back tattoo snaking up his neck. My footsteps speed up as my heart pounds aggressively in my chest. Ensuring it's him, I angle myself for a better view and try to see the back patch. I get a glimpse of Sinister and stop moving, my body frozen in fear. Maci stares at me, worry etching lines in her flawless face.

"Synne, what's up? You look like you've seen a ghost."

"Not a ghost, a demon disguised as a beautiful man." Taking her arm, I lead her back toward the Custom Ride tent. "C'mon, we need to go."

With quick steps, I glance over my shoulder. Hazel brown eyes make contact with mine, and I look away, hurrying my steps. Getting back to the Custom Ride tent, I gather my leather jacket draped over the chair Ink is now sitting in and toss my beer in the nearby trash. Walking up to Liz, I give her a hug.

"I gotta go," I tell her.

She pulls back from my arms.

"What? Why? Where are you going?"

"I don't know, but I can't stay here. My ex is here, so I can't be." I can hear the fear in my voice, so I know she does too. She grabs my wrist.

"Don't leave. You're safer here with us than out there alone."

"Synne!"

The deep baritone of Levi's voice growls my name, and I flinch, closing my eyes, wishing this wasn't happening. Turning to face him, I widen my shoulders, refusing to let him see my fear. Reaching across the table, he snags my arm, jerking me against the table, and brings me close so I can hear everything he whispers.

"If you don't want your friends to get hurt, you're going to come with me without a fight."

Two more Sinister Sons are on either side of Levi—Joker, with his two red, two black diamonds on his neck and Ty, with his long, black hair in a ponytail—their arms over their chests in the standard biker pose. I can see the butts of their guns, just inside their vests. They're giving me stares like Levi's, and it sends a cold prickle down my spine.

"Let go of her arm," Liz snaps.

Levi's glare turns to her.

"Your ol' man clearly needs to teach you how to respect the patch. This is between me and my ol' lady, so stay the fuck out of it."

Yanking my wrist out of his grip, I rub at the mark he's left.

"I'm not your ol' lady anymore. What we had is over. You need to leave."

Levi cocks his head, his lips forming a frightening scowl.

"We're not done unless *I* say we're done, and we're definitely not finished with what we started."

Ty pulls back on his vest, revealing more of his gun, then tilts his head.

"Let's go, Synne."

The presence of a man comes up behind me. I glance over my shoulder and see Ink pulling back his cut to show his gun.

"We got a problem here?"

Levi scoffs at Ink.

"Stay out of this, Prospect. You're in over your head."

He's right. There's three of them with guns and only Ink with a gun and me, Liz, and Maci. Ink puts a hand on his gun and comes forward.

"You're stepping into the Kings' territory. I'd say it's the other way around."

Levi switches his menacing gaze to me.

"Step out of the tent, Synne unless you want your friends to get shot."

Levi and the other two Sinister Sons put their hands on their guns. Liz steps back, putting her hand on my arm. Maci whimpers behind me and steps back. In my periphery, I can see her pull out her phone.

"Synne!" Levi barks, and I jump. Ink starts to draw his gun, but I put my hand out, stopping him.

"Don't. Not here."

Ink's eyes dart between me and the three Sons.

"Don't go with them," he says under his breath.

My heart thuds so loud, I can feel it in my ears. Inching around the table, my movements are hesitant, my body beginning to tremble.

"Tell Nix goodbye for me."

Ink reaches for my arm, but it's too late. Levi yanks me into his arms, his grip so tight, I wince from the pain. He shoves me forward as Joker and Ty keep their eyes on the others, their hands still on their guns.

Levi keeps his iron grip on my arm, forcing me through the sea of leather and chrome. He veers to the right in the direction of the campgrounds, and I swallow the lump in my throat. Maybe, just maybe, I can plead with the man who once had affection for me.

"How'd you find me?"

"Got lucky. Been looking for you for a while. Figured I might catch a break here where all the bikers and chrome lovers come to fuck and play."

"Why bother looking for me? You don't even want to be with me."

Levi keeps his tight hold as he leads me on a dirt path through a small stretch of woods.

"You never should've left in the first place."

Jerking my arm from his grip, I glance over his shoulder at Joker and Ty, their expressions cold and careless, and it hurts to see it. They were once my family, but that doesn't matter because I was never a patch member, never their brother. I was nothing more than Levi's property to them. I see that now.

"What do you want from me?"

Levi sniggers, lifts my chin, and takes hold of my waist, bringing me tight against his solid frame as his affectionless eyes bear down on me.

"To teach you a lesson. You don't walk out on me or the Sons. Not with everything you know, not after disrespecting me like you did."

Shoving at his chest, it does little to put distance between us. Fisting my hair, he yanks my head back.

"I think we need to fight and fuck for old times' sake. I've missed it these last few months."

Fear rips up through my chest, and I shove harder, but he just laughs, the sound rumbling out of his chest and across his lips with a frightening timbre.

"Don't tell me you don't want my cock in you. You used to beg for it."

Hands trembling, I stretch my arms out, then kick him in the groin. He doesn't expect it and buckles, loosening his grip. I take off running, but Ty catches me by the hair, and my face whips sideways from the force of his backhanded slap. Shoved into Joker's waiting arms, he wraps his muscled arms through mine, locking me against his body. I can only use my legs at this point, kicking out at Ty. He grabs my ankle and slams his hand down on my shin, bringing tears to my eyes. Levi comes into view, his glare terrifyingly angry.

"You're going to wish you hadn't done that."

Levi fists my hair, pulling so hard I grimace and am forced to follow his lead. In my periphery, I see movement in the trees and hope with all my heart someone has seen what's going on and is getting help.

Tears sting my eyes as I'm forced by my hair into a clearing where Levi and the other two Sons have set up camp. Levi shoves me into an open tent and bends down, coming into the tent with me and zips it behind him. Joker and Ty are moving outside the tent, no doubt keeping guard as Levi follows through with whatever horrible plan he has.

Withdrawing his gun from his side, he points it at my face, and I crawl backward, away from the barrel.

"Take your clothes off."

The calm tone of his voice is more terrifying than if he was yelling. He's too controlled, too collected, giving me a bone-chilling view of the dangerous outlaw, the side of him he kept well hidden from me.

Leaning forward, I try to stabilize my shaking hands as I untie my boots. I can survive this. I've been with him so many times before, it's just another fuck. When he's done, when he's relaxed, I'll go for the gun and get the hell out of here.

As he unzips his pants, he watches me with a fierce stare that's half hatred and half arousal.

"Hurry the fuck up."

Releasing his dick from his pants, he strokes it in his fist, the barrel of his gun still aimed at my face. Lifting my shirt and bra off, I tuck my thumbs into my jeans and peel them and my underwear off my sweaty hips and legs. He glances down, briefly looking between my legs.

"On your back. Spread your legs."

With one hand, he lowers his pants farther down his hips. Coming forward, he keeps the barrel of the gun aimed at my face. So many emotions are exploding through my body—fear, hatred, anger, disgust. I hate that I loved this man, hate that he thinks I'm still his property to fuck as he pleases. I hate that I'm not fighting him, but I know if I do, he'd beat me and hurt me far worse than forcing me to have sex at gunpoint.

Spitting in his hand, he puts his fingers at my opening and slides them in as I pinch my eyes closed, tolerating his touch. When he's satisfied with my body's response, he comes forward, putting his cockhead to my lips and moves it up and down my opening, gathering my slickness.

"Don't pretend you don't want this dick," he mutters. "I know how much you love it."

He shoves forward, invading me, and I bite my lip, grimacing from the unwanted force.

Outside the tent, there's a ruckus, voices shouting, then grunts and the sound of fists contacting skin and bone. I recognize one of the voices—Nix. Levi pulls out, his face in a rage.

"There're guns surrounding your tent, and your brothers no longer have theirs. Bring her out, *now*."

Levi lowers on top of me, his voice a menacing whisper as he pushes the barrel of the gun into my temple.

"Tell your friends you're leaving with me or I'll kill you."

Hearing those words from his lips, in that soulless whisper, has my chest constricting, my leg muscles tightening. Beads of sweat pool on my forehead, and I wipe them away as Levi glares at me, tugging his pants up and zips them.

"My ol' lady needs to get dressed. We'll be out when she's done."

Levi cocks his head, his gaze challenging me to say a word. I don't, and he grabs my pants, shoving them at me.

"Hurry up."

Body clammy, I have to wiggle into my pants. My bra and top stick to me, making for an uncomfortable redress, but at least I'm back in my clothes and no longer being forced to take his dick. Scowling at him, I reach for the zipper of the tent, but he yanks me back, making me wait behind him. Putting his gun back in the waistband of his pants, he takes my hand. Raising his other one, he holds it out as we exit the tent.

Coming into the sunlight, I look around at every Kings member outside of the tent. Jake and Dominic have Joker and Ty on the ground, their boots on their chests and guns in their faces. Every other member has a gun raised and aimed at Levi. When I look at Ink, I mouth, *thank you*.

Nix takes one look at me, and his eyes narrow to slits, then his face reddens, his gaze sharp and focused on Levi. Rage is like a fragrance emanating off him. It's palpable, far more potent than the rage I saw in Levi. For a moment, I have hope I won't have to leave with Levi.

"Why the hell are you in my camp, interrupting me fucking my ol' lady?"

"Cut the bullshit. I know damn well she doesn't want to be here." Nix tilts his head, motioning for me to come to him.

I take a step, and Levi drops his arm, gripping me. He laughs, and I cringe.

"She wants to be here. Tell him, Synne. Tell this dumb fuck who you belong to."

Staring at Nix gives me confidence. There's no worry or doubt in his eyes. He knows I don't want to be here. I look at Levi, who's staring at me with a warning glare.

"Don't ever touch me again," I snap. "I'm not your damn property."

Levi's shoulders go back, his jaw shuddering, the only sign of the anger he's restraining other than his deadly stare. Jerking out of his grip, I leave his side and go to Nix, who puts his arm out and moves me behind him.

"We can do this the easy way or the hard way. Let her go, get on your bikes, roll out of here, and never come back. Or leave on a stretcher and lose your bikes."

Levi's nostrils flare, and he locks his gaze with mine.

"This isn't over, Synne."

"Yes, it is." Nix's voice is laced with acidity and certainty. "You come back for her, you'll be met with a bullet between the eyes." Nix takes several steps forward, putting the gun in Levi's face. "It wouldn't be the first time I had to put a man down."

"Fine." Levi curls his lip, keeping his eyes on me and Nix. "Keep the cunt. She's a nagging bitch, anyway."

He spits at Nix's feet, then storms toward his motorcycle. Jake and Dominic lift their boots off Joker and Ty, and they get up, spitting blood into the grass, wipe their mouths and go to their motorcycles. The three of them speed off down the dirt road, and I finally take a breath of relief.

Nix comes back to me, tucking his gun in its holster. Putting an arm around my neck and the other around my lower back, he brings me to his chest. For several moments, I breathe in his masculine scent—a mixture of sandalwood and something spicy. The aroma alleviates my rattled nerves, helping me regain my composure. Neither of us says anything at first, needing time to collect our emotions.

"Thank you for coming for me. I'm not your girl, yet you just put yourself and crew at risk to protect me. I don't know how to repay that."

Nix lifts his hand, caressing my cheek, rubbing over the tender part of my skin where Ty backhanded me.

"You do mean something to me. It's why I've been an ass trying to push you away. When Ink called and told me your ex took you, there wasn't a second thought about coming for you."

I'm not the kind of woman to cry, but my eyes are damp and there's a flutter in my belly as I stare up at him and see affection in his eyes.

"I care about you too, might even like you a little."

Nix's sexy smile skirts his lips as he caresses his hand down my hair. The touch warms me, and I move into his open arm. With me at his side, he faces the other Kings members. They've thrown Levi's and the Sons' camping equipment into the fire ring and torched it, the smoke curling as it rises into the air.

"For the rest of bike week, the entire club goes everywhere together." He looks down at me. "Including you."

"So much for staying away from you."

"We'll figure it out. I don't want you out of my sight." He kisses my head, then lowers his hand to my back. Together, we walk out of the campsite while Wesley picks up a jug of water and dumps it over the fire, dousing the flames and charred gear.

Back at our camp, the first thing I do is take a shower in the camper, washing off Levi's filth. Under the warm water, I have time to think about what happened. If not for Nix and the Kings, Levi would've finished forcing himself on me and even worse, would've either beaten me and left me to die or taken me back to the Sons for them to torture, rape, and kill me. I owe Nix my life, and I don't know how to begin thanking him.

Leaning against the shower wall, his words replay in my mind, *You come back for her, you'll be met with a bullet between the eyes. It wouldn't be the first time I had to put a man down.* That threat was no joke, and Levi knew it. I could see it in his eyes. Levi might be the outlaw, but Nix is the stronger, maybe even deadlier man. Levi's never killed anyone, not that I know of, but what do I really know about him anymore? Maybe there are multiple bodies buried in deep, unmarked graves because of him.

Stepping out of the shower, I grab a towel and dry off, then find fresh clothes. Liz is outside the little bathroom waiting for me, a shot of liquor in her hand. She outstretches her hand for me to take it as I rub the towel in my damp hair.

"Thanks."

Downing it, I set the empty shot glass on the counter.

"Need more?"

"I'll take another, yeah."

Liz studies me as she pours another shot of vodka.

"You all right?"

"I'm coming down from the adrenaline blast, but yeah, I'm all right."

"Nix told me your ex had you in his tent. If you ever want to talk about it with me, you can. I've been in a situation like that."

There's a brief flicker in her eyes that hints of something painful. I imagine whoever caused that pain is the man Nix was referring to when he told Levi he's killed before. That makes sense and leaves me with more questions.

"He barely got his cock in me." I take the shot glass from her hand and down it. "I promise I'm all right. I've had that cock in me hundreds of times before. Having him shove it into me isn't going to scar me." I slide the glass toward the bottle of vodka she's holding. "It's what he was going to do after that terrified me."

Liz opens the cabinet and gets herself a shot glass. Filling it, she tilts her head back and swallows it quick.

"What do you think he would've done?"

"I think he planned to take me back to the Sinister Sons. I wouldn't have made it out alive."

Worry pinches her brows inward.

"Think he or the Sons will come back?"

"I don't know. Nix scared him though. I could see it."

"Hopefully, that's enough to keep him away."

"I hope so. What your brother did for me..." My cheeks warm at the thought. "I was with Levi for five years, and I don't know that he would've protected me like that."

The corner of her mouth pulls back slightly. "My brother is really protective of the people he cares about."

"I like him, more than like him, but I keep my walls up because I've had to. I grew up around rough men who didn't show their feelings very often, and with Levi being a cheating asshole, I learned to protect myself by not allowing myself to open up emotionally. I want to be open with Nix, but the threat of the Wild Royals is real, just like the threats from Levi were today. How do I do it?"

Liz steps closer, the corner of her mouth lifting into a reassuring smile as she places her hand on my shoulder.

"You let us in. All of us. In the Kings, we're a family who looks out for one another and protects each other. You can trust us. Nix, my husband, the rest of the Kings, they're good men. They protect the women they love, they don't hurt them."

Wrapping my arms around her, I hug her. It feels good, so good to have a friend like her. Liz releases me and touches my cheek.

"Would you like me to cover that with makeup?"

"Yeah, I don't want to be walking around with a bruised face."

Walking back to the bathroom, I hang the towel up to dry. Sitting on the toilet seat, I relax as she works on my makeup.

"What's everyone doing?"

"Dominic and Ink are getting patched tonight, so they're preparing to celebrate."

"Good, they could use a reason for fun after the shit that happened today."

Liz stops dabbing the concealer sponge on my cheek and looks me in the eyes.

"What happened isn't your fault. I don't want you to feel that way. You had every right to leave him. You don't owe Levi anything."

"Thank you. You don't think the Kings will harbor any animosity toward me for what happened?"

"No, they won't. None of them would do the shit Levi did, and they know Nix wants you."

Those words cause a flutter in my belly. I must be grinning like a fool because Liz looks at me and winks, her smile cheeky.

"Yes, he wants you. You two should stop fighting it."

"What about the Wild Royals?"

Liz puts her hand under my chin and turns me to face the mirror. Our gazes meet, her green eyes glistening with the pain of the past and worry for the future.

"I know my brother and the Kings are planning something. What the Royals did to Jenna won't go unpunished. The Royals will get what's coming to them."

I can hear it in her voice—the hope for retribution. She wants it as much as they do. With a look in the mirror, I give her a smile of approval for a flawless cover-up, and we leave the camper to join the party. The Kings have created a four-wall barrier around camp with the camper, motorcycle trailer, and both trucks. Inside, they have their bikes parked in a circle and inside that, the tents, coolers, and firepit. It's smart, protective, and means they plan on partying hard tonight.

Nix is sitting in a camp chair, bullshitting with Jake and Dom. Erika is on Dom's lap, cuddled against him, keeping warm. His hand is on her hip, caressing her as he talks. Seeing that creates a longing in me that takes me by surprise. I want that, to be loved and protected as she is, a feeling I struggled to have with Levi.

Nix catches sight of me and motions his head for me to come over. Putting his hand out, I take it, and he brings me onto his lap and puts his arms around me. Nuzzling his face into my neck, he kisses me with a tenderness I didn't expect but appreciate.

"I love the way you smell—cinnamon and vanilla. It's perfect for you—spicy and sweet."

With him stroking my neck and head, I lean back, giving in to the delightful sensation and the warmth of the liquor in my belly. With his green eyes sparkling from the firelight, I stare at him, taking in the details of his handsome face. Above his short, dark beard, there's a tiny scar on his cheek, and I raise my hand to it, running my finger over it. As he looks at me, I see the desire in his eyes, the longing, the want. Coming forward, I kiss him, giving in to the buzzing electricity that swims between us. His kiss is powerful, sensuous, but not overbearing and forceful. He takes his time, tasting me, savoring me, drawing out my desire. Several moments later, we break apart, and he rests his head against mine.

"You're the only thing that takes the pain away."

His words shock me, catching my breath. When he raises his gaze to mine, I accept it and all the emotions with it. Kissing him again, I rise from the chair, keeping hold of his hand and lead him to the camper. Inside, I close the door behind us, and he presses me to it, his body welcome against mine. With our kiss, I drift into euphoria, my mind clear, my body taking control. His fingers curl around the back of my neck as he slips his tongue between my lips. Gripping each side of his vest, I pull it back from his shoulders, and he moves his arms behind him, letting it slide down before he tosses it on the couch. Unable to pull away from our kiss, we stay united as I tug his black tank out of his jeans. Taking hold of my wrists, he stops us, reading my eyes. My lips tingle, needy for his kiss to return.

"If you're not ready, I understand."

I answer with my lips to his and back him to the

bed, and he drops onto it. Crawling over him, my hands reach for his belt. Undoing the skull belt buckle, I unzip his jeans and open them.

"You take away the pain for me too."

Sitting up, he lifts my shirt off, then his. The touch of his warm lips kiss along my neck and shoulder as he squeezes my ass in his hands. I arch forward, his erection pressing into me, and I moan from the pleasure.

"I want you." The moisture of his lips coats my ear, then across my cheek as he places his lips to mine. Heat, warm and inviting, fills my body. Between my legs, it's a blaze of desire.

"You can have me."

Guiding me off his lap, he has me stand as he takes off my pants and underwear. Keeping his sensuous gaze on me, he lifts his hips and removes his jeans, briefs, and boots. With his hands on my hips, he brings me forward and onto the bed with him. As I lie atop him, he turns us and spreads my legs apart with his knee. Warm, strong hands caress my body as his kiss adds to my pleasure. Moving his hips to the right, he centers over me, his stretched cock lying between my wet folds. Rocking his hips forward, he slides his length up my opening, covering himself in my slickness. Rocking back, he aligns himself and slides in, the warmth and feel of him filling me, satisfying me, bringing me the physical and emotional gratification I need.

At first, he thrusts slowly, taking me on a sweet ride

of freedom—freedom from my anger, my guilt, my shame, my fear. As my hips rise to meet his, our desire for more of that freedom quickens our pace. With each of his powerful thrusts, my moans are a crescendo, my body and mind lost to the passion, the heat, the need for release.

With several more thrusts, he takes me to the peak of freedom, and I let go, freefalling into a cavern of exquisite bliss. With another thrust, he loosens his hold on me, nearing his climax.

"I'm on the pill."

With my whispered words, he tightens his hold, thrusts deep, and releases inside me. My legs tighten around him as he pushes into me again, continuing the little pulses of pleasure leftover from my orgasm. Staying inside me, he holds me close as his passionate kiss and intimacy brand my heart.

I'll never be the same after this. Nix has cracked me open and exposed a hidden, delicate part of me.

CHAPTER THIRTEEN

NIX

I DON'T THINK either of us was ready for the intensity of what we just experienced, yet I'm already thinking about how much I want her again. Lying on my back, I stare up at Synne, admiring her beautiful face as she leans over my chest, appreciating my ink.

Dragging my eyes down her body, I follow her ink and discover the bluebird in flight on her arm and just below it, the name Jay. It amazes me how much pain she's suffered at the hands of other men, yet she's still so strong. It's fitting for her to bear the phoenix branded on her skin because that's what she represents —a woman who's risen from the ashes of despair and learned to live again. I respect that about her, fuck, I admire her for it. There's something about her, about the fire inside her I'm drawn to. Each time I'm with her, that fire burns away the darkness surrounding my soul, and I crave more of it, need more of it.

"What you did for me..." As she caresses her finger over my skull and crown tattoo, her silver ring reflects off the outside firelight, drawing my attention to it before I look back at her emotional expression. "It's not something I'll ever forget. You saved my life."

Putting my hands on her arms, I pull her body on top of me and caress her back, making sure she sees the sincerity in my eyes.

"You don't owe me anything. I don't ever want you to feel like you do. I meant it when I said you mean something to me. There's no way in hell I was letting that piece of shit take you."

A shadow of a smile flashes across her lips.

"You mean something to me too. The first thought I had when Levi forced me to go with him was that I might not see you ever again, and it upset me because I want to see you more. I'd like to spend a lot more time together."

Running my hand down her back, it rises over the curve of her ass, and I squeeze it as I lift my head to kiss her.

"I would too."

As I rub my fingertips up and down her back, she stares at me, her smile peeking out as she bites her lip. In her eyes, I see desire developing, mixed with her affectionate gaze.

"I'd like to stay in here all night, talking and fucking," I wink, and she grins. "But I need to get out there and perform my duties. Dominic and Ink are becoming full patch members tonight."

"How do you feel about me sleeping in your tent tonight?"

"I thought that was a given." Sitting up, I bring her with me and kiss her forehead. "I want you with me."

With a smile swelling her cheeks, she gathers her clothes. Picking up my shirt, she tosses it at me when she catches me staring at her ass. Lower on her shin, I notice a bruise. Putting my shirt on, my brows draw together in thought, worry pinching my chest. After we're dressed, I take her hand and bring her back to the bed.

"You sure you're all right?"

My hand grazes her cheek, where her bruise is covered by makeup. Her eyes fill with recognition, and her hand raises and takes mine before kissing it.

"I am. It would've been far worse had you and the Kings not arrived when you did. I'll be okay. I promise."

Looking off, I release the breath trapped in my lungs. When I look back at her, there's a question in her eyes.

"If you decide it's something you need to talk about, I'll listen."

A smile sneaks up one side of her face.

"Thank you. It means a lot to me that you would."

Coming forward, she straddles my lap, caressing her fingers into my shoulders, pleasuring me with her touch.

"It would take more than what Levi did to break me.

127

And with the way you make me feel, it doesn't leave room to dwell on what happened."

Cupping her ass, I pull her in closer to kiss her. Resting my head against hers, I indulge in the massage she's giving my muscles. Her cinnamon vanilla scent fills the air I breathe, and I take another slow breath, savoring it.

"I'm glad we got to you when we did. I never would've forgiven myself if he'd hurt you more than he did or if he'd taken you back with him."

With her soft fingers, she lifts my chin and stares into my eyes, her words as potent as her scent. "You carry the burden of everyone else's pain as if it's your own. You're a good man, Nix. You shouldn't be so hard on yourself."

What this woman does to me is startling. With the way she looks at me, the way she touches my soul, she's tearing down the wall of anger, guilt, shame, and rage I have built too high to climb over myself. But as that wall crumbles and hope emerges, so does fear. I'm afraid this won't last. One way or another, I'm afraid I'll lose her, and I'll be left broken beyond repair.

With her hands on each side of my face, she kisses me, and I continue the kiss, deepening it, cherishing this moment—a moment where I'm able to forget all my emotional turmoil and have a taste of freedom.

Leaving the camper, I have my arm draped over Synne's shoulder with two new vests dangling from my hand. She takes a seat in my camp chair while I draw the attention of the Kings. Everyone makes a circle around the fire, either standing or sitting.

"The Kings have been through a lot over the years. We've gained and lost many great men. But one thing that holds true today is our brotherhood. I know every one of you has my back, just as I have yours. Our brotherhood has taught us to be better men, better spouses, and better brothers to one another. What this club has brought us more than anything is family. Looking around at each of you, I know you can be counted on when we need each other, to help if a brother is down and out, to step in and be a voice of reason when we're at our worst. Which makes tonight an important night.

"Dominic, Ink." When I look at them, Erika moves off Dominic's lap and stands behind his chair, a smile tilting her lips. "I've come to respect you both and believe your loyalty to the Kings has been well earned. Tonight, the Kings welcome you as official club members. Come get your colors."

Setting his beer down, Dominic rises and comes forward. I hand him his vest and tap his back as I hug him.

"Respect the patch, wear it with pride. We are a family, and I'm honored to call you my brother."

Dominic shifts out of his prospect vest and tosses it

into the fire before sliding into his new vest. He glances down at the new patches and gives a half-cocked grin.

"It's a damn good group of men. I'm honored to be a part of the Kings family."

Ink fills his spot as Dominic receives pats on the back and welcoming words from his brothers.

Ink sheds his prospect vest and tosses it in the fire, then gathers his new vest from my outstretched hand.

"Thanks, Pres. This means the world to me."

Putting it on, he lets out a long, savored sigh as if he'd been waiting on this moment for a while. Bringing him in, I tap his back as I hug him.

"Respect the patch, wear it with pride. We are a family, and I'm honored to call you my brother."

"Thanks, brother."

William shakes a whiskey bottle toward the campfire, and as the liquid hits the flames they surge upward, dancing in the dark night.

"Now, it's time to fucking celebrate!"

Axel flips on music from his truck, and shot glasses fill hands as the women start to dance.

CHAPTER FOURTEEN

NIX

WIPING my hand down my face, I blink a couple of times then reach for my phone. Heat is thick in the air, and I expect it's later in the morning. Grabbing my cell phone, I check the time, and sure enough, it's nearly ten a.m. Synne stirs next to me, and I put out my arm for her. She lies on my chest, draping her hand over my side as she looks up at me with drowsy eyes.

"What time is it?"

"Nine forty-six."

As I caress her back, she caresses my side.

"I need a shower," she proclaims. "I have your cum all over me."

Laughing, I lean down and kiss her.

"Hearing that reminds me of how good last night was."

With messy, wild hair and a lopsided grin, she sits up and searches for her clothes.

"It was hella good, and I'm a little shocked at how many positions we accomplished inside this small space."

Sitting up, I spot her underwear peeking out from the sleeping bag and pull them out. Dangling her blue silky thong from my finger, I rub her back, getting her attention.

"I think the whiskey made us more creative," I wink, and she snags her underwear from my hand.

"*Very* creative." Leaning forward, she kisses me, and I consider having her again. If it wasn't for our desperate need for water, food, and a shower, I would. One thing for damn sure is how good it feels to be inside her.

"I'm gonna round up the guys. We need to have a good meal after last night. When we're finished, it should be about time for the first journey ride. Would you like to ride with me?"

Sliding her underwear up her thighs draws my attention to her pussy. My eyes graze over her trimmed patch, and my cock jerks. Before it gets hard, I pull my gaze from her and find my briefs.

"Ride passenger on your Harley?"

With a chuckle, I raise my hips and release my briefs, the waistband making a quiet snap as I pluck my thumbs from it.

"Yeah." Putting my arm on my bent knee, I read the surprise on her face and wait to see what her answer is going to be.

"Yes, I'll ride your pussy pad because I know what it means to be asked." With her finger and thumb on my jaw, she brings us to one another. Putting my hand into her crazy hair, I hold her close as I claim her lips.

"I'm particular about who I let ride with me. There haven't been many."

"Are you trying to tell me I'm special?"

"You are."

As I caress her cheek, she leans into my touch, kissing my thumb as it rubs over her lips.

"If I wasn't so thirsty, hungry, and sticky, I'd show you how much I appreciate that compliment."

My brow rises, the corner of my mouth turning up.

"How about we share a shower?"

"It's tiny"—she shrugs a shoulder and grins—"but we can make it work." With a wink, she puts on her shirt, and I frown as she covers her breasts.

"You'll see them again soon."

"Good thing. Those tits are luscious." Filling my hand with one, I kiss her, and she leans into me before straddling my lap.

"We're not going to make it out of this tent if we don't stop teasing each other."

Pressing her up against my cock, I squeeze her ass cheeks and nibble her bottom lip.

"You shouldn't have climbed on top of me." Tugging her hips forward, she bites her bottom lip as I rock her back and forth. Her breathing heightens as she moves her hips, pressing herself tighter against me.

Laying her beneath me, I reach into my briefs and pull out my erection. Moving her underwear to the side, I slide into her, and she grips my shoulders tight as she moans. With her arms around my neck, she hangs on as I thrust into her. Bending her knees farther toward her chest, she gives me better access, and I push harder and deeper. My mind goes clear, and I let the exhilarating sensation take over as my cock swells inside her tight pussy. Sweat beads across my brow and the scent of sex fills the tent. With one last thrust, I release inside her. Closing my eyes, I let the pleasure roll over me.

A hand taps the tent, and my eyes snap open to see the pleasured look on her face before I turn toward the sound.

"Liz has coffee made," Jake tells us.

Rolling onto my back, I glance over at her, and she's smiling ear-to-ear, turning on her side to face me.

"That was damn good morning sex."

With a prideful smile, I watch her finish dressing, my body and mind still reeling. She unzips the tent, and the breeze blows in, cooling the sweat on my bare chest. Finished sliding into my jeans, I tuck my feet into my boots as she climbs out of the tent. I come out behind her, my jeans still unbuttoned, and my boots untied. Axel and William catcall, and she flicks them off as she walks to the camper, grinning.

Jake steps up to me and hands me a coffee cup.

"You look drunk on sex. Must've been a good night."

"And morning," I add, lifting the cup to my lips.

Looking at me sideways, he smirks.

"Yeah, I know. We heard you riding that pussy loud and clear this morning."

Rubbing the back of my head, I let out a breath.

"I'm in deep. I want more with her, but the timing couldn't be shittier."

"We'll get shit handled. Don't walk away from her." He puts a hand on my shoulder. "She's good for you."

Trevor and Audrey step out of the camper, carrying bacon, ham, eggs, oil, and a skillet. Trevor dips his chin at me, a smirk curling the corner of his mouth.

"Mornin' Pres."

The corner of my mouth upturns. They were in the tent next to us. Guaranteed they heard Synne's ass slapping against me last night in between their own fuck fest. Audrey trails behind him, glancing at me with a humored smile before sitting in a camp chair next to Trevor. With her blond hair braided down her back, Trevor gives it a tug, bringing her face up so he can kiss her. With a wink, he leans in and whispers something that makes her giggle. Seeing the love between them forces me to face the truth, I don't want to walk away from Synne, not with the way she makes me feel.

Turning toward Jake, I put my back to Trevor and Audrey.

"He hasn't got cold feet, has he?"

Glancing over my shoulder, Jake ensures our conversation is private, but still lowers his voice as I did.

"Nah, he's got the ring in his pocket. He's doing it at Lookout Point."

"Did he get her a good rock? Not some shit out of a crackerjack box?"

Jake lifts his coffee cup, forming a grin behind it. "Liz gave her approval, so he's in the clear."

"Good, that woman deserves it. She's been loyal to him for years."

Jake's phone dings, and our attention goes to his pocket. Pulling it out, he checks the screen. Staring at it, his eyes brighten and his smile reaches his ears.

"Aunt May send a video of Liam?"

"Yeah," Jake turns his phone for me to see and my mouth automatically forms a smile as we watch Liam work a scoot-crawl motion as he reaches for his Harley Davidson bear. Once he grabs hold of it, the bear's ear goes right in his mouth and gets chomped on. Drool dribbles out of Liam's mouth and he kicks his feet in triumph.

"Damn, that's cute."

"I know it, brother. Liz is missing him bad and wants videos at least twice a day, so now May's sending them to me too." He glances at the video one more time, his mouth quirking before collapsing the video and pocketing his phone. "Every video is like that. It's making me miss him just as bad."

"Nix, Jake," Audrey calls behind us. "Breakfast is going to be ready soon."

Trevor sits back in his camp chair, chewing on a slice

of cooked bacon as Wesley lifts a Dutch oven filled with biscuits off the fire. The camper door opens to Synne, her damp hair draped over her shoulder and fresh clothes covering her creamy skin. She and Liz are laughing at something, and it draws my eyes to Synne's smile. Looking in my direction, her bottom lip gets caught between her teeth as her cheeks gain more pink. I love seeing her body react to me this way. Carrying two cups of coffee, she sees I already have one and lowers her hand. Walking past me, she leans in, kisses me, then moves on to join the crew.

"Let's eat." Jake's voice snaps me out of my Synne-induced trance, and I join everyone, taking a seat. Next to me, Synne makes me a plate as I lean back in my camp chair, finishing off my coffee. When she hands it to me, I take it and kiss her in appreciation. Glancing at an empty camp chair, I look beyond it to the weathered blue tent behind it.

"Where's Ink?"

Wesley, being closest to Ink's tent, stands up and walks to it. His fingers tap the edge before his deep timbre rumbles out a morning greeting.

"Rise and shine. Breakfast's ready."

Movement stirs in the tent, and a few minutes later, when I'm nearly finished with my breakfast, Ink and the brunette stumble out of the tent looking rough. Sweaty hair is plastered to the woman's face, her mascara smeared below her pale eyes, and the fishnet leggings she had on last night are missing. Just in her jean shorts and tank top, she tries to smooth down her hair and put it in a ponytail. With a brief glance at us, her cheeks turn red, and she veers toward the trail that leads back to the main drag. Ink snags her wrist and brings her back.

"Don't worry about it. Have breakfast with us."

The woman glances at me questioningly, and I nod, pointing at Ink's chair.

"There's plenty to go around."

"You can use the camper shower if you need to," Liz tells her as she takes the empty seat next to her.

With nervous eyes, she smiles at Liz. "Thanks."

Ink squats down next to her chair and makes a plate. Liz hands the woman an empty plate, and she glances at Ink, giving a smile that speaks volumes about their night together. He winks, and she watches him with a brighter and much less nervous gaze. Ink sits on the ground, and Dominic hands him a beer, which he accepts, tipping the beer in the air. "Thanks."

The breasty brunette smothers her biscuits with sausage and gravy, causing my lips to tilt.

"You from around here?" I ask her.

"Alabama," she replies, drawing out 'bama' with her southern accent.

I flick a glance at Ink and catch his frown.

"Just here for Bike Week?"

"Yeah, a few friends and I came for the first time last year. We've been hooked since. We're staying at another camp nearby."

"You ride?"

"Yeah, but I don't have a bike yet. I thought maybe I'd find a deal while I'm here."

"Shouldn't be a problem. I think I saw a Yamaha V Star 250 somewhere with a for sale sign on it." Synne sets her plate aside and scoots her chair closer to me. Leaning back, I put my hand on her bare leg. With a quick glance my direction, she lets me know she likes it with the curl of her full lips. "It's a good starter bike for a woman."

"It was only a couple years old. Silver color," Synne tells her. "I saw it at the Yamaha tent past the food vendors."

"Do you ride?" the brunette asks Synne.

"Yeah," Synne points to her ride parked right along with the Kings' bikes. "Harley Sportster 883."

Pride fills my chest, and I give her thigh a gentle squeeze, drawing her attention to me. I lean toward her ear.

"Hearing you talk bikes makes me want to bend you over mine."

When I pull back, her cheeks are flushed, and she winks, giving me a smirk that hints at how much she'd like that.

"You two been together long?" the brunette questions, pointing her fork between Synne and me. "Y'all are a really cute couple."

"Hear that, Pres?" Jake chuckles, tossing his and Liz's empty plates into the fire. "Y'all are *cute*."

Synne gathers our plates and tosses them in the fire, their edges turning black as the fire consumes them. Leaning forward, I shake my head, then stroke Synne's hair before I stand and toss the paper coffee cup in the fire.

"Fuck off, Castle."

"Sure, I'll fuck right off into your sister," he quips.

Half the crew laugh, the other making noises of humored shock.

"Jake!" Liz slaps his arm and Jake laughs. Taking her hand, he brings her forward so he can kiss her.

"Peach, baby. Your brother already knows how much I love your pussy."

Liz's cheeks glow red, but the corner of her mouth tilts. "You better love my pussy," she playfully replies, leaving her chair to climb onto his lap.

"You know I'd break skulls for it," he murmurs before pulling her in close to kiss her.

Synne looks at Jake and Liz with a tilted head and wanting stare before glancing at me with emotion in her eyes. I slip into the camper as the thought fills my head.

We're already there, Red. You're already mine.

Leaving the cool shower, I rummage through my pile of clothes, grabbing a fresh T-shirt and jeans before pulling on my vest. Securing my Glock in my hip holster, I exit the camper and find Liz sitting behind Synne, braiding her hair.

Arms crossed, I lean against the camper as memories flood my mind. As teenagers, Liz and Jenna would sit in the living room, watching a movie with a bowl of popcorn and braid each other's hair. It's something they did even after Liz returned from college, a bonding experience between them. Watching Liz and Synne creates an ache in my chest the same way it creates something warm. Liz is becoming attached to Synne, just as I am.

Guilt hammers my gut, and I drop my head, remembering Jenna's beautiful face. Locking down the painful emotions straining to erupt, I walk to my bike, avoiding the two of them. Revving it up, I let the powerful vibrations rumble through my body and silence my heart.

Synne looks up at me, just then, and those gorgeous hazel-green eyes capture me, and it takes all of my willpower not to walk over to her and slam my lips to hers, obliterating the pain clawing its way into my chest.

"*You okay?*" she mouths.

Dragging my gaze from hers, I nod to Max and Axel, giving them the signal to get on their bikes. They join me, and we put rubber to the road.

—SYNNE—

"WHAT WAS THAT ABOUT?" I ask Liz, my chest clenching at the hardened stare on Nix's face.

Liz's hands graze my back as she folds strands of my hair over the other. Lowering her voice, she leans closer.

"He needs some time to himself. That look wasn't toward you. That was a look of holding back emotions. Seeing me braiding your hair surely brought back painful memories for him."

"What do you mean?"

"Jenna and I braided each other's hair. It's something he's seen many times."

"Oh..." My voice trails off as discomfort winds its way into my belly. "Do you think I'll always remind him of her?"

Liz stops braiding, her hands resting on my back.

"I don't know." With a sigh, she moves her hands again, finishing the braid. "I don't think so, but I can tell his feelings for you make him feel guilty."

My head lowers as she wraps the hair tie around the end of my hair. With a sideways glance, I look in the direction Nix left. My gaze falls to the tire tracks in the dirt as my stomach quivers.

"He deserves to be happy, yet he fights it like he doesn't deserve it."

Liz rubs my shoulder, and I turn to her, seeing moisture pooled in her eyes.

"He needs you in his life. I know you make him happy. Just be patient with him."

As the rest of us at camp clean and prep to be gone for the day, Jake gets a call. I know he's talking to Nix when I hear him say *Pres*. Jake hangs up and puts his finger in the air, circling it.

"Wrap it up. It's time to ride."

Frowning, I traipse to my bike and put a water bottle in the saddlebag.

"Synne," Jake calls.

Looking his direction, my hand falls to my hip, awaiting what he has to say as Liz climbs on the back of his bike, giving me a sympathetic expression.

"You're not riding solo. Nix is coming back for you."

Liz and I look at one another, our smiles matching twin curves between our sun-kissed cheeks. Jake revs up his bike, and in the distance, I hear the three bikes returning. Nix is the first to come through the clearing, his sunglasses covering his face. Unable to read his expression, I wait while he stops next to me. He doesn't cut the engine, just lowers his glasses and winks.

"You getting on, gorgeous? Or you gonna make me work for it?"

Grabbing the water bottle, I secure it in his saddlebag before climbing on. Lowering my sunglasses, I lean forward and wrap my arms around him. Putting his hand on my leg, he caresses me, and the sensation brings back the rush of feelings I've been getting accustomed to all morning—the kind of feelings that tell me I'm already in deep with Nix.

Beneath me, his Harley vibrates between my thighs, the power of his bike more intense than mine. It growls into the air as he speeds off, gliding us through the wind with expert skill. Around us, the Kings' Harleys create a chorus of deep roars. Ahead of us is wide open pavement and the sun high in the sky. The breeze brushes over my face in a cool embrace. It's nearly as blissful as riding my own bike. Admittedly, it feels good to be against Nix's back. The strength of his body leading us and his Harley down the road gives me a sense of security. Nix is the kind of man who protects the ones he loves, and maybe someday, I can know what that love feels like.

As the sun's rays stream between puffy clouds, the Kings follow the road up winding curves, challenging their riding skills. Reaching the top safely, Nix leads the crew to an overlook parking area. The Kings park their bikes in a row, the rumbling engines quieting as the women step off first. Walking to the waist-high stone guard along the cliff, I look out at the lush green treetops and blue-gray mountains behind them, their tips hidden in the clouds. Nix comes up behind me, wrapping his arms around my waist and setting his chin on my shoulder. I welcome the warmth of his chest on my back, nestling further into his arms.

"You okay?" I ask quietly.

"I needed some time to think on the road. I figured you'd understand being a rider."

"Completely. You seem to be feeling better."

Turning me in his arms, he places a hand on top of the stone guard and the other hand on my waist, his body caging me in, his vibrant green eyes expressive of his relaxed state.

"I am. You said something that stuck in my head. I

want to live, and I don't want to keep feeling guilty about it."

Putting my hand inside his leather vest, I lift his shirt, running my fingers along his abs. Pupils dilating, he tugs my waist toward him.

"I want what's between us to be more than a fling. I want you to be my girl."

Squeezing my ass, he tugs me tight against him, his gaze a mixture of arousal, hope, and mischief. Lowering my hand, I rub against the knot in his jeans, and his eyes close briefly, indulging in it before shooting open and staring at me with sharp intensity.

"I'll take that as a yes?"

Giggling, I grab his shirt and yank him to me, firming my lips against his. Wrapping a hand around my neck, his other hand remains on my ass, gripping a cheek as his tongue slides between my lips and sets fire to my libido. Tiny embers of arousal kindle at my nerve endings, my whole body alight with desire. Between my legs, I'm becoming wet as he pushes forward, pressing his growing erection into me as my ass meets the stone wall. Letting a breath escape us, he's quick to bring our mouths back together, and I welcome him, just as needy for the taste of him.

To our left, Audrey squeals, and we put space between us and look over. Trevor is on his right knee, holding a ring out to her. The corner of Nix's mouth pulls back in a grin as he watches. Audrey screams, "Yes," and Trevor rises and puts the ring on her finger, his smile as bright as the sun. Jumping into his arms, he holds Audrey and spins her, his lips meeting hers.

Nix looks at me, his beautiful green eyes studying my face as they allude to his thoughts. I believe he wants the kind of love we just witnessed, and there's no denying, so do I. Coming forward, his warm breath feathers my ear, and I soak in his masculine scent of sandalwood, spice, and leather as his warm body covers mine.

"I'd like to hear you say it."

"What?" I bite my lip at the husky drawl of his voice. "That I'm your girl?"

Warm lips nibble my neck, then lick the shell of my ear, sending pleasured goosebumps down my arm.

"Yes."

Covering the view of me from the others, he slips his hand into my shorts, and my head falls back as his fingers find my clit with adept precision. Swirling his finger around it, he draws a hiss from my lips. With one swift movement, he thrust a finger into me, and my fists tighten at the pleasured sensation. Not wanting it to end, I glance over his shoulder to ensure no one has caught on to what we're doing.

"More," I encourage with a quiet breath.

When my eyes meet his, his grin is lascivious. Another finger is added, and he thrusts harder, my legs widening for him to go deeper. Gripping his vest, I bring his lips to mine, concealing my moan. When we pull apart for a breath, he glances over his shoulder and is clearly pleased to see the others busy in conversation or enjoying the view of the mountains.

"Keep going."

Silently, he answers with flicks between my clit and plunging into my pussy.

"We should come back here tonight and finish what we've started."

With his sensuous bite to my neck, the mix of tantalizing pain pushes me into the orgasm I've been chasing.

"Fuck, yes."

My head tilts back, the warm sun on my skin as my arousal coats his fingers. Nix chuckles, lines creasing his eyes as he smiles with satisfaction. Withdrawing his hand, he puts his fingers to my lips and watches with heated arousal as I suck his two fingers.

"Damn baby, you have me hard as a rock."

"I'd suck you off if we didn't have an audience."

He looks over his shoulder at the scattered groups of his crew, then back at me.

"They're not paying attention. Even if they notice, they'll mind their own business."

The thrill of sneaking public oral sex turns me on. Keeping my eyes on his, I unbutton his jeans.

"It's going to get really obvious when I'm lowered in front of you slurping your cock."

Unzipping his jeans, he guides my hand to his thick, hard dick.

"I really don't give a fuck right now. I want to feel

my girl's mouth around me."

Lowering between him and the wall, I pull his erection out from his briefs and wrap my mouth around it, not wasting time, sucking hard and fast. Nix's hand holds my head as he uses the other to brace his weight on the wall. With my hand at his base, I stroke him as I try to fit as much of his length in my mouth as I can. Crunching of gravel sounds behind us, then the boots stop, turn on their heel, and remain there. A moment later, there are more boots crunching gravel, and I stop briefly to see a few of the Kings members making a wall for us. With a grin, I return to pleasuring Nix, and he looks down at me with an arousing intensity that makes me wish we could finish this sex-scapade with a good, hard fuck. Pumping into my mouth, his grip on my head tightens momentarily. Several more thrusts, and his body stiffens, his cock squirting cum into the back of my throat. Licking him clean, I stand as he puts his cock back in his pants and zips them.

Bringing me in close, he caresses my cheek, his satisfied smile curling the corner of his mouth.

"I love how you're not afraid to live on the edge."

"Never, especially not when there's a chance for us to pleasure each other."

Grazing his fingers under my chin, he raises it.

"Tonight will be a night just for us. I'll give you a hell of a lot more pleasure."

Watching my lips part and curl toward my eyes, his own smile widens. Wrapping an arm around me, he leads us back to the rest of the crew. Max is the first to hear us coming and looks over his shoulder, a knowing smirk tilting his lips.

"Y'all enjoy the view?"

Nix taps Max's shoulder. "Best view I've ever seen."

Axel, Wesley, and William share the same grin, and all the guys laugh.

"Damn, Red, you're not shy about pleasuring your man, are ya?" Axel jokes.

William points to the corner of his mouth. "I think ya got a little something right there."

I flick him off, and their laughter echoes into the air.

"Careful, William, she's liable to kick your ass," Wesley teases.

William puffs a breath and tilts his head. "No, shit. She left Ink with a bruise. It's all right, though. We need the queen of the Kings to be a tough chick."

Nix looks down at me, his mouth slanted as he caresses my side.

"Queen of the Kings?" Staring up at him, I wink. "I think I could get used to that title."

Nix lowers his hand and squeezes my ass, pointing at his Harley with the other. "Your chariot awaits."

"That's the best kind of ride there is."

"Hell yeah, it is," Wesley replies.

The guys nod in agreement.

Tearing through the wind, the Kings' Harleys put rubber to pavement and continue the journey ride through the wooded roads. All around us are lush green trees, and in between are mowed fields and ranch houses. Passing a black wooden rail fence, the scent of paint wafts through the air as two blond horses chew the grass around their hooves.

In the distance, hundreds of rows of grapevines can be seen before a log cabin winery comes into view. A few cars are parked to the right of the building with a handful of people walking toward the entrance. With the stretch of road ahead of us clear, Nix shifts and rolls on the throttle. Wind whipping over us, the engine roars, and we speed down the road, the sensation exhilarating.

The journey ride continues several miles through another patch of woods, up a hill, and to a short road on the right with parking and a covered pavilion at the end. Under the shade, we take a rest and refresh.

Stretching on my toes, I kiss Nix on the cheek and slap his ass before leaving him to meet up with Liz, Audrey, and the other women. Audrey's eyes glimmer in the sunlight as she beams a smile at us. Putting her hand out, she shows us a sparkling round diamond on a white gold band with little diamonds along the band.

"I'm engaged," she raves. With long fluttering lashes, she glances at Trevor. "I love that man."

"I'm happy for you. The ring is beautiful."

"Thank you!"

Stepping onto a picnic table bench, I take a seat on the table, my feet resting on the bench as I sip my water. Audrey joins me, sitting on my right as Liz takes my left side. In front of us, Maci, Erika, and the new girl with Ink remain standing. Erika sheds her property jacket and wipes the sweat from her brow. Setting the jacket on the picnic table, she accepts the bottle of water Liz holds out for her. One of the many things I like about Liz is, being a nurse and a new mom, she's practically the mother of the group, always attentive to everyone's needs.

"Did your aunt May send the morning video of Liam?" I ask her.

"Of course!" She pulls her cell phone from her jeans pocket and flips through the screen. A moment later, a video of a squishy baby with brown eyes fills the screen as he giggles and kicks in his activity sit-and-play. "Isn't he cute? I miss his slobbery kisses and that laugh. It reminds me of Jake's."

Maci leans over and watches the video. Stepping back, she grimaces. "No, thank you." Smoothing her hand over her belly, she lifts her shirt, revealing abs and a dangling gold belly ring. "I wouldn't want to lose this figure."

Liz rolls her eyes and pockets her phone. "That might change if you find the right guy."

Lowering her shirt, Maci's mouth pulls down. "William is the right guy."

"Don't get too attached," I warn her. "Playboys and commitment don't go hand-in-hand."

With a huff, she turns her attention to me. "What do you know?"

Liz chuckles as she smooths the loose strands of her dark hair and tucks them behind her ear. "She knows from experience, and so do I. Jake was a playboy for years. We had a rough patch at the beginning. Committing wasn't in his nature."

Putting a hand on her hip, she juts it out. "If Jake settled down, William can too."

"Maybe," I reply, "but he has to want to. Not all playboys want to."

Maci throws a hand in the air, her pink cheeks becoming more flushed. "You can't compare the guy you dated to William. They're different people."

The sound of motorcycles in the distance draws our attention to the road. A group of five women riders pull into the parking area and cut their engines. They acknowledge our group with waves or a dip of their heads, then get into their saddlebags for drinks or pull their cell phones out to check messages.

Max briefly points their direction, dipping his chin toward them. William and Axel follow behind as the three of them walk over to the women. Pointing to the women's bikes, they initiate conversation.

Maci is on her toes, peering over our heads to watch William. Everyone has their phones out, and it seems like numbers are being exchanged, but you can't tell for certain who's actually doing the number exchanging.

With her face turning a shade darker, Maci huffs and stalks over to the group. We watch as she puts a hand through William's arm and juts out her tits toward him.

Into his conversation with the group, he doesn't break from it to give her attention. She glances back at us, then drops her shades down over her eyes, but I saw the dejection in them before she did.

Erika hops onto the picnic table next to Liz and sits back on her elbows. "She might be his property, but I don't think he's hers," she says aloud.

"He's not," I reply. "He's keeping her close enough that she sticks around, but far enough, so he can still fuck who he wants."

"What about Ink?" Bama asks.

My gaze switches to the busty brunette and her hopeful expression.

"He's into you," Liz tells her. "And I think Ink is looking for a commitment, but don't you live in Alabama?"

With her thumbs in her jean shorts pockets, she shrugs. "I'm open to possibilities."

Audrey flashes Bama a brief, empathetic smile. "These guys aren't long-distance types." She throws a thumb over her shoulder at the Kings. "They want a woman who's going to be around, loyal, and who likes to fuck... *a lot*. I know, I used to be in your shoes. Trevor was already in the Kings when we got together. I knew I had to make a move if I wanted to keep him."

"But I just met him. I'm not going to move across several states for the guy." A shadow of disappointment darkens her pale eyes as she frowns. Glancing at us, she studies our expressions to see what we think.

Audrey brushes her hair off her forehead, then leans back on the picnic table like Erika. "I understand. I only had to move a couple of towns over. Having to move several states is a lot different."

"Just enjoy your time with him," I tell her. "You never know where things will lead."

The frown lines on the outside of her mouth fade. "Thanks. That's what I want to do."

Maci's voice raises, and I look over to see the women back on their bikes, getting ready to leave. Maci and William are off to the side, arguing as Max and Axel leave them and join the rest of the Kings under the pavilion.

"Chill the fuck out, Maci. I was just talking to them. You can't lose your shit every time I talk to another woman!"

"Maybe if you didn't try to fuck other women, I wouldn't get so jealous!"

"I gave you a property jacket. What the hell else do you want? My balls in a fucking bag?"

"Ah, shit," I hear Axel say behind us.

"I want you to fuck me and only me, not every other bitch who draws your attention!"

"I haven't fucked anyone else, but if you keep nagging at me and acting like a bitch, I will."

A slap whistles through the air and William's head jerks to the right.

"Don't call me a bitch!"

William puts his hand on his cheek and glares back

at Maci, his expression evident of shock, far more than anger.

Nix steps out from the pavilion, his voice booming. "Enough! Maci, join the women. You both need time to cool off."

Maci turns toward Nix, her blue eyes glaring. William turns away from her, and she grabs his leathers, ignoring Nix. "Don't leave. We're not done."

William shoves her hand off. "Yes, we are."

Stepping off the picnic table, I lean against the opposite pillar from Nix. "Maci, get your little ass over here."

Whipping her head toward my voice, her shoulders drop, and she huffs but follows my request. Nix looks over at me and dips his chin in thanks.

Maci storms past me and sits on the bench on the other side of Erika. "Fucking asshole," she mutters.

"What brought that on?" I face the women and lean against the pillar, my water bottle loosely dangling from my hand.

"He was flirting with those stupid hos and completely ignoring me." With her shades down over her eyes, she covers the tears falling down her cheeks. "I don't want to break up," she says quietly, sorrow in her young voice.

Erika drops onto the bench and puts an arm around Maci. "You two need some space though or you're just going to fight again."

"If you really care about him, you need to talk to

him and tell him how you feel. Give him a chance to earn your trust, and if he doesn't, then you need to walk away," Liz tells her. "Do you have any reason to believe he's cheated on you?"

"I don't know." Raising her sunglasses, she wipes at her tears. "No, I guess. He's got a password lock on his phone, probably so I can't read his messages. He flirts all the damn time. It drives me nuts."

The scuffling of boots draws my attention as the men work their way to their bikes. Nix walks up to Max's side and says something private. I assume it's about Maci as Max's eyes draw toward her. He shakes his head yes and moves on. Nix turns to us.

"Maci, you'll be riding back with Max."

Maci sniffles beneath her glasses, and I see more tears stream down, but she keeps her face stoic. "Fine."

The rumble of more motorcycles can be heard in the distance and grow louder as the bikes turn into the parking area. The recognizable Wild Royal patches come into view, and my body stiffens.

"Fuck."

The Kings leave their bikes and form a wall with Nix, blocking the Wild Royals from us. Over their shoulders, I watch the scene and draw my pocketknife from my side. Liz tells the women to lower themselves onto the benches. In their wide-open eyes, their fear is unmistakable.

The Wild Royals cut their engines, blocking the exit. The Kings' backs tighten as I hear the hard thuds of the rival MC boots pounding the ground. Several of the Kings draw their vests or jackets back, revealing their guns.

"*Reed Alverez*," Nix singsongs, his voice mocking. "It seems you're as much a dumb fuck as your cousin was."

A man with lengthy, slick, raven hair, a full beard, and a belly full of too many beers steps forward with *President* on his vest. Throwing his arms in the air, a callous smirk stretches the man's lips, and he runs his tongue across them as he snickers.

"We're not the ones blocked in with nowhere to go, *Pres*."

"Both our crews got women to protect. Let's keep this shit knuckles and knives. No guns," Jake orders.

Reed glances over his shoulder at the curvy, long-haired woman who was riding passenger with him. Around him, his crew is lined up for a fight, just as the Kings are.

"Just this once," Reed agrees. "No guns."

"Which one of you bastards shot the bullet meant for me?" Nix asks, his tone acidic.

A few of the Royals snigger.

"Here I thought the cunt was back from the dead, but that must be the new redheaded pussy you replaced her with."

Reed points over Nix's shoulder at me, and Nix loses it, charging him. Jake and Trevor hold him back, and Reed laughs, spreading his arms out.

"Blood for blood, Wilson. That's how it works. You

know that. Had you minded your own business, Tolito and your whore would still be alive."

Nix throws off Jake and Trevor and gets in Reed's face, towering several inches over him, but Reed is a wide man, visible on either side of Nix.

"The blood war started long before us when your uncle murdered mine and raped my aunt. Your whole family is nothing but filthy trash. You want blood for blood, I'll fucking give it to you."

Nix unleashes his rage, his fist slamming into Reed's face, jerking it to the side. Three Wild Royals descend on Nix, and the Kings rush in to protect him. The brawl between the two MCs is a circle of black leather and fists.

"Fuck this." Bama's boots scuff behind me, and I turn to see her reaching for her cell phone as she backs away from us. As soon as the operator answers, she's asking 911 for help and describing the scene. Maci joins Bama, giving her directions.

Voices rise, and blood spatters the pavement. A glint of silver reflects in the sunlight, and I lunge forward, shouting at Axel.

"Behind you, Axel, knife!"

Jake slams his hand down on the Wild Royal's arm, and the blade drops from his grip. Jake does some kind of fancy roundhouse kick and knocks the guy on his ass. Axel punches the guy behind Jake, and William is a wrecking ball plowing into the Wild Royal in front of him and takes him to the ground. My eyes stay on Nix, making sure no blades come his direction. He and Dominic are back-to-back, crunching bones that come in contact with their fists.

Sirens sound in the far distance, and the men push off each other, putting space between them as they take off for their bikes. The Kings' Harleys start and they wave for us to join them.

Bama backs up to the pillar at the end of the pavilion. "I'm not coming." With wide, frightened eyes, she clenches her phone in front of her like it's a safety barrier.

Liz and I race toward her.

"Yes, you are," I grab her phone and ensure the call has ended.

"You're not ratting out the Kings to the cops." Liz grabs her arm, and I grab the other, tugging her along. She resists us, and I put myself in front of her, staring her dead in the eyes.

"You can rejoin your friends when we get back to camp, or you can stay here, tell the cops what happened, and become the enemy of an outlaw motorcycle club."

Without resistance, she runs with us to the bikes and gets on the back of Ink's. Kings and Wild Royal motorcycles speed off the opposite direction of the sirens.

CHAPTER FIFTEEN

NIX

D<small>RIVING INTO CAMP</small>, I cut the engine and help Synne off the back of my bike and into my arms, making sure she's okay. She does the same, checking me over for knife wounds. Looking at my busted lip, she frowns.

"You're gonna need ice for that."

"Nah, babe, I'm fine."

Pulling her thighs forward, I bring her closer, inhaling her scent in an effort to calm my rage.

"But it does ruin the plans I had for eating your pussy."

She chuckles, and I give her a forced smile. Putting my head to hers, my jaw locks as Reed's words replay through my mind, my shoulders tensing. Synne must notice the change. Putting her hands on my shoulders, she massages, her strong hands alleviating some of the tension. My right shoulder is especially sore after the punches I threw. She must've been watching because she gives that shoulder more attention.

The rest of my crew parks their bikes, and I look them over for obvious injuries. Maci jumps off William's bike, blood-stained on the right side of her tank top.

"Liz!" she shouts as she helps William off his bike. Synne hops off mine, and I rush to William, taking his arm and putting it around my shoulders.

Liz is off Jake's bike as fast as she can. "Bring him into the camper."

William stumbles into the camper, but at least he's still lucid. Dropping onto the bed, face first, he raises his shirt. Blood coats his skin and is soaked through his shirt from the three-inch knife wound on his ribs and back. Liz sits on the bed next to him, eases a towel under him, then pours hydrogen peroxide on the wound. With the first aid kit open next to her, she takes out the needle and cleans it with alcohol. Threading the needle, she begins the suturing. William grimaces but remains still. Minutes later, she has the wound closed up, and William looks like he's ready to pass out. Jake comes forward and hands him a whiskey bottle.

"Here, it'll help."

Liz puts a bandage over the wound and tapes it. "Don't do anything to tear open my stitches." She gives him a pointed look as she puts her supplies away.

William turns on his back and slowly sits up, only grimacing once. Chuckling, he takes a chug of whiskey. "If you're tellin' me I can't fuck or ride my Harley, that's not gonna happen, sister. Thanks for patchin' me up though."

Maci pushes forward and sits next to him. Wrapping an arm around her, William raises the bottle and takes another chug of whiskey.

"You all right?" he asks her, concern filling his eyes.

"Yeah, better now that you're okay."

"Would've been worse if Dom hadn't fucked the guy up. Let's head out there. I need to thank him."

William and Maci exit with his arm still draped over her and the whiskey bottle dangling from the other. No doubt they'll be fucking again by night's end.

Liz washes her hands and puts the first aid kit away as Jake and I leave the camper with a second bottle of whiskey. The Alabama chick is marching past us as we come out. Ignoring us, she continues on with rushed steps, heading right for the trail that leads back to the main drag.

"Sarah!"

Ignoring Ink, she keeps her pace and disappears down the trail.

"I don't think the MC life is for her, after all," Synne tells him. "We had to convince her to get back on your bike."

Brows furrowing, Ink's mouth downturns into a frown, and he takes the whiskey bottle William hands him, swigs twice, and hands it back. Moving to the camp chair, he drops into it and kicks at the charred wood in the firepit.

Looking around at my crew, they look exhausted from the fight. Slumping into their camp chairs, they pass the whiskey bottles around as Liz checks each of us for wounds.

Every man who has a woman has her draped around them, rubbing or kissing on them, and Synne's no exception, standing behind my chair, massaging my shoulders. Lowering, she puts her arms around my chest. The silky touch of her skin rubs against my face, the cinnamon scent I'm coming to love filling the air.

"You all right?" she whispers.

Putting my hand on her arm, I caress it, tilt my head to the side, and kiss her.

"Ladies, can you give us Kings some time to talk in private?"

Synne's hands stop kneading the tension in my muscles. She stands and directs her head toward the camper.

"Let's cool off inside."

The women glance back at us with concern but follow Synne's lead. Once the door of the camper is closed, I outstretch my hand and take the whiskey bottle Wesley hands me.

"It's time to put our plans into action." Taking a couple of swigs, I pass the bottle to my right and hand it to Dominic. "Find the weakest link. Get the information we need. *Tonight.*"

Dominic takes the bottle, swallows a mouthful, then lowers it, his expression stone cold.

"Consider it done."

Dominic hands the bottle back to me, and I take another swallow. Standing from my camp chair, I pitch the nearly empty bottle into the firepit and watch the glass shatter into hundreds of tiny shards. Staring at them, the remaining bit of liquid soaks into the dark embers around them, my gaze is frozen, looking at what seems like a reflection of my own damaged soul.

"We're going to make them suffer like she suffered."

THE KINGS GET rowdy as Axel rolls up to the start of the men's bike races. As the road captain, he has the fastest bike out of all of us, thanks to some of my custom installs. Next to him is an equivalent model with similar speed; I'm eager to see how Axel's bike performs against it. When the flag drops, the two bikes take off and hold steady next to each other, challenging their riding skills, then it changes to their bikes' performance when Axel shifts and rolls on the throttle. The space between the two bikes becomes a massive gap, and Axel takes the win. With our fists and beer bottles in the air, we cheer him on.

Soon, our attention returns to the starting line as Trevor rolls up with his red devil, the nickname he gave his ride. With Axel in the race, I'm certain Trevor won't win, but Trevor does have a good shot at the badass bike contest. The custom paint job I did on his ride looks killer. Trevor and his opponent go head-to-head, and with the weight of Trevor's bike, he takes a loss. He doesn't care though, it's all an excuse to show off our bikes and indulge in our need for speed.

Trevor rejoins our crew, and we all get revved in anticipation of Axel's next race. He pulls up with his glossy black and shiny gold Harley. Next to him is a red, white, and blue ride with an American flag attached to the sissy bar. The bike is pretty badass, but like Trevor's ride, it looks like it's more for show and cruising than racing. The race flag drops, and the red, white, and blue Honda is left behind as Axel gains speed and roars through the finish line. With another triumphant win, the Kings seem to have forgotten the stress of the fight from earlier today. Maci returns with Audrey and an ice-cold bucket of beers. They're joyously welcomed as the men grab fresh cold bottles and pop the tops. It's another two races before Axel is up again, but this time he meets his match and loses the race. Shortly after, he joins us on the wooden bleachers, and we give him a congratulatory beer and pats on the back in celebration of his wins.

As I sit back down, I pull Synne onto my lap, and she loops an arm around my neck and steals my beer. Tilting her head back, she chugs several long swallows, then hands it back to me half empty. Setting it aside, I finger at the frayed strings of her jean shorts, and she nibbles that plump pink lip of hers.

"Are we still on for tonight?"

There's hope in her sensuous gaze—hope for time alone with me, hope for pleasure—and I want to fulfill every dirty thought running through my mind.

Sliding a finger farther up her shorts, I tease the soft flesh of her pussy, and she spreads her legs just a bit wider for me to feel her slickness. As soon as I do, my cock stretches, and all I can think of is how much I want that slick heat surrounding my dick.

"I always keep my promises."

With her legs spread between mine, I reach farther up and circle her underwear against her clit. Her head falls back against my shoulder, and she sucks in a breath, doing her best to keep her face impassive, but her rising chest gives away how much she craves more of my touch.

Grabbing a fistful of her hair, I lick along her ear before I whisper, "Will you let me fuck every hole?" Facing me, there's a lascivious twinkle in her eye. "You like that idea, don't you?"

Staring at her hazel gems, I catch her leg as she swings it over mine and angles her body to face me. My hand goes right to her ass as she sucks along the shell of my ear and bites at the lobe. Goosebumps race across my flesh, and my cock goes full length.

"The thought of you fucking my mouth, pussy, and ass turns me on like you wouldn't believe. We should ditch the crew and begin our night together. I'm so damn horny for you."

Pulling her ass across my erection lights up her eyes.

"I feel the same." Bringing those full pink lips closer, I slip my tongue between them, my cock now painfully erect and desperate for her pussy. "Give me a minute to handle this, then we'll go back to camp."

Sneaking her hand down between us, she massages my hard-on. My head drops, my eyes pinching closed as I battle the mix of pain and pleasure.

"Keep it up, and I'll bend you over this bleacher and fuck you in front of everyone."

The playful challenge in her eyes feeds my raging libido. Putting my hand over hers, I wink.

"You're askin' for it, aren't ya?"

"I wouldn't stop you if you did."

My head lowers, a chuckle rumbling out of my chest.

"Damn, babe, you're full of surprises, and I love it."

Reaching over, I snap my fingers and get Trevor's attention. When he looks, I point to Liz. "Get her for me."

Liz leaves Jake's side and comes to mine.

"What's up?"

"You mind if I use the camper tonight? Synne and I need time alone."

Liz and Synne exchange glances, both of them flashing smirks at one another.

"No problem. There's an extra tent in the camper. Leave it out for us. I'm not sleeping in your jizz covered tent."

Synne tightens her lips, holding back her laughter. My smile draws up the side of my mouth.

"You're not wrong about that. I'll leave the tent out. Knock if you need anything else inside."

Leaving us, she returns to Jake. He looks over at me, and I slide Synne off my lap now that my erection is down enough to walk around without my jeans looking like a horizontal teepee. With my arm around her, I motion for Jake and Dominic to join me. They follow us off the bleachers to a private spot at the back corner of them.

"We're headed back to camp. Just the two of us. We'll be in the camper for the night. I don't care how late it is, I want to know when you're back and how things went. Check in and report with Max as we planned."

"We have this handled. Nothing to worry about." Dominic's confidence eases the nerves tickling the back of my neck.

"We'll have each other's backs. In and out like silent predators," Jake shares.

I accept Jake's fist and clamp mine around it, then tap him on the back.

"Be safe, brother."

I offer the same to Dominic and am pleased with his acceptance of the gesture. In the last few months, the friendship we started has come to feel like a true brotherhood between us. I'd trust this guy with my life, and I believe he'd do the same.

Jake dips his chin at Synne. "Take care of him."

Synne moves in closer, and I wrap my arm around her. Reaching between my legs, she grabs my dick, taking me by surprise.

"He'll be very well taken care of, I assure you."

"That's my cue." Winking at Jake and Dominic, I match their grins and slap Synne's ass. With my arm draped around her shoulder, I lead us out of the racetrack as the cruisers finish, and the sport bikes begin. Sliding my hand into her tank, I rest my hand over her breast. She doesn't stop me or pull away, and I bring her in close to kiss her in appreciation. Synne is comfortable with her sexuality, and I appreciate that about her. She isn't shy in showing her attraction to me, and I don't ever want her to be. If she's always this open about intimacy, we're going to have a damn good relationship.

Every so often, she glances up at me, and each time, I steal a kiss. After the third kiss at the edge of our camp trail, we stop walking, and I hold her face to mine as I deepen the kiss. Looking down at her, I lose myself in the flecks of gold and green amid the light brown in her irises.

"You're beautiful."

With a soft expression, her lips part, and she reaches up to touch my hand caressing her cheek.

"The way you make me feel... I'm happy you asked me to be your girl."

"I am too."

Taking her hand, I lead us through the trail into the opening with our vehicles and tents. Unlocking the camper, I open the door for her and wait for her to enter first. Inside, she gathers two cups from the cabinet and fills them halfway full of liquor. Handing me one, she watches me behind the glass as she tips it back and empties it. I do the same, moving forward as I set the glass down on the counter. Caging her between me and it, I remove the space between us, my whiskey flavored lips meeting hers.

Sliding her hands beneath my vest, she peels it off my shoulders and down my arms. I catch the vest and toss it onto the table. Putting my hands on her hips, I bring her with me, leading us to the bed. Snaking her hands up my shirt, she works it up my chest, and I toss it on the floor as my ass lands on the bed. She takes a step back and slowly undresses, letting me admire every curve of her hot as fuck body.

Unzipping my pants, I loosen my erection and fist it in my palm, pumping it as she lowers her hands, fingering her pussy. When she steps forward, I replace her fingers with mine, her silky wetness coating them like I want her to coat my stretched cock.

"Ride me, baby."

Bringing her forward, I lie on my back as she straddles me. One hand grips her hip as she slides onto me, her eager pussy taking me fully without having to ease in. With her pussy clenched around me, I palm her tit, my thumb giving extra attention to her tight nipple as she pulls off my cock, then comes forward again, taking all of me. My head falls back, and my right hand drops to her hip, gripping her as I continue to thrust my hips up, matching her rhythm. The slick heat of her pussy and the sensation of pure unadulterated pleasure coursing through my veins draws my orgasm through my shaft. Exploding into her, I continue to grip her hips, pushing deep into her. She lowers on top of me, and I wrap my arms around her, caressing her hair and back. Together, our paired lips move in affectionate languid motions, our hands caressing the other, their strokes silent words of affection.

"I care about you. Probably more deeply than I'm ready to admit. I want you to know you're not a replacement. Who you are, what we have, is different from what I had before."

The tip of her finger swipes down my cheek and across my lips as her gaze stays locked on me. The gloss of her eyes and the way she swallows her first words exposes her vulnerability as if I've uncovered a deep well, pooling with emotion.

"I don't give a fuck what that asshole said. You're different, so different from the rest. You love deeply and protect those you care about fiercely. I know I mean something to you. I can feel it here." She rocks her hips forward, the friction stiffening my cock. "And I can feel it here." Lips like candy and spice, sweet and invigorating, drop to mine, and I don't back off for air.

With my arm around her, I turn us, putting her on

her back. Pushing forward, my stretched cock invents new sounds of arousal from her lips.

"This rounds for you."

Mouth tilted and hungry for more of her, I kick my jeans and boots off. With one hard thrust, my cock is surrounded by slick heat. One thrust after the other, her lips solicit sounds expressive of her mounting pleasure. Pulling her knees together, I raise her legs, holding them toward the ceiling. Her palms fist the blanket as her ass is raised off the bed, my cock driving in and out of her clenched pussy. Her arousal soaks my cock, and her bottom lip disappears between her teeth, just before she releases it and cries out in satisfaction. Freeing her legs, they drop like deadweight as her palms open and let go of the blanket. Face flushed, her eyes widen when I raise one leg, drape it over my forearm, grip her hip, and slam forward, thrusting as hard and deep as before. I've yet to cum, and if I'm lucky, I'll get another orgasm out of her before I do.

Raising her arms, she palms the wall, spewing *fuck me* between her moans. Watching her tits bounce adds to my arousal, and a moment later, reaching my orgasm, I drop her leg and lean over her as the pleasure courses through me. Another orgasm makes her pussy spasm around my dick, and I can't help smirking at the equally exhausted and pleasured expression on her face.

"Next time, I'm coming in this tight ass."

Using the wetness from her pussy, I finger her hole. Spreading her legs wider, she gives me better access.

With her wayward grin, there's no denying she wants me to stick my dick where my finger is. Closing her eyes, she indulges in the pleasure I'm giving her. With each stroke of my finger, I swipe my thumb over her clit, and her body shudders. The more I finger her hole, the more she moans, her body stretching. Fisting my cock, I work up another erection as I add another finger in her ass.

"Can you handle me, baby?"

Hazel eyes glance down at my growing erection, a questioning thought furrowing her brow.

"Yes. Just go slow at first, your cock is fucking colossal."

Laughter rumbles out of my chest. Withdrawing my fingers, I take her thighs and flip her over. At first, I slide into her pussy, taking her from behind, massaging her back and ass cheeks as I thrust slowly. Pulling out, I hold the head to her ass, pushing in gently, then pull out when I feel her tense. Several more times, I ease in, stretching her, the friction already pumping blood to my cock, teasing at another orgasm.

Moans progressing, her body relaxes, taking me fully. With my cock buried to my balls, I fist her hair, pulling her head back. Sucking at her neck, the skin puckers after my bite. With her breathing heightened and her ass squeezing my cock, I quicken my pace, the tight, ribbed friction making me groan as my cock swells inside her. The sound of her ass slaps against my pelvic bone, and my eyes close, the rush of ecstasy taking over my body as I cum inside her.

My body falls above her, my arms on either side of her as I pull out and kiss her shoulder.

"Fuck... your ass feels even better, and I thought your pussy was incredible."

Beneath me, she rolls onto her back, her beautiful smile etched into my memory.

"That felt so damn good. We need to make it a regular thing."

My chin drops, the high of sex still lingering in every limb as a smirk curls the corner of my mouth.

"This is why you're mine. You're beautiful, strong, and kinky as fuck. You've reminded me what it feels like to want something good again."

"You're not broken." She leans up on her elbow as I drop to my side, my fingers tracing the tip of a tattooed feather on her hip. "You might be scarred, but you're still capable of having happiness."

My fingers stop, my eyes jumping to hers.

"I'm not the same man I was. Losing Jenna did break me. There's only one thing left that can give me closure."

"You and the Kings... you're planning to retaliate, aren't you?"

"That's club business, and club business is private."

"Yet you discussed it in front of me. I believe you know you can trust me."

Lifting her fingers, I bring them to my lips.

"I do, but that doesn't change the fact I want you kept away from certain things."

"Am I truly better left in the dark or better off being prepared for what's to come?"

Rolling onto my back, I place my arm behind my head, staring up at the ceiling panel and the tiny nick in the corner, wondering what the right answer is. Turning my face to hers, I place my thumb on her tender lips, and she kisses it, her gaze as penetrating as it was before.

"I've made a lot of mistakes. I don't want to lose you too. I need you. Which is why I won't ever share the worst of me. I don't want you to ever stop looking at me the way you are now."

Leaning over my chest, she cups my jaw in her hand.

"I want to be with you, which means accepting all of you. If we're going to do this, we need to let each other in."

Raising my head, my lips press to hers, my affection for her escaping between each breath of passion.

"You're already in, deeper than I was prepared for."

CHAPTER SIXTEEN

DOMINIC

IT'S BEEN a while since I've shed blood. I can't deny I've missed it. It's why my cousin, Jake was my only choice for backup. If things go south, I know I can rely on him to handle the situation and do what it takes for us to survive. Crouching behind the wooded vegetation, twenty yards out from the Royals' campsite, we watch them throw back hard liquor and listen to the sounds of their boisterous partying. Sitting on the edge of a truck tailgate is a thickly bearded man I've come to know as Rex. His legs are spread, his dick hanging out as a bike bunny blows his load. She must do something to piss him off. He shoves her off him and backhands her. She drops on her ass, her fists digging into the dirt. Dropping down from the tailgate, he fists her hair and shoves his cock down her throat as he tips his beer bottle back.

"That fucker. He's the one," Jake snarls. "He's on the

inside. He'll have the information we need, and he's a woman-beating drunk, who owes me blood."

"Get comfortable. We'll wait until they're passed out, then take him."

It doesn't take that long. Twenty minutes or so after Rex forces the bike bunny to finish the job, he walks toward the woods to take a leak. We got lucky with this dumb fuck. Signaling to Jake, I motion for us to move through the woods after him. Pulling the knife from its sheath on my belt loop, I step as quietly as my boots allow. The blade of my knife tucks under the base of Rex's shaft as my arm whips around from behind and covers his mouth. The man jolts, and Jake is there in front of him, the barrel of a gun pointed at his head.

"If you ever want to feel another pussy, you'll keep your mouth shut." Rex opens his mouth against my palm as if he's going to shout, and I tighten the blade on his dick. A hoarse whimper vibrates against my fingers. "Be smart. Don't test me. I'll cut it off, slit your throat, and leave you here, drowning in your own blood."

Jake puts a boot forward, pressing the gun deeper into Rex's forehead.

"By the time the gunshot registers to your brothers we'll be long gone. Cooperate, and you live." Jake uses his free hand and pulls a set of cuffs out of his jeans pocket. "Put these on."

Rex catches them and makes an "oomph" sound when my blade tightens on his balls. Complying, Rex cuffs his own wrist, and Jake fastens the other. Clasping his palm over the cuffs, Jake jerks Rex, and I shove the blade against his throat as we march forward. Several feet ahead, we lose the light of the campfire, so I flick on my cell phone flashlight to guide us.

"What the fuck is this, Castle?"

Gripping the back of his neck, I shove him forward, and he glances over his shoulder, glaring at me.

"Unless we ask you a question, don't make a fucking sound."

Behind us, a male voice calls out Rex's name. Rex turns toward the voice, his lips moving as if he's going to shout for help. The butt of Jake's gun slams into Rex's skull, and the man's body twists awkwardly before collapsing on the ground.

Without having to say anything, Jake holsters his gun and tucks his arms under Rex's as I tuck my hands under the man's knees. Together, we carry him out of the woods, my cell dangling from my mouth, lighting our path.

—NIX—

SYNNE'S BODY is half covering me, her leg wrapped around mine like two snakes mating. Stretching my arm out, I do my best to reach for my vibrating cell without waking her.

"What's the report?" I whisper to Max.

"Job's done. Dom and Jake are on their way back. We're meeting by Axel's tailgate."

The call disconnects, and I set the phone aside as I attempt to slide out from under Synne. My efforts are futile as she mumbles inaudible words, then her eyes blink a couple of times as she raises her head to look at me.

"I need to meet with the Kings. I'll be back soon."

"What time is it?"

"Three-thirty."

"Where are you guys going?" Her bottom lip puckers as I sit up and drop my legs off the side of the bed.

"Nowhere. We need to talk about some things."

"About the job Dom and Jake were doing?"

"Don't ask questions I can't give answers to." Leaning over, I kiss her, and she drops back down on the bed, the silver glow of the moonlight highlighting the round shape of her tits. Palming one, I caress over her nipple, and it hardens under my thumb. "I'll make it up to you when I get back."

Wrapping her hand over mine, she moves it between her legs, and I rub at her clit until she's breathing harder.

"That's a promise."

A shadow of a smile dances over her lips.

"I'm holding you to it."

Before my cock gets any harder, I pull my hand away

and comb the floor until I find my jeans and boots. With them on, I leave the camper, using my cell phone as a flashlight. Around the tailgate of Axel's truck are my crew, and in the moonlit distance are two familiar figures walking toward us. Axel leaves his flashlight on and sets the phone on his tailgate, giving us more light.

Jake and Dom approach, my eyes dropping to the bloody knuckles of Dom's fist.

"I'm glad you're back, brothers. How'd it go?"

Jake hops onto the tailgate and removes his ball cap, rubbing the back of his head as he lets out a tired breath.

"We left him with his clutch and throttle hands, minus half a digit."

Dom chuckles, then accepts a bottle of water Ink hands him. Moving between our circle, Ink hands one to Jake too.

"We got the information we needed," Dom tells me, twisting the cap off the bottle and chugging half of it. "Their largest drug supply is being held in a repair shop. It's distributed, loaded into vehicles, then driven to the drop points. It's perfect for our plans."

"Good. And the Royal?" I question.

"Rex won't be talking, texting, or writing for at least six weeks. We broke his jaw and several fingers."

"Fuck," Ink mumbles, twisting one hand over the other.

Dom glances at Ink and grunts as if Ink needs to toughen up.

"Where is he now?"

"Unconscious and lying in a ditch outside a bar," Dom shares. "It'll look like he got in a drunken bar fight."

"You guys did damn good. Get a good night's rest. Tomorrow, we'll begin plans for stage two."

"Where's Peach?" Jake asks, hopping down from the tailgate.

"In the spare tent," I point toward it, and Jake veers off, his mind set on one thing now, his woman.

The crew splits, and I return to Synne, who's half-covered under the blanket. Once I'm naked, she lifts the blanket for me to join her.

CHAPTER SEVETEEN

NIX

WITH JAKE'S HELP, we roll my reaper onto the patch of pavement for the badass bike show. With the kickstand down and the *Custom Ride* tag hanging from the handlebars, I take the key and leave the bike. Three motorcycles down, Trevor and Max have prepared Trevor's red devil for the show. Leaving the bike row, we move to the side of the crowd and rejoin the rest of our crew. Once the announcer says the show has started, our crew weaves in and out of the show bikes, admiring the custom work put into each road machine.

A familiar trike with custom front and rear tires, custom handlebar grips, and a killer black and blue teardrop paint job catches my attention, and that's because I did every inch of bodywork on that bike. The owner, Jim, is standing behind it, answering questions from a fellow rider, and when he sees me, a grin slices through his lips and curves his mouth. Jim's white-haired ponytail flops off his shoulder as he turns his head toward me, opening his tattooed arm out as I approach.

"This is the guy who did all the custom work. If you want anything done right, you go see Nix at Custom Ride," he tells the man. "No one does a better job."

Shaking the older man's hand, I enter into a conversation about what he rides and what he's looking to upgrade on it. My crew doesn't go far, keeping an eye on my back as I'm busy talking business. In my periphery, I catch Royal back patches and the cold stare of Reed glaring at me over his shoulder as he and a few Royals pass by. My gaze follows Reed's as he looks Synne up and down. She flicks him off, never peeling her gaze from his for a second. That's my girl.

Reed motions to one of his guys, and under his arm is Angela, her expression sullen, her eyes full of fear. Reed blows a mocking kiss at me, then grabs Angela, jerks her to him, and grabs her ass. She doesn't fight it like the woman I knew would. Reed shoves her back at the other Royal, and he puts his tongue down her throat. My stomach lurches when I see him pass her to another Royal, and that son of a bitch does the same thing. They're passing her around like she's the whole club's pussy. Evidently, she got back together with Rex, and with him missing or in the hospital, she probably thinks it's her only way to remain protected.

Giving the potential client one of my cards, I excuse

myself and motion to my crew. Jake and Max flank my sides as I walk along the bike row.

"They're using Angela as their club whore now that Rex is out."

"Think they suspect us of fucking Rex up?" Max asks, his tone uneasy.

Keeping a distance, I pretend to look at the motorcycles while watching Reed and his crew.

"Nah," Jake replies. "Unless he used his toes to spell Kings, they don't know who beat the shit out of him."

"I agree. That shit with Angela is a show of dominance. He has the woman who used to be mine."

"What do you want us to do?" Jake stops next to me, glances over his shoulder to check on Liz, then leans back on his heels, arms crossed as he awaits my answer.

"Get one of our girls to follow Angela into a bathroom. We'll offer her protection and cash to get out of town."

"What about tonight's job?" Max tucks his thumbs into his vest as he looks at me questioningly. "We can't escort her out of town and get done what we need to."

Running a hand over my facial hair, I click my tongue in frustration.

"You're right. We'll tell her to meet us tomorrow night."

"IT CAN'T BE ME," Liz shakes her head, the lines around

her mouth tight. "The moment she sees me enter the bathroom, she'll bolt."

"She's right." Jake shrugs his shoulders. "Angela will think Liz is coming at her to fight."

At the edge of the massive crowd of motorcycle enthusiasts, our crew has claimed a picnic table, and I'm standing at the end next to Jake, Liz, Erika, and Dom. Glancing at Erika, I consider her as a choice, especially after what happened to her sister.

"What about you, Erika? Could you talk to her?"

Erika starts to speak, but Dom puts an arm around her. Her words fade, and she looks up at him with questioning eyes as he shakes his head no.

"She's not getting involved."

"All right. Fair enough."

Synne, who's been listening to our discussion, lowers her beer and stands from the end of the picnic table.

"I'll do it. I'll talk to this chick."

My back goes rigid, and I nearly bite the inside of my cheek as my jaw clenches.

"That's not a good idea."

"Why?" Synne raises a brow, her lips thinning as she frowns. "Because she's your ex?" My crew watches as Synne squares off to me. "Doesn't matter. She needs help, so I'll talk to her, let her know what you're offering. I'm not going to lose my shit because you used to fuck her."

Coming forward, I jerk her to me and rest my hands on her lower back. She softens, her tough exterior melting a coat. Dom, Erika, Jake, and Liz move away to give us space.

"I don't like the idea of you being anywhere near her. She's a conniving bitch and will probably say something to piss you off or make you upset with me." With her hands on my arms, she slips them under my T-shirt sleeves and caresses my biceps, the sensation easing some of my tension. "Plus, I feel like shit sending my girl in to talk to my ex."

"Don't overthink it. I'm just taking a message to her. Having run from the Sons, I can offer her some decent advice. And if the Royals see me follow her in, it'll look like the new girl is threatened by the ex."

Leaning my head against hers, I caress her back, and her muscles relax.

"I'll never be able to say no to you, will I?"

Breathy laughter escapes her lips, and she licks them, leaving a sheen of moisture on my lips after I've kissed her.

"Not if I can help it."

Lifting her chin, I stare back at the intricate blend of colors in her eyes.

"To be clear, I don't have any love for that woman, but I don't want to see her used and abused either."

Eliminating the space between us, she slips her tongue between my lips, the passion she exudes stretching my cock.

"I know. It's why you're the amazing man you are."

Putting my hand through her hair, I kiss along her

cheek and throat, leaving an imprint of my lips on her neck.

"Be careful," I whisper. "Max and Axel will stay with you. Don't go anywhere without them." I nibble her earlobe, and she releases a pleasured sigh. "I'm going to be a stressed-out motherfucker until you return to me. You know that, don't you?"

"Yes," she whispers back. "But I love how much you care."

With my fingers wound in her soft crimson waves, I kiss her temple. "I care a lot... more than you know."

As I let go of her, she pulls me back in for another kiss, and as we stand there, lips locked, my crew whistles and hollers their approval. My mouth is upturned in a grin as she withdraws. When she pivots to walk away from me, I slap her ass, and she glances over her shoulder, a grin etched on her stunning face.

"Max, Axel, go with Synne." Axel tosses his empty Coke in a nearby trashcan as he stands from the table. "Don't let her out of your sight."

Max gives a tap to his vest. "You got it, brother. She'll be protected."

The three of them disappear into the crowd as I heave an exasperated sigh.

—SYNNE—

ON EITHER SIDE OF ME, Axel and Max are watch

187

guards. Axel is the taller of the two with rusty brown hair, a full, lengthy beard, and more tattoos than I can count. His dark jeans have a chain running from the front to the wallet in his back pocket, and he doesn't wear anything under his vest so he can show off all his artistic ink. Max is shorter and beefier, his brown hair currently buzzed. Sharp brown eyes are always scanning his surroundings. There's an air about him that suggests he's ex-military, and if you don't recognize it, there's a small patch on the lower right side of his vest that proves it.

Around us, the bustle of bike week is active, the scent of beer, brats, and funnel cakes in the air. Stepping up to a food vendor truck, I put my order in for a root beer and a barbeque pulled pork sandwich, then Axel and Max put in their orders. Once we get our food, we keep moving through the crowd, keeping our eyes peeled for Royal patches. Finding a few open spots at a picnic table, we scarf down our food, licking our fingers clean. Max's Coke is halfway to his mouth when he lowers it and points a finger behind me.

"I've got eyes on the Royals. Angela is with them."

"Good. Let me know if she walks off."

Axel chucks our containers in the nearby trash. "We could be following them all day. We don't have all day."

Eyeing him sideways, my brow rises.

"What are you suggesting?"

Axel points at my drink. "Make her have to go to the bathroom."

My nose wrinkles as my tongue smacks the inside of my cheek. "The girl's going through enough. She doesn't need my drink dumped on her too."

Max swings a leg over the bench and straddles it as he rests his chin in his hand and his elbow on the table.

"She cheated on Nix with one of our brothers. And before she did, she was continually making advances on the rest of us." Max glances at Axel, and they share a private exchange.

"I think she wanted to be the Kings' club pussy, but that sure as hell isn't what Nix wanted." Axel runs a hand through his smooth hair and angles his head toward me. "I wouldn't be surprised if she wanted to be the Royal's club pussy."

Disgust churns my stomach and my lip curls. "Maybe she wanted to be with all of you, but it doesn't automatically mean she wants to be tossed around and abused by the Royals. I have eyes. I saw the way they were shoving her around."

Axel fusses with the silver ring on his thumb, twisting it clockwise. "Yeah, maybe you're right."

Max swings his leg back over the bench and leans his body across the table toward me.

"We need to figure out a way to speed this along. We don't have all day."

They're anxious, and I know it has to do with the retaliation they're planning. Whatever crazy plan they have in place, I don't want to be the one to interrupt those plans and endanger them. Looking over my shoulder, the side of my mouth pulls down as I watch Angela get manhandled as the Royals wait in line for food.

"All right, I'll figure out something to get her to the bathroom."

My cup is half empty, but there's enough liquid to do the trick. With each step I take toward her in line, my stomach knots. Regret is forming in sweat bubbles across my back and neck. Raising my cup, I make a path toward her, her back facing me. I'm so close now, I could throw the drink and keep walking, but my feet slow, my hand tightening around the cup. When I stop, a man bumps into me, trips forward, and dumps two full cups of beer onto the back of Angela and the Royal standing next to her. Like a flash of lightning, I whip around and rush into the mix of people walking. Briefly glancing over my shoulder, I catch the Royal barking at the other biker, his anger coming out in spittle onto the other man's face. Angela's arms are up in the air, and she looks just as angry. Another chick with the Royals grabs a couple of napkins from the condiment stand outside the vendor booth and tries to help dry her off. Angela accepts the napkins, says something to the woman, then veers off toward the nearest women's bathroom. I'm grateful it didn't have to be me. It'll make this conversation much easier.

Axel and Max are watching from the picnic table. I signal to them, then head toward the same building as Angela. On each side of the building are men's and women's restrooms. Slipping inside the women's, I find Angela at a mirror with a wad of paper towels.

"Fucking asshole," she grumbles.

Pulling another towel from the dispenser, I run it under water, then approach her.

"Here, let me."

Almond-shaped brown eyes narrow in on me and I lower the towel.

"Aren't you Nix's new girl?" Her tone is dripping with acid, and her eyes are like daggers, trying to slice through me.

"I am, but that doesn't change the fact you have beer dripping down your back and need a second set of hands."

Her lips press together as spots of color enter her cheeks. "Why the hell would you offer to help me? Haven't you heard what a whore I am?"

Closing the paper towel in my fist, I cross my arms. "Look, I'm not here to hassle you. You looked like you could use a hand. Take my help or don't."

Poking a tongue into her cheek, she inhales a long breath. "Fine. Could you wipe between my shoulders?"

"Yeah." Standing behind her, I move her damp ponytail to the side of her shoulder and wipe the towel down her back to the top of her faux leather camisole. In the dingy smeared mirror, her intelligent eyes watch me, studying me.

"You're hotter than the last redhead." As she says it, her voice vibrates with irritation.

"I guess that's a compliment."

A frown draws her lips down. "Maybe it shouldn't be. You know what happened to the last woman he dated, don't you?"

Wiping left to right, I clean the beer off her shoulder blades. In the mirror, I share an uncomfortable glance with her as my stomach tightens.

"I do."

"You need to keep Nix away from the Royals. They want blood. My ol' man is missing. They think the Kings had something to do with it."

Keeping my face stoic, I move to the sink and run the towel under the water again.

"I don't know what happened to your ol' man, but based on the bruises you've covered with makeup, it's probably better he's missing."

Angela goes silent, disengaging from the conversation. With her towel in hand, she wraps it around her ponytail and pulls it down over her dark red hair. Another woman walks into the bathroom, and the tension between us amplifies. We're both quiet until she comes out of the stall. She glances at us then quick steps out of the bathroom as if she knows she's interrupting something awkward.

Angela moves away from me and dumps her wad of paper towels in the trash. Adjusting her top, she thins her eyes as she stares at me.

"Why are you still here?"

Leaning against the porcelain sink, I cross my arms. "I have a message from Nix."

Throwing her black nail polished hand in the air, she huffs. "All right. What is it?"

Looking back at her, I can see why Nix was attracted to her. She's curvy in all the right places, has sass, and a face that would attract most men. She was probably even prettier before the stress lines, bruises, and layers of makeup.

"He's offering you an out."

Eyes widening, her head tilts to the side. "What do you mean, an out?"

"A protection escort and cash so you can get out of town and have a fresh start."

Her eyes narrow to slits and her shoulders square off to me.

"Why now?"

"He saw how the Royals were treating you. If you knew Nix well, you know he protects the people he cares about, even exes."

Moisture pools in her eyes, her expression softening as her shoulders slump.

"Nix was good to me. I never should've screwed him over." With a sniffle, she wipes at her nose, glances at the tiled floor, and drifts off in thought. A moment later, she returns her attention to me, her eyes covered in a glossy sheen. "I want out, but I don't know how to do it."

Seeing fear in her gaze, I lower my arms and step closer, putting a hand on her bare shoulder.

"I've been in your position. I ran from my home, my club, and my ol' man. It was the most terrifying thing I've ever done, but I'd do it again. I wasn't safe there. If you're no longer safe with the Royals, you need to do what's best for you and get out while you can. No woman should ever have to take a man's abuse."

Pulling away from me, she snags another paper towel and dabs the corner of her eyes.

"What's the plan? How does Nix suggest I get out?"

Glancing over my shoulder, I ensure no one is coming into the bathroom. With nervous eyes, Angela looks over my shoulder too.

"You'll have to find an opportunity to slip away from them tomorrow night. Once you do, come to the Kings' camp. Nix and the Kings will give you an escort out of town. They mentioned taking you to a bus station and giving you enough cash for a month's rent plus necessities."

She's quick to wipe away a single tear rolling down her cheek. "I can't believe he's doing this for me after everything I put him through."

"You know how he is."

Wiping at another tear, she smears her makeup, revealing more discoloration on her cheek. My heart sinks at the sight.

"And you're okay with this?"

"Yes." The sincerity in my voice is raw, and I know she senses my worry for her.

"I'm sorry for being a bitch when you came in here."

Behind the tough exterior, there's a damaged woman doing everything she can to hold that wall up, but I can see it breaking down, and it hurts to see it.

"Don't worry about it. I get it." My posture sags as I offer a half-smile. "You should probably get back and keep up appearances."

Letting out a slow, labored breath, she nods. "At least I only have to put up with their shit for another day. Tell Nix I'll be there. I won't fall back on my word."

"I believe you. I'll see you tomorrow."

CHAPTER EIGHTEEN

NIX

THE ANNOUNCER IS about to share the badass bike contest winners, and I'm sitting on a wooden bench, my leg tapping like a piston. I can't give him my attention though, not when I'm scanning the crowd, watching for Synne to return with Axel and Max. The moment I see her red hair emerge through the crowd, air expands my lungs and releases the breath I was holding. With my arms out, I hug her to my chest and kiss her.

"How'd it go?"

Ink scoots down the bench and makes room for Synne to sit next to me. She settles with my arm resting on her hip.

"It went good. I'll fill you in later."

The microphone crackles just before the male announcer shares the news the crowd is eager to receive.

"Third place goes to Jim Callahan of Memphis, Tennessee for his Capone custom trike!"

The edginess that had my muscles knotted like a rope loosen. Even if I don't win, I'm proud a customer of mine placed third. Jim steps up to the wooden platform and accepts his motorcycle trophy and an enlarged showcase check in place of the real one he'll receive once he steps off the platform. A few photos are taken, then he's asked to wait behind the announcer while the other two winners are revealed.

"Second place goes to Nix Wilson of Nashville, Tennessee for his custom grim reaper Harley Road Glide!"

Whoops and clapping hands echo around me as I stand and walk to the platform. Pride erupts in the form of a grin as I accept the motorcycle trophy and take hold of the cardboard check. Bright flashes of light temporary blind me, and a moment later, I'm being congratulated, patted on the back, and escorted to stand next to Jim. Outstretching his fist, I knock mine to it, and he dips his chin at me.

"Well done, son."

"Thanks, man."

"First place goes to Roy Dunham of Gadsglove, Alabama for his custom American flag Harley Road King!"

Not entirely surprised, I give congratulations as the pepper-haired man lines up next to me after accepting his trophy and photo.

"It's a badass bike. Killer paint job," I praise.

Roy gives a nod and points to my ride.

"I was worried when I saw yours. That's some talent in that detail work."

Jim leans toward us and pipes in. With a finger extended from his trophy hand, he points between me and him.

"It's his work. He did my trike too."

"Well, I'll be damned. I'll have to get your number if I'm ever in need of custom work again. It'd be a good excuse for a ride up here."

A cute blonde, showing off as much cleavage as her lacy shirt will allow, interrupts the conversation and requests photos of us with the bikes. My crew sticks around and bullshits as I'm given direction to stand next to my bike, just like the other two men. The photographer takes single shots of each of us, then group photos. At the end, each of us take the real winnings via a check in an envelope. Opening it, I discover how much the pot is this year. One thousand, two hundred and fifty is a real good take home. Tucking the check back inside the envelope, I fold it and slide it into my back pocket. The cute blonde bounces up to me, her smile beaming.

"Hey, good lookin'."

If I was still single, I would've considered a one-night stand with this chick, but knowing what's waiting for me with Synne has my interest at zero.

"Sorry, sweets, my crew's waiting for me."

"I could join you. I'm free now that the show's over." Baby blue eyes hint at experience, not innocence. Coming closer, she stands straighter, giving me a perfect view of her creamy tits as she thumbs her jeans pocket, flashing me a lascivious grin. Chuckling, I shake my head.

"You're cute, but—"

"He's taken."

Synne steps up and my arm goes out to curl her under it.

"Hey, baby," I greet, kissing her cheek.

Disappointment draws the blonde's mouth into a frown. Releasing a resigned sigh, she turns on her heel.

"Congrats on winning," she utters over her shoulder.

"I can't leave you alone," Synne quips.

"All the more reason you should stick close."

Beneath my arm, her muscles relax. Turning me to her, she tugs my vest, bringing my mouth to hers, reminding me why I'm ready for time alone with her again.

Lying on the camper bed, I twist my cell phone in my hand. Glancing at the clock on my screen for the third time, I stop thinking about worst-case scenarios and scoot out from beneath Synne. As usual, my movement wakes her, and she pops her head up, the silver moonlight accentuating the stress creases at the corner of her eyes.

"You're leaving, aren't you?"

With two fingers under her chin, I pull her to me and merge our lips.

"I have to. The Kings have business we need to take care of."

Turning on her side, she bends her elbow and rests her head in her hand.

"This is about the Royals. I know it is."

She fingers a loose thread in the blue blanket, her mouth pulled down in a frown.

Gathering my jeans, I step into each pant leg, my heart heavy with the way she's reacting.

"I'm sorry. It's better for you if I don't share details."

Laying her hand flat on the blanket, her eyes angle toward me, revealing the concern in her sleek irises.

"When will you be back?"

Buckling my pants, I sit on the edge of the camper bed and tug my boots onto my feet.

"Don't know. Whenever our business is finished."

The silky touch of her fingers wrap around my chest as her warm, naked breasts flatten against my back.

"I'm worried."

Bringing her hand to my mouth, I kiss the inside of her palm.

"About what?"

With her hand in mine, I turn toward her and bring her into my arms.

"When the men I care for leave to do something dangerous, they end up hurt, and I end up hurting too."

"We're not attacking the Royals. There won't be a gunfight."

Across her warm skin, I caress my hands, but her muscles refuse to loosen.

"But what you're doing is still dangerous. You don't have to tell me details for me to know."

I kiss her forehead, and she inhales deeply, letting it out slowly. With how difficult this is for her, it's making it even harder for me to leave.

"Nix, please."

"Baby, I have to go. I'm sorry."

Moisture glistens in her eyes as I stand and leave her on the bed.

"Try not to wait up."

"I will be waiting. I'm going to be a nervous wreck until you return."

Leaving my vest behind in exchange for a long sleeve black shirt, I lean down, giving her a quick kiss goodbye, avoiding the worry in her eyes that matches the stiffness in my chest.

Outside the camper, there are more discussions happening like the one Synne and I just had. Audrey is whisper shouting at Trevor, and Dominic is giving Erika a look that says don't argue. Giving the signal, my crew says their goodbyes, and we climb on our bikes. Axel's truck is behind us, the truck bed cover concealing the boxes of supplies we need for tonight.

Leading my crew into town, I turn my high beam down and shift into first, coasting into the parking lot, two buildings down from Hacker's Automotive. I never knew the automotive shop was owned by the Royals until Dom extracted that vital piece of information from Rex.

With everyone knowing what their role is, my crew steps off their bikes and get to work. Covering their faces with black ski masks, Ink and William haul out the paint guns from the back of Axel's truck. They're the first to go in to black out all the security cameras. With the job done, Dom gathers the lock pick gun. With his mask over his face, he gets us in the front door, then enters the security code Rex gave him into the panel. The tiny light flashes green and we close the door behind us. With a duffle bag over my shoulder, I move past the familiar odor of grease and mechanic supplies to the door of the auto parts room. Knowing there are drugs stored in this room, I'm not surprised to find it locked. Waving Dom over, he picks the lock on the dingy white door, and we slip inside. Max and Axel help us go through auto parts boxes, and it doesn't take long for us to find the cocaine bags.

Max does a sweep of the chemicals, finding exactly what he needs. Motioning for us to step out of the room, he and Axel dump ketone solvent in the room and continue several trails into the garage where Jake, Wesley, Dom, and I have set out the explosives. Whistling to the men, I motion for them to finish up and leave the building. Ink, William, and Trevor, the lookouts, give the all-clear. All of us return to the truck, and I gather the remote-control detonator.

"Head back to camp. I'll finish it from here."

This was the part they all fought me on when we made this plan, but they know they have to go. We can't have any motorcycles associated with the explosion. Jake pats me on the back.

"Careful, brother. We'll see you soon."

Jake taps Max's shoulder, giving him a nod and the same farewell, then he and Axel climb on our rides, leaving the truck behind for us. With their engines long gone, Max and I keep to the shadows and move closer to the repair shop.

"On three," I tell him.

Crouching down behind a large, foul-smelling commercial dumpster, we watch the building as I count down. Without hesitation, I press the red button, and moments later, an explosion echoes into the night. Flames lick the sky and debris litters the horizon. Running back to the truck, two more explosions pierce the silent night, and we waste no time getting out of town.

CHAPTER NINETEEN

NIX

PUSHING THE CAMPER DOOR OPEN, I stretch my arms and yawn. The aroma of bacon and eggs fills my nostrils as I leave the scent of fresh-brewed coffee. Having slept in, my crew is slow to move around, and there's a noticeable tension emanating from the women. They know we went off to do something dangerous last night, and the worry is evident in their questioning gazes.

The tension isn't something that's addressed. My crew settles into camp chairs, talking about the day's events while filling their plates with food. With our usual morning routine underway, the stress drifts away, replaced with the enthusiastic chatter of my crew and Maci declaring she's entering the bikini contest. William runs a hand down his face.

"Fuck. You're gonna make me have to fight someone," William grumbles.

"You got nothing to worry about." Maci's voice goes

up a notch, and her smile is like a bird's feathers when they're about to fly, its tips raised at their highest point. "I'm all yours, baby."

William gives her a wink and outstretches his arm, dropping Maci onto his lap. The two lip-lock and a few of us chuckle.

Synne kneads my shoulder as she sips from a coffee cup. In appreciation, I take the plate Wesley hands me and give it to her. Golden hazel eyes glitter in the sunlight as she takes the plate offered. She drops into the seat next to me, and I take the second plate served to me. Leaning back in my camp chair, the warm sun pebbling sweat on my skin, unease creeps across the back of my neck and shoulders. So many thoughts are running through my mind, I'm lost in them. The thought at the forefront is—do the Royals know yet?

To the left of me, Axel clears his throat, gathering my attention. Silently, he hands me his cell phone. On the screen is a Nashville news article about a chemical explosion at Hacker's Automotive. A photo shows charred remains after the local fire department put out the remaining flames. Handing it back to him, I give him a thankful nod. My gaze sweeps the rest of the Kings, giving them an affirmative dip of my chin—the Royals know now. The tension among the women grows, and Liz, being the smart woman she is, starts searching on her phone. Only she won't find anything related to the Royals because the repair shop was a cover for them, unassociated with their club, at least in regard to law enforcement.

"After the bikini contest, we should enjoy the concert they have tonight and take it easy," Trevor suggests.

"I like that plan," Max agrees, dipping his coffee cup toward Trevor.

"Axel, you got another journey ride we could do before the bikini contest?" I ask him.

"I do. Y'all in?"

The answer is unanimous.

RIPPING through the breeze with the rumble of my Harley beneath me, I feel centered, relaxed, and I know part of it is the relief I've received from exacting revenge. Knowing the damage we've caused to the Royals' drug business lifts the corner of my mouth. It isn't enough for taking Jenna's life, but it will make them suffer. It'll cause trouble with their drug supplier when they don't have the cash to hand over to them, and if I'm lucky, maybe Reed will take a bullet for it.

This ride is what I need. A couple hours of peace, freedom, and time to clear my head. Riding the Harley next to me is Synne, her fiery red hair blowing in the wind, a peaceful look on her face. It's a damn good feeling to have her in my life, and the fact she's a rider who loves it as much as I do is something I never expected but am grateful for. She's filled the dark, empty cavern in my heart and stitched the scarred halves back together. I want to do everything I can to protect her and avoid the mistake I made before. I won't underestimate the Royals. I know Synne's going to be a target, and once we return from bike week, it's time I move to another house. She won't be safe at mine.

After a peaceful ride, returning to camp is rough. I don't want the false feeling of security to end. On the road, my problems are left behind. It's part of the addiction to riding and why it's so hard to cut the engine and climb off.

Standing next to my saddlebag, I chug a bottle of water and listen to Maci try to talk Synne into participating in the bikini contest. Synne glances at me, a humored smirk on her face.

"What do you think, Nix? Should I show a little cleavage for some cash?"

Chuckling, I grin at the thought of Synne in a skimpy two-piece.

"I'm not going to complain, babe. I know where we stand, and you have a hell of a shot at winning with those gorgeous tits."

Maci's expression contorts, and she glances at William.

"Why don't you say shit like that to me?"

William rolls his eyes. "Thanks a lot, *Pres*. I spent all morning trying to convince her not to participate."

With a shrug, I swallow the last of my water.

"Put a ring on it and she won't bitch so much," Trevor quips.

Audrey slaps his shoulder, and he laughs as he wraps her up in his arms.

"That doesn't apply to you," he coos in her ear.

I know Trevor means it. None of the women here bitch and moan like Maci. The girl is claws deep in William, yet she still struggles to hold on to him. The guy's not ready to settle down, but the girl's trying so hard to get him to. I don't blame her for being bitchy when William is one foot in, yet one foot out. But I give the guy credit, he's only had eyes for Maci the entire time we've been at bike week. Maybe he's warming up to the idea of being a one-woman guy.

"What about you, Liz? You want to join us?" Maci asks, resting an elbow on Synne's shoulder.

"Fuck, no!" Jake blurts as he drops into a camp chair, pulling Liz onto his lap. "My ol' lady is *not* going to parade her hot ass on stage for other men to enjoy. That ass belongs to me and only me."

Liz shrugs her shoulders. "You heard the man."

Erika glances at Dom. His thoughts are written all over his stern red face. Erika busts out laughing. "I wasn't even considering it, but I'm getting a kick out of your reaction to the thought."

Dom's facial muscles relax, and he lifts Erika up, tosses her over his shoulder and slaps her ass, making her squeal and laugh. "You can go on stage, just like this, your body attached to mine, so everyone knows who you belong to." His smile stretches wide as he slaps her ass again, and she laughs harder. "Let's practice, Sparrow. Who do you belong to?"

He slaps her ass a third time, and she half laughs, half screams, "You!"

The rest of us have our bellies rolling with laughter as he sets her down.

"Damn straight," he smirks.

Erika stands on her toes and smiles against his lips as she kisses him.

"What about you, Audrey?" Maci asks.

"Hell, why not? I haven't done anything wild and fun lately."

Trevor slaps a hand to his forehead.

"This is payback for my shitty comment, isn't it?"

Audrey leans in and kisses him. "A little, but it'll be fun too."

Trevor sucks in a breath and tilts his head. "Fuck it. I'll pay all you bastards twenty bucks each to holler as loud as you can for my girl," he jokes.

"Thirty-five for y'all to holler for Synne," I add in, upping the ante.

Maci is quick to look at William, and he bites. "Fifty to holler for Maci. It was her idea."

Her face lights up.

"Done," I reply. "Fifty it is."

William's head drops into his hand. "Jesus Christ."

The crew laughs, and William looks up at the sky. "I walked right into that."

"Now that you owe four hundred bucks, I better enter the contest and win," Maci gleams.

William's eyes are wide as his hand flies in the air. "Fuck yeah, you better."

"Well, I guess I won't enter if Maci is taking home the cash," Synne announces, her voice playful.

"Me either. You got this, Maci." Audrey puts her hands under her boobs and bounces them as she pouts her lips and winks.

"I feel swindled," William groans, his eyes dancing between us. "You two are still entering," he points at Synne and Audrey. "There's still second and third place cash winners."

"Fair point," Synne praises. "I'm in."

Audrey pulls her braid over her shoulder and removes the hair tie at the end. "I'm in and claiming the shower first."

When she disappears inside the camper, Axel and Wesley walk toward Axel's truck. "We're making a beer run," Axel announces. "Want anything else?"

"More coffee," I call back.

With a hand through his hair and a head nod, he climbs into his truck—a truck now empty of all evidence, thanks to Max and me destroying it last night.

Between the girls showering, I get a call for a custom order, a new client who attended the badass bike show. After booking him in my calendar, I take a seat in my camp chair and bullshit with the guys while we wait for the girls to finish making themselves look glamorous—Liz's words, not mine.

Maci is the first to walk out in a black bikini with silver swirls and so many strings going every which way, it's a fucking maze on her chest. It definitely draws the eyes, that's for damn sure. Her bottoms are super short jean shorts, but I assume the bottom half of that bathing suit has just as many mesmerizing strings to look at once her shorts are off. She kept it light on the makeup, which is nice. Her face is prettier without the extra colors and sparkles. Long curls spiral around her face, a small portion of them clipped up to the side by her ear. Admittedly, she looks pretty hot.

The next woman out the door is Audrey. She has her hair pulled back in a high and tight ponytail with the long length of it straight and sleek. She's in a bold red bathing suit with gold beading. The little bit of fabric barely covers her tits and looks smokin' on her tan body.

The last one out is Synne, and the moment my eyes land on her, my cock swells. Beneath her wild curls is a green bikini with tiny straps and slits of fabric covering her tits and pussy. It's the kind of bathing suit I like— not a lot to it and comes off easy.

Several of us whistle at the girls, and they grin and strike poses as if they're already on the stage. I can't peel my eyes away from Synne's creamy tits about to fall out of the slivers of fabric. Following the lines of her flat stomach, my eyes linger over the narrow V-shape between her legs, and I lick my dry lips.

"Fuck, Synne. I've changed my mind. You look too damn hot to go on that stage."

Coming over to me, she straddles my lap, and my hands wrap around her bare ass. Damn it, it's a thong bikini.

"What if I promise a private show after, just for you?"

"I'm back on board, baby."

Squeezing her ass cheeks, I wiggle her over my growing erection, and she leans forward to whisper. "I want you to fuck me with this on, then tear the fabric off with your teeth and fuck me even harder."

A low groan filters out of my mouth, my dick becoming rigid.

"We got time before the contest starts."

Lifting her up with me, her legs stay wrapped around my waist. Jake and William whistle as I carry her into the camper. Putting her up against the wall, I devour her mouth as I unzip my jeans. Folding them down over my hips, I free my stiff cock, swipe her strip of fabric to the side and thrust into her pussy. Her wet heat surrounds me, ready and waiting for my dick to fill it. Keeping hold of her ass, my thrusts are forceful and eager, wanting to be balls deep as long as I can. Latched onto my shoulders, she moans loud and unashamed, stroking my ego and my desire as I take her harder.

"This pussy..." is all I manage to mutter as the familiar sensation of an orgasm tightens my balls.

"So fucking good," she mumbles as her body shutters, her orgasm spilling onto my shaft.

Another couple thrusts, and I lean my head against the wall as I cum inside her, the euphoria momentarily controlling me.

As the sensation fades, I lower her legs, and she unties the left knot, the bathing suit bottom falling to the floor. Putting my fingers between her legs, I gather her sticky sweetness and rub it on her clit. She falls into me, feathering my lips as she rides another wave of pleasure.

Against my lips, she smiles. "You make me feel so good."

"So do you, baby." My fingers slide down lower and thrust into her pussy. She inhales a sharp breath, her fist gripping my vest. "You sure you want to go to the contest? I'm thinking we continue this into round two."

She lets out a groan mixed with breathy pleasure.

"I promised them I'd go."

Withdrawing my fingers, I look down at her glistening eyes and the way she bites her lip with needy want. I know what her body craves, but she's trying to be a good friend.

"Later then, I'm tearing this bathing suit off and fucking this ass." Palming her cheek, I squeeze it hard, and she leans into me, her tongue slipping between my lips as she grips the back of my head and holds me hostage to her intoxicating kiss.

"You can have me, anytime, anywhere."

Biting my lip, I moan as my cock presses between her pussy lips, the wet friction increasing the arousal I'm already having trouble containing.

"Get cleaned up before I change my mind and hold you captive in this camper."

Reluctantly, she pulls away, her hand caressing my arm and lingering in my hand. While she freshens up in the bathroom, I squeeze past her to take a shower. By the time I'm out, she's outside with a pair of black shorts and a pink tank top covering her suit. The crew is putting away camp gear, preparing to head to the show and concert. While they collect what they need, I shoot a text off to Axel to check on him and Wesley. Moments later, he sends a text back that all is good, and they'll be arriving in a few minutes.

The time goes quickly, and when they arrive, we help them unload the truck and put the beer and ice in a cooler. As we put supplies in the camper, Maci whines that it's getting late. Checking my cell phone, I remember Synne telling me Angela promised to show up tonight. With that in mind, I search the camper for paper and a pen, find them in a drawer, and scribble a note for Angela.

~A

If we're not here, wait for us.

~N

Tearing a small piece of tape off the dispenser, I stick it on the note and paste it to the outside of the camper door. Synne sees it and her gaze becomes wistful as she stares at me.

"What you're doing for her makes my feelings for you even stronger."

Taking her hand, I lead her out of camp, the trail of fallen pine needles crunching beneath our feet, their earthy scent mixing with Synne's vanilla and cinnamon.

"Part of me wants to help someone I once cared for, the other part of me is doing it for you, knowing what you went through." Raising her hand, I kiss it and notice a sheen of moisture developing in her eyes.

"I'm thankful I met you."

"Good." Caressing my thumb over her hand, I lean over and kiss her head. "Because I feel the same about you."

CHAPTER TWENTY

NIX

I'M certain the majority of bike week attendees are here for the bikini contest. The place is packed with little room to move around. The cash winnings are going to be large with twenty-one entrants. In the front rows and to the right of the stage, my crew has settled in with camp chairs and a cooler. We throw back a few while the announcer talks about some of the proceeds going to a charity and how impressive it is to have twenty-one women in the contest. The attention of the audience is captured when they announce the details of the first contestant.

A fit woman in her fifties with long, probably dyed blond hair struts out onto the stage first in her tiny black bikini, riding boots, and a number one contestant sticker. Wesley perks up in his chair and whistles at her. It's loud enough to grab her attention. She glances at him, blows a kiss, then struts back off the stage, waving her farewell as the crowd cheers. Wesley's face is red and struck with shock.

"Got a crush, old man?" Max jokes.

"Hell yeah, did you see her?"

Liz leans against his chair and puts an arm around him.

"I'll sneak back with the girls and see if she's single."

"Would ya, doll?"

"Of course."

Before she leaves, she kisses Jake, then takes the path along the stage to where the other girls went to prepare for the contest.

As the beer gets low, the beautiful women keep coming, and the crowd gets louder. Number eleven is a hot, busty blonde, and when she enters the stage, she gets a boost from the crowd by taking her bikini top off and spinning it around in the air. Drunk men go wild and shout for her to take her bottoms off. With a glance at the announcer, he shakes his head no, and the men at the front of the stage boo him.

The flash-the-crowd trend continues for another four women, and the group of bikers to the left of us get more boisterous and give the gesture of eating pussy to the current girl on stage. When the next girl comes out and doesn't flash the crowd, the men boo her. As she leaves the stage, she wipes at her eyes. Next up is Synne, and my neck and shoulder muscles tighten so hard, I can't swallow. The bikers next to us start shouting, "Show us your tits!"

Synne is unfazed. She turns her ass toward us, bends over, whips her hair into the air as she stands straight. Looking at me over her shoulder, she winks, then struts off the stage like she owns it. A smile curls my lip. Of course, she handled their shouting like the badass she is and looked sexy as fuck doing it. Audrey enters the stage after Synne, and the men shout the same phrase. Trevor moves toward them in my periphery, and I put my hand on his chest and shake my head no.

"Audrey wouldn't want you to fight."

Audrey, being the snarky chick she is, pretends to take her bottoms off, then pulls a middle finger out instead. The bikers next to us begin to boo her but are drowned out by our whistling and cheering. With a kiss blown to Trevor, she struts off the stage, a grin curling her lips. Maci is next, and the one I'm the most worried about. As soon as she enters, the group of idiots next to us shout, "Take your top off!"

I know Maci wants to win, so she'll go that extra step. Turning her ass toward the crowd, she shakes it as she unties the strings around her neck.

"Yeah, baby. Show us what you got!"

William stiffens, his gaze flipping between Maci on stage and the group next to us, his face as red as a blister.

With Maci's top down, she turns toward the crowd, hooks her thumbs in a string on her bikini, and does an erotic dance for the crowd.

"Show us the rest!"

Her gaze flicks in our direction and I make eye contact. With a scowl, I shake my head no.

In the group next to us, a beefy, black-haired dude with a beer belly catches me telling her no and decides he doesn't like it.

"Fuck off, man. If she wants to show us, she can."

William quick steps up to the man and gets in his face. "Watch what you say, fucker. That's my woman up there."

The man doesn't back down, the beer in his hand sloshing as he gets in William's face.

"Watch what you say, fucker, or I'll lay you flat on your ass."

My crew is at my back as we step up to protect William. The patches on the man's vest read; *Oakland* for his chapter, *Tank* for his road name, and a standard *Member* patch.

"Unless you want a blood bath, Tank I suggest you back the fuck down."

Glancing at my vest, he reads the President patch and my name.

"Your buddy was in my face first, *Pres*. I can't help if his girl wanted to show off her tits and ass for us."

William clenches his fists, ready to throw a punch, so I move between them.

"My ol' lady was one of the women you shouted *show us your tits* at. You're lucky I don't dig your face into the ground with my boot." Stepping closer, I tower over him. "You have one last chance to respect the patch, or I'll make an example out of yours."

Behind him, his buddies are listening in and ready for a fight, eager desperation written all over their faces. As Tank's eyes narrow to slits and he contemplates a fight, the barking orders of law enforcement shout at us to break it up.

A black, metal baton gets shoved between us, followed by the same orders being repeated more loudly and aggressively. Gesturing to my crew, I motion for them to back up. Tank and his buddies remain there, ignoring the officers.

"Pussy," he shouts at me, spitting at my feet.

"What the fuck did you just say to me?"

"Let it go," an officer shouts.

My eyes flick to his hand on his taser. Now's not the time or place to finish this.

I point to Tank. "I'll be seeing you again, bitch."

My crew and I walk off as the officers bark more orders at Tank and his brothers. The sound of shouting and a taser going off whips our attention back to the drunk bikers. Tank is on the ground, two officers working to handcuff him.

With a smirk, I cross my arms and watch the dumb fucks get arrested, one by one.

"This is almost better than beating the shit out of him," William says.

"Oh, we'll get our chance," I assure him. "Jake, call

our bail bondsman friend. Find out when that piece of shit is going to get released."

"Will do, Pres." Jake lowers the brim of his ball cap, smiling like a wily cat.

The last two contestants have come and gone, and while the results are being tallied up, the women are lined up in a row on stage to be ogled. Maci looks nervous, and I don't know if it's about winning the contest or the shitshow going on below the stage. Tank and his brothers are escorted away in cuffs, and the crowd returns their attention to the beautiful women.

William drops into a chair with a thud, his face red, jaw tight, his gaze fixed on Maci. I think she seriously crossed the line with him this time. The announcer calls the third-place winner, and sure as shit, it's my Synne. She laughs as she steps forward. Finding me in the crowd, she shrugs a shoulder and smirks.

"Yeah, baby!" I whistle loud, and my crew joins me in cheering her on.

Synne puts two fingers to her lips, kisses them, then points right at me and winks. This woman... she rocks my fucking world.

The second-place is none other than the busty blonde who started the tit-flashing trend. She struts forward and playfully pretends to untie her top as she winks at the crowd. I'm thankful that hot little number isn't my girl; I'd look like William, steaming in the corner.

The first-place winner is announced, and Maci's face

lights up when they call her name. She comes forward, grinning and waving at the crowd like an experienced pageant queen. William doesn't cheer or whistle, just tosses back the rest of his beer and chucks it on the ground with a grunt.

Flower bouquets, a patch, and a small cardboard check are handed to each of the winners. The rest of the women are applauded as they exit the stage. A few minutes later, Liz, Audrey, and the first contestant rejoin our group. Liz introduces Deborah to Wesley, and the two stay to the side and chat. Wesley's face is a shade of red I haven't seen in years. It's good to see the ol' man get some action.

Liz settles under Jake's arm while Audrey receives congratulatory kisses and ass squeezes from Trevor. When the contestants are finished getting their photos taken, they head off stage, and we wait for Synne and Maci to join us.

Synne waves the check in her hand with a humored smile as she nears our group.

"Can you believe it?"

"With that ass, I can."

Her cheeks swell into little crimson puffs as she slides into my arms and looks up at me as if she adores me. That look right there cements the truth for me—I'm falling in love with her, and I believe she feels the same. Bringing her in tight to my chest, I kiss her head.

"You did good, baby, and you respected me up there."

Tilting her head back, she remains against my chest and kisses me. "Thank you."

Glancing over her shoulder, she checks on Maci, who's standing by William's chair, staring at him expectantly. Holding a beer to his lips, he tilts it in the air.

"What?" he snaps.

"You're not saying anything."

William rolls his eyes. "We're gonna talk, but not here, not now." The last couple of words are clipped. The man is fuming and knows he needs to cool down.

"Maci," I call. "Give the man some room."

With tears in her eyes, her attention whips to me. She starts to say something, then thinks better of it. Wiping at a fallen tear, she walks off, her patch and check dangling from her hand. Erika joins her, putting an arm around her.

"Let's go." I motion toward the girls. "I'm not gonna have our group separated."

"Let her go," William grumbles, his speech slurred.

"Get off your fucking ass, right now," Dom orders, motioning his hand for William to stand. "You can be pissed off, but you still have an obligation to look out for her."

"Fucking Christ," William spits. "This day's been nothing but shit."

Getting up from the chair, he moves slowly, putting it inside the bag. The alcohol is hitting him hard. Obviously, William's feelings for Maci are deeper than he shows. He's really pissed about the stunt she pulled on stage, and he's burying those feelings in alcohol.

William and Dom trail behind the girls while the rest of us gather the chairs and cooler.

"Let's get some food before the concert starts," I tell the crew.

TAKING the last swig of my beer, I toss it aside as Synne sways her hips, pushing her ass into my dick. Kissing her neck, I pull her tighter against me as the band belts out their melody.

"You looked sexy on that stage. That move had me wondering what else you can do."

"I have a few more moves up my sleeve I can perform, just for you."

Synne raises her arms and intertwines her fingers around my neck, and I grip her hip, tugging her to me as I push into her ass cheeks.

"I want to see you perform them in this slinky bikini."

Tugging at a string, I loosen the straps around her neck. She reaches into the back of her tank top and unties the back strings. Pulling the bikini top out from under her tank, she hands it to me.

"Or I can perform them naked."

Pocketing her bikini top, I slip a hand under her tank and caress her breast.

"I think it's time I take you to bed."

"As long as you keep to your earlier promise."

She turns in my arms and looks up at me, her grin inviting and lascivious.

"I'll more than deliver on that promise."

Sliding my hand up her thigh, I slip my finger into her shorts and rub over the minuscule fabric covering her pussy.

"I want you now." Her breath is a whisper of needy arousal.

Pulling my hand out, I palm her ass with both hands and lift her. She puts her legs around my waist, and I pull her tight against my hard dick and rock her over it until she's moaning as we kiss.

"Fuck, baby, I need to tell the crew we're heading back to camp. I'm about to fuck you here if I don't."

"I should've worn a skirt," she groans.

"You should've."

Letting her legs down, I adjust my hard-on.

"We're heading back to camp." Flicking a pointed finger between me and Synne, then toward camp, I gather the attention of most of my crew.

In the dimly lit mowed field, with the band blasting music into the sea of drunken people, every Kings member has a girl dancing or flirting with them, so I know they don't mind heading back either. The word passes between them, and when it gets to Wesley, he motions his head toward camp and asks Deborah to join him. I'm pleased to see her say yes. Max and Axel have their arms slung over the shoulders of the women they're with, so it's clear they're joining us as well.

Through the thick crowd, we move to the outside and try not to disrupt anyone having a good time. Across the main drag of bike week, the tall streetlamps light our way to the campsites. As we near the main trail to our camp, there's a law enforcement UTV with its red, white, and blue lights flickering. A small crowd of people blocks our view from the scene. Assuming a fight went south, I slow down and join the crowd to see what happened. One of the officers, a bald, middle-aged man, puts his hands up, ushering the crowd back.

About fifteen feet away, there's a woman's body lying in the vegetation. Crimson hair catches my attention, and I move sideways, trying to get a better look as my heart rate kicks up a notch. To the right of me, I hear Jake telling the girls to stay back, and that's when everything goes silent around me. My ears ring, and my hands shake as I move closer. Gaze fixed on Angela's battered body and torn clothing, nausea fills my stomach, and I cover my hand over my mouth.

"Son of a bitch."

"Sir, you need to step back. This is a crime scene."

Max comes out of nowhere and addresses the officer.

"We know who that woman is. That's Angela Kersee. She runs with the Wild Royals."

The bald-headed officer pulls a notepad and pen out of his chest pocket.

226

"I'll need you two to stay here and tell me everything you know about this woman."

Leaning forward, I put my palms on my knees and focus on my breathing as the nausea continues in waves.

"I can't do this." One knee gives out, and the hands I feel wrap around me are my sister's. Turning my face into her hair, I hug her tight as moisture fills my eyes, my words whispered against her ear. "I did this. She's dead because of me."

Pulling back to look at me, confusion fills her eyes.

"You're wrong." She says it so adamantly, I almost believe her.

"Take Synne and everyone back to camp. Don't say anything to anyone."

With an understanding nod, she disappears behind me. Max places a hand on my shoulder and gives it a squeeze as I stand.

"I'm here, brother."

"Thank you," I mutter.

My gaze keeps landing on the bits of cream flesh catching the light from the streetlamp. The rest of her skin is dirty, bruised, or cut. Looking away from her body, I breathe in deeply, then slowly let it out. My mind is adrift, but I'm still aware of the dull, painful tearing in my heart. Angela didn't deserve to die like this, and the fear that's coursing through me is that I caused this to happen.

The officer who asked us to remain for questioning is being patient, holding off questions while a second officer places yellow tape from the UTV to a tree, keeping the crowd out. Another UTV pulls up, the medical emergency skid unit that responds before the actual ambulance. The dark-haired officer who put up the yellow caution tape addresses them, and the passenger of the skid unit gets into the back and gathers a white sheet and a large medical kit. The two paramedics approach her body, and a short time later, they lay the sheet over her.

Watching the pristine, clean sheet cover her brings back flashes of Jenna's bloody, dead body being covered. I can't hold back the nausea anymore, and the last few beers I drank spew out. Max and the officer give me space to be sick.

The officer who set up the tape walks around and asks the crowd if anyone saw anything. The bystanders don't have any information to help, and most of them leave the scene after telling the officer they didn't see anything and just wanted to know what happened. Only a small group remains, the ones who found her and called 911. The dark-haired officer pulls out a notepad and begins asking them questions.

"Sir, are you well enough to answer my questions?"

The bald officer in front of me is holding out his notepad, his expression expectant of me to cooperate. He's studying me with curious, intelligent eyes, I'm sure wondering why my reaction to her has been so strong.

"Yes." Wiping my mouth, I stand straight and give him my attention.

"How do you know the deceased?"

The deceased. It's a cold description, but it's true. Angela is dead, her body decaying in the dirt while everyone else has been partying. The people who could help her didn't know, and the people who knew didn't care.

"Three years ago, I had a relationship with her. After our relationship ended, she started a relationship with a member of the Wild Royals."

The man's head tilts, and his brows raise as he writes. He's familiar with the club.

"Do you know who she was in a relationship with?"

"Rex Alverez."

"Did you see her or talk to her while at Bike Week?"

"Saw her, yes. She was with the Wild Royals during the badass bike show. No, I didn't talk to her."

"Based on how well you knew her, did she seem distressed when you saw her?"

"Yes, she seemed distressed."

"Thank you."

The officer looks at Max.

"How did you know the deceased?"

Max leans back on his heels, his thumbs in his vest. With his past experience in the military, he's able to handle this situation with a level of expertise and a calm composure I need right now.

"I knew her from when she was in a relationship with him three years ago." His elbow stretches out and points toward me.

"Did you see her or talk to her while at Bike Week?"

"Same as him. Saw her but didn't talk to her. From what I knew of her, she seemed troubled."

"Did she speak with anyone else in your club or camp party?"

"No," Max replies easily.

"All right. I need your names, phone numbers, and addresses in case we need to bring you in for further questioning."

"They did this." I point to Angela's body.

The officer's blond brows furrow. "Who did this?"

"The Wild Royals. We know as well as you do what they're capable of. They're animals."

"We'll be questioning them. As of now, we can't make speculations. Thank you for your time, and I'm sorry for your loss."

The officer leaves us and enters into a conversation with his partner. Over his shoulder, the dark-haired officer takes note of us. Max and I linger and watch as the ambulance arrives. Max taps me on the shoulder, his dark gaze empathetic.

"You shouldn't be here for this part."

Putting pressure on my shoulder, he urges me to turn away and walk with him. Reluctantly, I do, glancing over my shoulder at the stretcher being carried to her body. My chest constricts, and I look away, knowing the next part will only make the pain worse. Running a hand from my temple to my chin, I take a long breath. Max turns on his cell phone flashlight to light our way to camp.

"They dumped her here for us to find her," I tell him.

"It's some sick shit what they did to her. They need to pay for it."

"We'll find a way."

My words are a promise to Angela and to myself.

CHAPTER TWENTY-ONE

SYNNE

Opening the camper door, I step out to a cool morning with the dew still bubbled on the grass and vehicles. My eyes sweep the camp in search of Nix. When he returned to camp last night, he didn't say a word to anyone, just grabbed a bottle of whiskey and disappeared into the night. The only person who got a chance to speak to him was Max, and Max wouldn't tell me anything, only that I needed to give him space.

The first place I check is his tent, but it's empty. Walking around the outside of the vehicles, I search the ground and the tree line. As I pass Nix's truck, there's rustling in the bed.

Popping my head in, I find Nix wrapped in a sleeping bag with an empty bottle of whiskey lying next to his face. He's still sleeping off the alcohol. I feel sorry for him. When he wakes, he'll be stiff and hungover.

Returning to the camper, I brew a fresh pot of coffee, gather two aspirins, and fill my canteen with water. Once the coffee is made, I bring all three to Nix. Setting them on the tailgate, I climb in, and Nix stirs. Swollen, tired eyes blink at me, then look up at the sky in confusion. Looking around him, it sinks in where he passed out and slept. Without saying anything, he opens the zipper of the sleeping bag for me to climb in. I do, and he lies on his side, so I can rest my head on his arm.

Turning on my side, I caress his cheek, and he opens his eyes, the sorrow in them gut-wrenching.

"Are you okay?"

"No," he admits.

"Want to talk about it?"

"No." There's pain in his voice, and I'm worried about him spiraling.

"I brought you coffee, aspirin, and water."

"Thank you. I'm sorry I disappeared last night."

His gaze trails to the tailgate.

"I'll get them."

"Thanks."

Slipping out of the sleeping bag, I grab the coffee and the rest. He sits up, rubbing both hands over his face, and groans. When he looks at me, I have the aspirin in my palm and the water in my opposite hand. Taking them both, he tosses the pills in his mouth and chugs the water.

"I need to get out of this truck. It's killing my back."

Climbing down, I carry his coffee and the canteen. He trudges across the campsite to the camper, his head hanging low, his steps heavy. Wesley unzips his tent and dips his chin in greeting as he climbs out. Nix doesn't acknowledge anything around him. He slinks into the camper, kicks his boots off, lays his vest on the table, tosses his shirt, and drops onto the bed. Moments later, he's passed out, and I'm sitting on the edge of the bed watching him sleep, my heart aching for the guilt and pain I know he feels.

Taking the coffee, I leave the camper to let him sleep. Voices and activity stir around me as I sit in a camp chair, sipping the warm liquid. Liz comes out of her and Jake's tent, adjusting the shirt she just put on.

"How is he?"

I hand her my coffee, and she takes a drink as she sits next to me.

"Not good. I found him passed out in the bed of his truck. Now he's sleeping off his hangover in the camper."

Returning the coffee, she throws her hair up in a bun. "He's going to pull back. Don't hold it against him. It's how he copes."

"I won't, but I'm worried how much he's going to pull back." My stomach knots, the coffee suddenly unappetizing. "I'm afraid he'll break it off with me."

Liz goes silent, staring into the distance. I guess my concern isn't unwarranted. Another stressor is tickling at my neck. I spoke to Angela, and if the cops find out, I might become a suspect as the jealous new girlfriend.

Liz glances at her tent as Jake moves around inside. She puts a hand on her temple and rubs her fingers into it. "This is an awful way to leave bike week."

"It is."

Wesley leaves his tent, and in the opening, I see Deborah inside. I'm glad not all the women were scared off last night. The girl who was under Max's arm grabbed her friend, who was with Axel, and they took off before we returned to camp. I don't blame them. Learning there was a woman's dead body less than twenty feet from where you're standing is a good reason to send them back to wherever they came from. Deborah must have felt comfortable with Wesley, and from what I got to know of her last night, she has a lot of life experience.

Wesley seems in good spirits as he begins his usual ritual, starting a fire for breakfast. Ink pops out of his tent alone, looks at us, then my coffee.

"Got any more of that?"

"I do, it's in the camper. Nix is in there sleeping."

"Okay, thanks."

Walking past our fire pit and chairs, he heads to the camper. He's in and out quickly, holding a cup of coffee and a skillet with a half-empty bag of bacon and a roll of biscuits in it.

"He's still passed out, snoring like a freight train."

Liz blows out a puff of air. "He does that when he's had *way* too much to drink."

"Think we should load his bike up in the trailer?" Ink asks, setting the skillet next to the fire. "Maybe he shouldn't ride home."

Jake unzips their tent and climbs out. Walking over to the cooler, he grabs a bottle of water that's floating in the ice-melted water, pops it open, and chugs it.

"Let me talk to him first and see how he's doing."

"All right." Ink sets his coffee on the ground, gathers a handful of bacon, and slaps it into the pan.

Angling my head over my shoulder, I look toward the sound of William and Maci's tent as their voices rise.

"I'll drop you off, but once I do, we're done."

"William!"

"I mean it. That stunt you pulled on stage was the last of your bullshit. You disrespected me in front of my brothers, then caused problems for us with another club. I can't even look at you right now."

"Then why'd you let me sleep in here?" Her voice is tearful and pleading.

"Because we were drunk last night, and it was the right thing to do. I'll make sure you get home safe, but I mean it, don't text or call me or show up at my house."

The zipper whizzes as it's opened with forceful speed. William climbs out, his face red, his hand rubbing his cheek and facial hair. He glances at us with hurt in his eyes, then stomps toward the camper and disappears inside.

Maci remains in their tent, her hands covering her face as she sobs into them. Going to the tent, I squat down and lean my head in. Hearing someone, she lowers her hands to look.

"I wanted to win to impress him. I wanted him to see others want me, so he would," she cries.

"I'm sorry, love. You want me to take you home?"

Gathering a shirt to wipe her eyes with, she nods.

"All right. Gather your stuff. You mind riding passenger on my bike?"

"No, I just want out of here," she pleads.

"Okay."

Closing the zipper, I give her privacy to dress and load her backpack. There's an awkward silence among everyone as I walk to the camper. Inside, William has an arm stretched on the cabinet above him as he looks out the window above the sink, holding a steaming coffee cup in his right hand.

"You okay?"

Looking over his shoulder, he watches me gather my bike keys, wallet, and jacket.

"Yeah," he replies casually, but I can hear in his tone that he's not. "Where are you going?"

With my jacket in hand, I check on Nix, who's still asleep.

"I'm taking Maci home."

William drops his hand and turns toward me, resting

his ass against the counter. Without a shirt on, he's showing off his muscles and matching sparrow tattoos on his chest. He really is a gorgeous guy. I don't imagine it'll be long before he's dating someone new, not with those pretty blues.

"You don't have to. I can take her."

"For the sake of avoiding another fight, it's best I take her. She's a hot mess out there and wants to go home."

William throws a hand in the air and pinches his brows. "All right," he sighs. "Just be careful. You ever had a passenger on your bike?"

"Yeah, we'll be fine."

With an accepting nod, he crosses a boot over the other.

"I'll stay in here until you leave, so I don't upset her more."

"Thanks."

Leaning down, I kiss Nix's cheek, but he doesn't register it.

"I'll keep an eye on him," William assures me.

Leaving the camper, I slide my arms into my jacket and zip it. Maci stands from the chair next to Liz, her backpack full of her stuff. Her expression is hopeful as if I might have a message from William or that he asked for her to stay. I tilt my head toward my bike.

"Let's go."

As the words leave my mouth, her face drops, a frown forming her lips.

"I'll wash your bikini and get it back to you."

"Keep it," she tells me. "It looks better on you."

Sitting atop my bike, I raise the kickstand and fire it up. Maci climbs on the back and wraps her arms around my waist. It's a foreign feeling, but it's temporary, and I could use the quiet ride back.

CHAPTER TWENTY-TWO

NIX

LIFTING my head from the blanket, I wipe drool off my bottom lip. A dull, pounding ache is in my skull, and my mouth is dryer than the desert. Throwing a leg over the edge of the bed, I rest my head in my hands and rub my temples. As I stand, a dizzy sensation overwhelms me, and I have to put my hand on the wall to stabilize myself. I'm right back to the familiar aftermath of reaching the bottom of a Jack Daniels bottle.

Dragging my feet to the fridge, I gather a water bottle and empty it. Stripping out of my jeans, briefs, and socks, I traipse to the shower and stand under the warm water until my eyes feel like they're no longer covered by foggy goggles.

Stepping out, I'm quick to dry, grab fresh clothes, and an energy bar from the cabinet. Leaving the camper, I join my crew, who are all awake and tossing their finished breakfast into the campfire. Searching the group, I look for Synne, worry tightening my gut when I don't find her.

"Where's Synne?"

"She gave Maci a ride home," Liz tells me. "You feeling any better?"

"Why the fuck did y'all let her leave?"

Anger shoots up my spine and crawls across my shoulders like spindly spider legs. Pulling my phone from my pocket, I call her cell. When she doesn't answer, my fist squeezes the phone, and I blow out an angry breath.

"She's fine," Liz assures me. "No one knows she left."

"You don't know that," I bark at her. "Did anyone check the tree line for the Royals? Did anyone make sure she wasn't followed?"

Wesley, Ink, and William lower their heads, and Liz's face turns red with worry.

"No," she admits.

"None of you should've let her leave!"

Max stands from the squatting position he was in by the fire and tilts his head toward our rides.

"Let's go. We'll meet up with her. William," Max motions his hand for him to stand. "Lead the way. Take the route Maci would've given Synne."

"You don't know if she'll take that route back," Jake adds. "It's better if you wait for her to return or call you back."

"I can't fucking wait. I need to know she's okay." My

tone is sharp and unyielding.

Max's gaze sweeps the group and shakes his head to them in a warning.

"Let's get going, Pres. We're wasting air."

Pulling my keys out of my pocket, I rush to my bike. My cell rings loud, and I freeze, gather my wits then answer it.

"Synne, where are you? You okay?"

"Yeah, I'm good. I dropped off Maci then swung by my place."

"Stay there. Don't leave. Don't come back here."

"Why? What's wrong?" There's distinct fear in her tone.

"It's not safe for you to be riding alone, especially since we don't know if you were followed."

"All right, I'll wait here for you." She sounds annoyed, yet still worried.

"I'll be there soon."

Hanging up, I pocket my cell and put my hand in the air and circle it.

"Pack it up, we're leaving. Synne's waiting at her place for me."

NEVER HAVING BEEN inside Synne's apartment, I take it all in—an open floor concept with the living room, dining room, and kitchen all visible. A light gray couch with a white leopard print blanket draped over it sits below a red canvas five-piece wall art that steals your gaze with its pop of color on a silver and black background. To the right of her living room is a four-chair dining table with black chairs and a glass top. The kitchen has silver appliances with dark wood cabinets and light marble counters. It's a nice place. I feel comfortable in it, and the best part is, no one knows where it's located.

Taking the duffle bag off my shoulder, I set it next to her couch, then remove my vest, laying it over the back cushion as she walks into the kitchen and gathers two glasses.

"I'm assuming you'd like water and some aspirin."

"Yes."

Dropping onto her couch, I lie back with my arm over my eyes in an attempt to soothe the massive headache throbbing in my skull. She disappears into a door off the living room, opens a cabinet in what I assume is the bathroom, then returns with two aspirin, and drops them in my palm. I toss them in my mouth and thank her when she brings me a glass of water. Emptying it, I set it on her glass top coffee table and lie back down.

"You should sleep here," she insists.

"Planned on it," I quip.

My arm drops to her hip as she climbs on top of me.

"You were really worried about me today. It meant a lot."

Caressing her side, I apply pressure and lower her down to me.

"I meant it. I can't lose you too."

Splaying her hands over my chest, her worried gaze meets mine. "Do you want to talk about what happened?"

"No," Putting a thumb into the waist of her pants, I push down. "I want to be between the legs of my woman, forgetting about all the shit outside these walls."

My mouth forms over hers as our kiss heats from the unruly passion always simmering between us. Raising her tank, I pull it off and reach for the back of her bra. It disappears as I fling it behind us. Gathering her tits in my hands, I massage them, pressing my thumb over her hardened nipples. Her hips rock forward and back, riding my dick and stretching its length. Unbuttoning her pants, I fold them down over her hips and watch as she wiggles out of them. I go for my jeans, but she stops my hands and takes over. Opening my fly, she folds my pants down and pulls out my erection, stroking it in a firm grip that curls the corner of my mouth. Another two strokes and my pre-cum is at the tip, swollen and throbbing for her to put her mouth on it. Warm, wet lips wrap around it, sucking hard, clearing my head and heart of its misery.

My head falls back, and I close my eyes, indulging in the peace she's giving me. The sound of slurping and sucking fills my ears as the sensation of her warm mouth and tight lips draws my orgasm through my cock. Gripping her shoulder, I spurt cum into her mouth and groan at the relief and pleasure coursing through me.

Looking down at her, I catch her wicked smile as she crawls over me. Caressing my palm over her ass, I toy with her tight hole, and she releases a moan before I bring her lips to mine, strengthening her needy whimpers. Sliding her thighs farther up my legs, I drop mine over the side of the couch and sit her up with me. Pushing to the edge of the couch, I lift her, carrying her to her bedroom.

Laying her on her green comforter, I spread her legs, step between them, and lift her ankles. Putting her legs over my shoulders, I watch her smile widen with anticipation as I lower between them. The taste of her meets my lips, and I'm quick to slide my tongue between her folds, taking her on the same high she gave me. With every raspy breath and moan that slips from her perfect mouth, I grow harder. Pulling back from her pussy, I wipe my mouth before gripping her legs and sliding her body closer to me. Lying down above her, I thrust hard into her soaking wet pussy as she grasps my shoulders, bucking her hips toward me.

Her tight walls clench around my cock, working me toward another orgasm as I pound into her G-spot, her pleasure exploding onto my dick, trembling her body beneath me. I follow behind her, a groan filling the air as she clenches her walls, drawing out the last of my cum.

Collapsing on the bed next to her, my jeans around my knees, I curl her into my arm and kiss her. She wraps a leg around my hip, her chest tucked into mine. It's in this moment, I'm aware of how much I need her, how much peace she brings my damaged soul.

Looking down at her magnetic gaze, I caress her cheek, letting my hand get lost in the loose strands of her long, red hair. It seems like minutes we stare at each other, giving slow, loving kisses in silence. But inside, my heart is shouting what it feels for her—love.

"Nix..."

"Yes, baby?"

"I've fallen in love with you."

There's no control over the smile that forms the shape of my mouth. Putting my fingers under her chin, I raise it, kiss her soft lips, and gaze back at the hope and fear in her eyes.

"If perfect moments exist, this is one of them because I'm in love with you too." Beneath my thumb, I caress her velvet lips, lips that bring me soothing pleasure. "I honestly don't deserve a woman like you, not with the mistakes I've made, but here you are, better than any woman I could've imagined, better than I deserve."

The soft touch of her hand caresses my face, following the muscles of my body down to my chest, where she rests her hand over my heart.

"You deserve me and so much more. You're a good man, a better man than any I've known. You love and protect with your whole heart, and I'm grateful your heart wants me."

Placing my hand over hers, it hurts me to see the adoration in her eyes. She believes I'm a good man, and I feel guilty for her mistaken belief.

"I'm not a good man. My decisions have led to the assault and death of people I care about." Turning on my back, I avoid looking at her beautiful eyes and the emotion I see in them. Straddling my waist, she places her hand on my jaw and forces me to look at her.

"Good men feel guilt and pain for those they care about. Evil men don't care."

There's truth to what she's saying even if it's a struggle to accept it.

Laying her chest on mine, she brings her lips within kissable reach.

"You need to forgive yourself. Angela's choice to join the Wild Royals was hers and hers alone. Their choice to hurt her was wrong, and what they did was out of your control."

"They hurt her because she wanted to get out. I offered her that out, and now she's dead."

"If you hadn't offered her an out, she would've taken another opportunity to get out. I know. I've been in her shoes. I was lucky you came for me when you did. If you hadn't, I would've been killed. You couldn't save her, but you saved me."

247

The need to touch her is uncontrollable. I wrap my arms around her, kissing her until we're desperate for air.

"I'd do anything to protect you. *Anything* to keep you safe. There are no lengths I won't go to. No man I won't kill if I have to." Lifting my head to hers, I hold her face in my hands. "I need you, Synne. More than I've ever needed any woman."

When her lips lower to mine, I turn us over, putting her on her back. Kicking my jeans and briefs off, I lie above her, holding one hand around her neck and the other around her hip as I bring us together, my cock sliding into her warm pussy, the world around me forgotten as I slowly take her.

ON THE FLOOR, my cell is buzzing in my jeans pocket. Synne slides off me as I roll off the bed and grab it.

Jake's voice comes through the receiver. "Tank is out tonight. What do you want to do?"

"Let it go. We have enough beef with other MCs as it is."

"I agree. You gonna be around the club or shop tomorrow?"

"Nah. I want time alone with Synne. William can take care of current orders until Synne and I get back."

"Got it. Give me a call if you need me, brother."

"Thanks. Take care of Liz and Liam."

"Always."

Tapping the end call button, I set the phone on the wooden nightstand next to her bed.

"What was that about?"

"The drunk MC that was asking y'all to show your tits on stage is getting out of jail. We were going to pay them a visit to finish what we started."

"I'm glad you're not. It's not worth it, and I'd rather you stay here with me."

Caressing my hand along the shape of her body, I massage into her hip, pulling her closer to me. Lying on my side, I rest my head on my hand and bent elbow, watching her eyes light up from my touch.

"I'm not going anywhere, babe. Except to get us food. You hungry?"

"I'll cook. I have food in the fridge."

"I'm looking forward to trying out your cooking."

Her breasts fall together, drawing my eyes as she leans forward and kisses me.

"I'm a pretty good cook."

Sliding off the bed, she grabs my T-shirt and slips into it, the bottom barely covering her pussy. When she turns around, my cock jumps as I stare at her ass cheeks peeking out below the fabric.

"I'll make chicken Alfredo. That sound good?"

Tossing my legs over the side of the bed, I chase after her. She squeals as my arms wrap around her and lift her. Dragging her back to the bed, I toss her on it, face down. Over her shoulder, she locks eyes with me as I lift her ass in the air.

"I'll eat whatever you cook after I fuck this ass."

My fingers slide between her wet pussy lips, and she moans, rocking forward and back over them as she pulls my shirt over her head. Using the slickness of her desire, I massage her tight hole, slipping a finger in, stretching her to take me fully. As I add a second digit, I slip my hard cock into her pussy, easing in and out, fucking her ass with my fingers as I watch her take pleasure from my cock. When her moans are at their highest, I pull out of her pussy and press my cockhead to her ass. Slowly, carefully, I ease in. Her fists clench the bedsheet, and I massage her ass and back, helping to relax her muscles. Sliding in and out, I thrust deeper each time until she's relaxed, and her breathing is heightened. When she's ready, I grip the side of her hips and quicken my pace, fucking her harder. The sound of her ass cheeks hitting my pelvis are drowned out by the blood pumping through my body, my euphoria blurring everything around me, the sensation of my swelling cock taking me to the highest peak. My grip tightens, my groan deep and guttural as I cum hard, holding her ass tight to me as I release inside her.

Opening my eyes, I gently pull out, grip her shoulder, and bring her upright against my chest. Putting my arms around her, I suck at her neck, biting and kissing as I massage a breast in one hand, her clit with the other. In my arms, her body quivers, a sigh of relief escaping as her orgasm coats my fingers.

Moving my hand from her breast to her jaw, I turn her face toward me, my lips taking hers.

"Synne..." Her name rolls off my tongue like a whispered caress against her lips. "It's the perfect name for a woman as sinfully beautiful as you are."

There's a glimmer in her eyes as they blink up at me. Between us, the passion is palpable, drifting in the air, pooling around us like warm water. Holding her close, I linger in this moment, afraid of losing the sensation filling my heart.

"The way you make me feel... I didn't know it could be this good."

"Levi was a piece of shit. He should've made you feel like this every day. You deserve it."

Turning to face me, she puts her hands around my neck, her warm breasts pressed against my chest.

"I want you to stay with me more than just tonight."

Putting an arm around her back, I lower her to the bed, kissing her as I lie above her.

"I'm not going anywhere."

IN THE KITCHEN, Synne shakes her ass to rock music as she flips pancakes. I'm sprawled out on her couch, watching her dance in only blue panties and another one of my shirts. I've been here for two days, and she's washed my clothes, cooked every meal for me, and had the great idea of us going on a ride together. The last two days have been blissful, but I can't keep it up. I have to get back to the shop soon. William already texted this morning, letting me know we've had several custom orders come in since bike week ended.

The problem is, I don't want Synne coming back to work with me. I don't want her sitting in a place the Royals know, a place she's easily accessible. I'm stuck between a rock and a hard place—I enjoy having her work with me, and I can keep an eye on her while she's there, but at my shop, she's a sitting target.

Leaving the couch, I rest my elbows on the edge of the counter across from where she's cooking. She turns down her phone, so we can talk.

"Butter or syrup?" she asks, removing two plates from the cabinet behind her.

"Both."

"Good, me too."

Tension coils in my gut as her brows pinch inward. She's studying my face, and clearly, unease is written all over it.

"We need to talk about work."

"I assumed we'd be going back in today."

"I am, but I want you to take some time off and stay clear of the shop for a while."

The fluffy round pancake slides off her spatula onto an empty plate before she sets the spatula down, staring at me in confusion.

"This is about what happened to Angela. Are you worried the Royals will attack me at Custom Ride?"

Rubbing my index finger and thumb over my facial hair, I stare back at her intense gaze and the tight lines around her eyes.

"They're capable of anything. I can't risk something happening to you."

"I have to come back sometime. What's a week going to do?"

Sliding the spatula under another pancake, she drops it on top of the other.

"It's not going to do anything. It might be a good idea for you to take the week and look for a job somewhere else."

Her arms drop to her sides, the spatula dangling from her hand.

"Are you firing me?"

"Yes."

Shoving the plate forward, she sets the spatula on the counter with a thud, her cheeks growing red.

"I love working there, especially with you. You shouldn't fire me because you're worried about something happening to me."

Reaching over the counter, I grab her hand, holding it in mine. Rubbing my thumb over it, I attempt to soothe her rising temper.

"This is about more than a job. I enjoy working with you too, but I can't risk anything happening to you. I'll do anything to keep you safe even if that means giving up seeing you at work every day."

Her other hand holds her weight as she leans against the counter. Looking off, her nostrils flare above her tight, flattened lips.

"I don't want to work anywhere else. I don't want to hide."

Withdrawing my hand, I stand straight, my shoulders widening.

"Did you see what they did to Angela?" I snap, my tone sharper than intended. "They stabbed her and beat her to death, no doubt raped her too. I'm not going to let that happen to you. I don't want to be an asshole about this, but you're not coming back to the shop or the clubhouse until I say so."

"You're scared, I get it, but I—"

"I'm not fucking scared, Synne. I'm being smart about this. I've known the Royals a hell of a lot longer than you have. I've lost two women I loved because of them. I'm not losing a third. You can be pissed at me, but I'd rather you be angry than dead."

Moving away from the counter, I grab my vest off the back of the couch and loop my arms into it. Dropping onto the couch, I grab my boots and shove my feet into them.

"Nix?"

"There isn't anything else to say. Find another job."

Her hand touches my shoulder, and I stop tying my boot as the soft grip of her hand turns into rubbing.

"I don't like having to find another job, but I'll stop fighting you on the subject. I can see how much it's upsetting you."

Putting an arm out, I pull her onto my lap, her legs straddling mine as she faces me, her hands rubbing the tension in my neck.

"I don't think you realize how much you mean to me."

"I'm not used to someone caring so much."

My forehead leans against hers as I lift my T-shirt and rub her back.

"It's not easy for me to tell you to get another job, I want you there with me, but this is what I warned you about. I can't have happiness, not as long as the Royals are alive."

Her next words are cut off by the ding in my pocket. Leaning back, I dig my cell phone out and read the group text message from William.

Clubhouse. Now. Royals are here.

"Shit!"

Pushing Synne off my lap, I grab my keys off the coffee table.

"What's going on?"

"Stay here until you hear from me. I mean it, Synne, don't leave this apartment."

Before she can argue, I'm closing the door in her face and running down the apartment building hall to the stairs.

CHAPTER TWENTY-THREE

NIX

WHAT I WALK into is a fucking hurricane of chaos. Tables are flipped, chairs broken, glass beer bottles shattered and scattered on the bar, tables, and floor. Jeff is nowhere to be seen, thankfully, but William isn't as fortunate. Two Royals have him tied down to a chair, his right eye and top lip busted, blood dripping onto his gray cut-off sleeved T-shirt.

As I take in the scene, Jake and Max enter behind me, their expressions revealing the same emotions I'm feeling.

"What the fuck are you doing in our clubhouse, destroying property and disrespecting one of my members?"

Reed kicks a chair out of his way and sits on one of the upright tables, one boot still on the floor, the other leg bent as he carelessly rests his ugly ass on the surface.

"It's all over the news, *Pres*. Our shop went up in flames and with it, ten kilos of cocaine."

"Sounds like a personal problem," I bite back, my arms crossed over my chest.

"Nah, you see, Rex took a hell of a beating, but the man still managed to get a message to us." Reed puts his pinky in the air and wiggles it. "With his little finger, he dipped it in hospital puddin' and wrote *Kings*."

The rest of my crew billows into the clubhouse, forming a wall around me, their hands on their guns.

"Rex has a grudge. Just because the son of a bitch woke up from a beating and assumed it was us, doesn't mean it was."

Reed puts his hands in the air and smirks. "You got me there, Wilson. He does have a grudge, but I still believe him. He's my second cousin, after all, and my men know better than to lie to me. It's a lesson you could use."

"The only lesson that's gonna be learned today is the hard beating we're gonna give you for damaging our clubhouse and throwing around bullshit accusations."

Reed steps off the table and motions his finger toward the two assholes on either side of William. The taller man with black and gray peppered hair holds William's shoulders as the shorter, beefier man with blond greasy hair slams a fist into William's face. Blood spatters across the floor, and my rage forces my arms to my sides, my fingers grazing the metal of the Glock on my hip. Between heartbeats, I raise the gun and apply five pounds of pressure. The bullet clips the greasy blonde's shoulder, tearing a hole through leather and flesh.

"Fucking Christ!" he screams, his arm dropping like deadweight. Next to me, Dom has his gun out and pointed toward Reed's head. My aim switches, adding another barrel at Reed as several more guns are drawn around the room.

"Fun's over. Get your crew and get the fuck out."

Reed slowly moves off the table, motioning for his crew to exit. As they approach, we make room for them, our guns still raised and pointed at them as they keep theirs pointed at us. Reed stops at the end of my barrel, his gaze cutting past the gun to me.

"You got seven days to deliver fifty thousand, a down payment for the full seven hundred and fifty you cost me and my crew. If you don't pay, you'll be burying another pretty redhead."

My teeth clench, my finger on the trigger. My breath is unmoving as the anger boils inside me.

"You touch her, you die."

Reed scoffs as he turns toward the exit. With them out the door, I lower my gun and breathe. Ink and Trevor rush toward William and untie him from the chair. Jake and Max approach, but I walk away from them, my anger still uncontrollable. With my gun in my hip holster, I rest my fists on the nearest standing table, my knuckles turning white. Reed's words replay in my mind, tormenting me. Gripping the table, I roar as I flip the table through the air, and it crashes into other toppled tables and chairs several feet away.

"I can't take this shit anymore!"

With my heartbeat pounding in my ears and sweat beading down my back, I stomp toward the bar, gather an intact bottle of whiskey, loosen the top, and swig. The men gather around the bar, passing the bottle around. When it gets to William, he wipes his bloody mouth and keeps the bottle, swallowing as much as he can in one gulp. The guy's gonna need it for the pain.

"We don't have fifty thousand to give them," Wesley says aloud.

"They don't need money, they need taken out," Dom says to me.

My gaze sweeps between the crew, their expressions a visual representation of anger, fear, and the crash of adrenaline.

"We're done suffering at the hands of the Royals," I say to them. "We're finishing this once and for all. I need to know who's in."

I DIDN'T THINK I'd be meeting Mr. Galloni again so soon, but life has a way of throwing unexpected obstacles at you on a regular basis. You have a choice.

Don't deal with the obstacle, but that'll only cause you more problems later. You can try to get a handle on the situation, do the best you can, and hope for the best. Or you can make a plan and blow that obstacle to smithereens. I'm tired of trying to get a handle on things. The Royals have pushed me to this point—the point of no return. Once I commit, I'll have to take the consequences as they come. My only regret will be losing Synne.

"It's a pleasure doing business with you again, Nix. The order you requested is complete." Motioning toward the blue moving truck behind him, two of his men in furniture delivery uniform shirts open the double doors and remain at the truck sides as Max, Axel, and I take a look at the contents—one wooden crate with everything we need. I give an approving nod, and Max and Axel gather the crate and load it into my Custom Ride trailer.

With day turning to evening, the building casts a dark shadow onto the parking lot, its gloom eerily similar to the despair that's crawled into my heart and dug its teeth in like a blood-sucking leech. I can't shake this feeling, not with what's coming.

Mr. Galloni studies my features, curiosity dropping his brow as he flicks a thumb across his clean, trimmed beard.

"Should you need my services again, you know how to reach me."

Outstretching my hand, I give him the envelope of

cash. Tossing it to one of his men, he waits for the man to count it.

"All there, plus extra," the burly man tells him.

Mr. Galloni's mustache curls with his lip. Putting his hand forward, he shakes mine.

"Thank you for your business."

"Likewise."

Putting my hand in the air, I circle it, giving the signal it's time to ride. The scent of exhaust fumes fills the air as we fire up our engines. Minutes later, we're on the road, my heart heavier as we move forward with our plan.

Back at the shop and clubhouse, we unload the crate and secure it in the parts room connected to the garage. Together, the crew and I head into the clubhouse. Jeff lines up shot glasses across the bar top, pouring liquor into each. With the last two days spent cleaning up the clubhouse bar, it's now presentable but filled with a lot fewer tables and chairs, a constant reminder of the Royals' visit.

Grabbing our shots, we lift them and meet eyes.

"Together we ride, together we live, together we die," Max says to the group.

The shot glasses are tilted as we swallow the liquor down and slam them on the counter.

"It's time, brothers."

They nod in approval as I withdraw my cell phone from my pocket. My chest constricts as I dial Reed's number.

"Got my money, Wilson?"

"Yeah, I'll get you your damn money. We'll meet you in two days, eleven p.m. at the address I text you."

"Nah, we'll come to your clubhouse to collect."

"The fuck you will. I have a business to run, and you've done enough damage. If you want your money, you'll meet where I say."

"You better have it, *Pres,* or there'll be hell to pay."

"See you in two days, asshole."

Turning back to my crew, I continue our plans.

"Trevor, gather three thousand from the Kings' account, have it bundled in dollar bills with twenties on top of the stacks. Ink, use cash and buy earplugs for all of us. Axel, use cash and buy bags of sand, around a hundred pounds. Wesley, get us a black duffel bag. Max and I will study the layout of the old warehouse and prepare the rest. We'll all meet here tomorrow at the same time and get everything ready. Go home, brothers. Love on your women and get the rest you need."

Most of the crew leaves, Jeff included, but Jake and Dom linger behind.

"We're going with you," Jake insists.

Dom crosses his arms in his familiar way that means the decision is final.

"All right. Leave your leathers in my office. We're taking my truck."

Driving into the old part of Nashville, where businesses once bustled and thrived over twenty years ago, we circle around rundown businesses with wood covered windows and graffiti painted on the aged red brick. The longstanding tobacco warehouse was my choice. I remember my grandfather worked there when I was a kid. The smell of leaf and smoke clung to his clothing and skin, wafting through the house when he came to visit us kids and my uncle Dallas, who raised us.

A flood from the Cumberland River damaged the first floor of the warehouse. Between property damage and the decline of the tobacco industry's support, the company had to shut down. It forced my grandfather into retirement, where he spent most of his time rebuilding motorcycles, and teaching Dallas and me everything he knew. Pulling into the cracked parking lot, I imagine my grandfather doing the same, preparing for a hard day at work so he could feed his family of two sons and a daughter.

It hit my family hard when Aunt May was raped and my uncle murdered by Tolito's father. It's something my grandfather never recovered from. He thought it was his fault. He started the Kings all those years ago, and it was his feud with the Wild Royals that led to that horrible day. Bear and Aunt May had a good life together, were thinking of having children, and that was all torn away by the cruel hands of the Royals. It's why it's my duty to end this. To finish the blood feud that's lasted three generations between my family and the Alverez's.

As the men climb out of my truck, my cell phone

dings in my pocket. Withdrawing it, I swipe the screen and read Synne's text message.

I know you've been busy with work and fixing the clubhouse bar, but if you need a break, I'm offering dinner... and dessert ;)

Guilt is a tightly knotted ball in my stomach. I miss her, more than I can cope with right now, but I have to keep my distance until this is over. It's the only way to keep her safe.

I can't this week, but I'll be over this weekend. I promise to make it up to you. You've been on my mind a lot. Miss you, babe.

After hitting send, I pocket my cell phone and join Dom at the tailgate of my truck. He's pulling one of the two crowbars out of the back while Jake and Max are doing a sweep of the area, searching for cameras and cops. I know there aren't any cameras. This part of town is nothing but vacant buildings, frequently used by street kids and those who are homeless, but it's still worth checking.

Dom and I work open the wood over the front door, prying and breaking pieces until the wood falls with gravity, and our boots catch it before it thuds on the ground. With the end of the crowbar, I bust through the glass window on the front door and reach in, unlocking it. Inside, there's an odor of mildew covered walls and rusty steel pillars. We angle the flashlights from our phones around the open space, my light landing on the red-brown tinted columns and dingy concrete floor.

"It's enough space and far enough away from the public to hide the sounds," Dom says to me, his light moving away as he inspects the area.

"Yeah. Now, we need to figure out coverage and how to exit quick."

CHAPTER TWENTY-FOUR

SYNNE

ALONG THE SIDEWALK to Jake and Liz's front door are pretty orange anemone flowers, the color popping against the cream siding and the coffee-colored front door. Stepping up to it, I press the doorbell and wait. Liz swings the door open with Liam resting on her hip, a wet, rumpled Harley Davidson teddy bear between his hands and teeth.

"Come in." She waves her hand and steps back, giving me room to enter. "The lasagna is just about ready."

Setting Liam in a baby playset, she moves to the kitchen, pulls two ales out of the fridge, and slides one across the island to me.

"You look like you need it."

"I do."

Taking the chilled bottle in my hand, I drop onto a barstool and use the bottle opener she hands me. With the top popped, I take a long swallow, my boot resting on the barstool footrest, while Liz slides a cookie sheet of garlic bread into the oven.

"I haven't seen Nix in several days. I feel like he's avoiding me. I told him I would look for another job, but I haven't found anything I want to do. I love working at Custom Ride."

Liz rests her hands and hips against the same counter as the oven, her eyes empathetic above a brief reassuring smile.

"He is avoiding you, but it's not because he doesn't want to see you. Last night, he crashed here. He and Jake thought I was sleeping, but I stood outside Liam's room, listening to them talk. They took turns holding Liam and promised him he would have a future without the threat of the Royals." Nervous tension tightens her brows and mouth. "They're planning something. Something dangerous and I'm scared for them." Her eyes dart to Liam, then back to me as tears pool in her eyes. "I asked Jake about it, but he won't tell me. He says it's better I don't know. Then said they're doing what they think is best to protect the Kings family, including us." She points to herself, me, and Liam.

My hand around the bottle tightens as my heartbeat races, causing an ache in my chest.

"What do you think they're going to do?"

"I think they're going to confront the Royals. I'm so scared they're going to end up in jail or killed." Tears fall from her eyes, and she looks toward the ceiling, wiping them away. With a sniffle, she tries to compose herself. "It's not the first time they've gone after the Royals. Two years ago, the previous president of the Royals abducted me. He tied me up..." She pauses, takes a breath, holding back tears before continuing. "He assaulted me and came close to raping me, but Jake and Nix got there before he could. Jake shot him, but because Tolito recorded everything, we had evidence of his assault."

My boot drops from the footrest. Leaving the stool, I walk to Liz's side of the island and hug her.

"I'm so sorry that happened to you."

Liz's arms wrap around me, holding me tight as she sniffles back more tears.

"I want to talk them out of whatever plan they have." She pulls back from me, her green eyes glossy, the skin around them blotched and puffy. "But I don't want my son to go through what we all have. They've terrorized my family for years. Nix can't take anymore. He's ready to snap."

Now I understand. *This* is why Nix is avoiding me. He wants me kept away from everything going on and whatever he's planning. His words playback in my mind —*I don't want to lose you too. I need you. Which is why I won't ever share the worst of me.*

Stepping back, I lean my weight against the island counter.

"Whatever they're planning, they're going for blood."

Liz's gaze flitters away from me, a heavy breath escaping her.

"I know."

The oven dings, and she rubs a hand over one arm, then turns to open it, sliding an oven mitt on. Removing the garlic bread, she sets it on top of the oven. Dropping the oven mitt on the counter, she turns back to me, wiping at a single tear.

"I don't want to lose them, Synne."

Moisture fills my own eyes as I look back at her. "I don't either. Can we talk them out of it?"

"No. When either one of them won't talk about something, their mind is made up, and there's no convincing them otherwise."

"What about Erika and Audrey?"

"Dom and Trevor are no different from Jake and Nix. They'll do anything to keep Erika and Audrey safe. Neither of them will be able to help talk them out of it, not when Dom and Trevor see the Royals as a threat too."

Liz turns away from me, putting the oven mitt back on, then grabs a second one out of a drawer and opens the oven to remove the lasagna. After setting the large baking dish on top of the oven, next to the garlic bread, she presses the off button on the oven.

"All we can do is wait, hope, and pray whatever they're planning goes the way they want."

Lifting the ale, I swallow several times, my body

rooted to the spot as my mind drifts off and my heart bleeds fear.

"And if it doesn't, we'll at least have tonight as a family."

My eyes blink, the bottle held midair as I stare at her confused.

"I insisted Jake bring everyone over for dinner."

My gaze jumps to the giant lasagna pan and the entire loaf of garlic bread on the cookie sheet, the pieces coming together. Harleys roar in the distance, the sound fluttering my stomach, knowing I'll see Nix within minutes.

Looking back at her, my mouth tilts. "Thank you for inviting me over."

"You're a part of this family too." She pulls me in for another hug, squeezing me in her arms. "Nix loves you. He's only keeping you away to protect you."

"I understand. Thank you for sharing everything with me."

Boots thud across the porch and we separate. She points to the cabinet and I gather enough plates for everyone. Jake is the first to walk in with Nix right behind him. Nix stops in his tracks, catching sight of me, and my heart skips a beat at the way his gaze takes me in. A smile curls the corner of his mouth, and he continues walking forward, coming into the kitchen. Going past Liz, he steps up to me. Without a word, his gaze roams my face, the glimmer in his eyes mesmerizing, holding me in place. Putting a hand around my waist, he lowers it to my ass and pulls me to him, covering my mouth with his warm, luscious lips. Beneath the heat of his kiss, warmth spreads to my center, my nipples growing tight as I wrap my arms around his neck. Gliding his hand up my side, he caresses, firms his grip, and slides his hand back down to my hip, leaving my body tingling and hungry for more of him. When he withdraws, my lips remain parted and prickling with the pleasure of his kiss.

My fingers delve into his hair as he adds another arm around my waist. When he squeezes my ass, I push into his dick, loving the feel of his length pressing back.

"I missed you," I tell him, curling my fingers in his hair.

Lowering his mouth to mine, he steals my breath once again.

"It's only been a few days since I last saw you, but it feels like it's been a hell of a lot longer."

"It does."

On the other side of the counter, Trevor catcalls as he passes by with Audrey. Nix glances over at him, giving him a smirk. The whole Kings' family is here and following Jake out to the back patio.

"I'm glad you're here." Nix's forehead lowers to mine. "I needed to see you."

"I get that you want to keep me away from all the shit that's going on, but it's been hard. I feel like you're keeping me at arm's length. Like you have something else going on that you don't want me to know about."

Nix kneads his fingers into my lower back, forming pleasured goosebumps along my skin.

"Trust me, baby. I want to be with you, but I have things I need to take care of. Knowing you're safe lets me focus on those things. Can you be patient with me for another few days?"

"I can, but I'd worry less if you shared with me what's going on."

"You know I can't."

Nix loosens his grip as Liz comes back into the kitchen.

"Sorry to interrupt you two love birds, but I need to get the food out there to all those hungry folks."

Jake opens the sliding door and joins Liz in the kitchen, giving her ass a slap as he walks past her.

"I'll get the lasagna, babe. Nix, can you bring out the beers? They're in the fridge."

Nix curls his fingers around my jaw, raising my lips to his. As he pulls away from me, his warmth leaves my body, and in its place is a deep and desperate longing to feel his touch again. Following him to the fridge, I attempt to gather the second twenty-four pack of beer, but he turns his head and kisses me.

"I got these, gorgeous."

Muscles, strong and contoured, swell as he carries a pack in each hand. When he catches me staring, he winks, reigniting the arousal that had just begun to settle. Going ahead of him, I open the sliding glass door, then return to the kitchen to help Liz gather paper towels and silverware. Jake makes one more trip inside to pick up Liam and tosses him in the air, smiling wildly as Liam giggles. With Liam tucked in his arm, he grabs the playset with his free hand and joins the rest of us outside.

Liz insists we say a prayer before eating, and as we all gather around the patio table and the extra folding table, Nix pulls me onto his lap, the warmth of his hand caressing my hip. He kisses my shoulder, and my stomach flutters. Leaning in close, I kiss his cheek.

"I love you."

Nix's eyes widen, a smile turning his serious expression into one of joy. Caressing a hand across my cheek, he slips his tongue between my lips, uniting us in a passionate embrace.

"I love you, Synne." Penetrating green eyes capture mine, emotion filling them as he holds my gaze captive. "You're the light in my deepest darkest hour," he whispers.

My lips part to reply but are cut off as Liz begins her prayer. She isn't shy about the undiscussed topic among us.

"Thank you for bringing us together and uniting us as a family. Thank you for the bonds of friendship we all share. Please continue to look after us, to protect our Kings family; on the road, in life, and against any future threats. Whatever choices are ahead of us, please give courage where it's needed and triumph where it's wanted."

Jake puts his hands on Liz's shoulders and kisses her head.

"Thank you, Peach. That was perfect." With a massage of her shoulders, he lowers his hands and points to the lasagna. "Let's eat this incredible meal she cooked for us all."

Around the tables, the men fill their plates with lasagna squares and garlic slices while we women glance at each other. It's clear we all fear the same thing—will this be our last meal together as a family? Will we see the men we love again?

WALKING INTO MY APARTMENT, my feet are heavy, my worry causing aches throughout my body. Saying goodbye to Nix tonight was gut-wrenching. Whatever they're planning, it's happening tomorrow. That much was clear by the hushed conversations about the things they prepared earlier today and the way Nix avoided it when I asked. When I stood next to my bike to leave, I couldn't let go, couldn't stop kissing him. At his insistence, I got on my bike, pulled him to me for one last kiss, and willed myself to leave. As I drove home, the ache in my heart grew stronger, my worry more intense.

Dropping my helmet, jacket, and keys by the door, I amble to the kitchen to pour a drink. It's the only way

I'll be able to sleep tonight. As the glass is set on the counter, there's a knock at my door. Going to it, I swing the door open, and Nix pushes through the threshold, his arms wrapping around me, his mouth crashing to mine. Kicking the door closed, he backs us to it and locks it, never taking his lips off me. There isn't room for words. Lifting my legs around his waist, he holds my ass to him as he carries me to my room. Laying me on the bed, he stays above me, caressing my thigh as he pushes his growing erection against my center. My moan spills out between our kiss, and he grabs my hands, raising them above my head as he pushes against me harder.

"Just saying the words isn't enough. I want you to feel how much I love you."

"Show me," I whisper as he's removing the clothes between us.

Trailing his fingers up my abdomen, he lifts my shirt and bra off, his lips locking onto each breast, hardening my nipples to rounded crests.

"I love the way your body responds to my touch."

Feathering kisses down my stomach, he unbuttons my jeans, folds them down, and pulls them off me, taking my underwear with them.

"I love how wet you get when you want my cock inside you."

Spreading my legs, he palms my clit, flicks it with his thumb, then massages it, my back arching as a rush of pleasure swims through my body.

"I love the look of satisfaction on your face when I make you come."

Taking his hand from my clit, he removes his vest, then lifts his T-shirt off, giving me a perfect view of his sculpted chest and abs.

"I love the way your eyes light up when you see me naked."

With a quick flick of his thumb, his jeans are unbuttoned. Stepping off the bed, he drops his jeans and briefs, kicking out of them and his boots. Coming back onto the bed, he spreads my knees and lies between them, his gaze carnal as he reaches down and wraps his fist around his thick cock.

"I love the way you bite your lip when you're thinking how good it's going to feel to have me fucking you."

Placing his tip against my pussy, he rubs it along my clit, my need for him coating his cockhead as I whimper for more.

"I love the way you moan for me."

Thrusting in deep, he pulls out and thrusts harder. My body screams with pleasure, little bolts of lightning igniting at every nerve ending. My arms reach for his neck, my legs wrapping around him as he holds himself up, thrusting into me with such fervor, my eyes pinch close and I cry out as he takes my body on a ride I'll never forget.

"Look at me, baby."

When I do, he collides his lips with mine, the

passion he exudes so intoxicating, I want to drown in it, be swallowed in this moment, frozen in the sensation of his love. I want this man to be my future, to love me like this for the rest of our lives, and I know he would. Nix's emotions run deeper than any man I know. He's an alpha in every meaning of the word, but beneath that protective exterior is a man with a heart that will love with everything he has and fight until he has nothing left to give. He's mine, my Nix, my white knight on a Harley.

"I love you."

Slowing his thrusts, he lowers on top of me, his hand winding into my hair as his other hand intertwines with mine. My legs stay wrapped around him as he rolls his hips, coming into me slowly, pulling out, and thrusting again, making love to me in a way he's never done before.

MY DRY MOUTH and urge to pee drag me out of my soft, warm bed, filled with the scent of Nix and the night we spent together. As my feet touch the floor, there's a hollow, empty pit in my stomach, quickly filling with sorrow. Nix is gone, and on my nightstand is a scribbled note.

BECAUSE OF YOU, I found happiness I didn't believe was

possible. Because of you, I developed hope for a future. No matter what happens, remember I love you.

MOISTURE FILLS my eyes as panic tightens my throat. Reaching for my phone, I dial his number. It goes right to voicemail, so I call Liz.

"Have you seen Nix this morning?"

"No, why? What's going on?"

"He stayed over last night. We didn't get a chance to talk. We had sex then fell asleep. When I woke up, he was gone."

"He would've gone back to his house to shower and change."

"I'm headed there now."

"Don't! Nix will lose his mind if you show up at his house. It's where he lost Jenna. *Please*, Synne, don't go to his house. Not today. Jake said they're meeting the Royals today, and we need to stay away from the shop and clubhouse. The Royals will be waiting and watching them."

"I have to. I have to see him."

"Listen to me." Her tone brooks no argument. "He needs a clear head for whatever is going down between the Kings and the Royals. If you show up and the Royals see you, they'll use you against him. For his sake, *please* stay home."

"I can't sit here all day worrying."

"You don't have to do it alone. I'll pack up stuff for Liam and come over to your place."

"What are we going to do? Try to watch TV we don't care about? Try to eat food we don't have an appetite for? I can't stay here, locked in this apartment, thinking about every horrible scenario. I'm going riding."

"Stay *away* from the clubhouse and shop," she reiterates, her tone forceful.

"I didn't fall in love with him so I can lose him. I'll talk to you later."

I disconnect the call and rush to the bathroom now that my body has remembered it needs to pee. Jumping in the shower, I wash all of me as quickly as I can, then with fresh clothes on, I head to the kitchen to get something to drink before gathering my riding gear. With thoughts of Nix constantly on my mind, I won't be able to accomplish anything today. Fear is a tight ball resting in my gut, and the only way it will loosen is if I see him. Maybe I can talk him out of whatever they're planning before it's too late.

With a cup in hand, I set it on the counter, open the fridge and fill the glass with orange juice. My doorbell rings and I jolt in surprise. Lowering the orange juice carton, I go to the door and am shocked to see Liz standing there in gray pajama pants, a pink tee that says, *I'm a drop the F bomb kind of mom*, her hair disheveled and half straightened with Liam tucked into a backpack carrier. Opening the door wider, I make room for her to enter.

"What are you doing here?"

"As soon as you hung up, I put him in a carrier and drove straight here. I could hear it in your voice. You were still planning to search for Nix. There's no way in hell I'm letting you anywhere near the clubhouse or shop. I already lost one best friend, I'm not losing another."

"Whatever they're planning, I have a bad feeling about it. I need to talk to him. I *need* to see him."

"Well, unless you plan on shoving a mom and baby out of your way, you're not going anywhere." Her arms cross, and she widens her sandal-covered feet, securing her stance.

I can't fight the chuckle that escapes.

"You and Liam are safe. I'm not going to shove either of you out of my way."

Liz swings her arm and shuts the door behind her.

"Good. Because I'm freaking out enough as it is. I can't handle fighting with you on top of it. Help me out of this carrier, then I'll tell you what Jake told me."

CHAPTER TWENTY-FIVE

NIX

JAKE DROPS his vest on my desk and lands in the chair across from me with a thump.

"Liz called. She had to stop your girl from rolling in here." Leaning back, he puts his hands behind his head, stretching as the chair balances on two legs.

Lowering the paperwork in front of me, I set down my pen and sit back in my chair.

"Seeing she didn't show up, I'm glad Liz talked her out of it. The clubhouse or shop is the last place she needs to be right now."

"I know it, brother. It's almost over. Soon, you won't need to worry about that shit."

Scratching my thumb across the facial hair on my chin, my brows flick upward. "I'm already worried about the aftermath.

"Leave no trace. That's the plan. As long as we stick to it, the aftermath should be minimal or none at all."

"Yeah." My chair turns as my gaze drifts out the window. "But that doesn't stop my mind from thinking of all the different ways this shit could go south."

The chair Jake's in taps the floor and drags my gaze to him.

"You thinkin' we should abandon our plans?"

Raking my hand through my lengthening hair, I exhale a resigned sigh.

"No. The Royals would keep coming for more money. It would never end, and Synne would never be safe—none of us would."

"Ever since you said it, I've known this is what we need to do. We're making the right choice... no matter what happens."

"You're right." Gathering the completed beneficiary paperwork, I place it in the folder with Liz's name on it and set it aside. "You got all your affairs in order?"

"Yeah. Liz gets everything—house, business, car, and Harley."

"Same," I nod. "With a special gift for Synne."

"What's that?"

"She gets the Reaper and my cruiser."

"Lucky woman," Jake quips.

A smile rounds the corner of my mouth but falls as my attention is stolen by the ringtone of my cell phone. Glancing at the screen, it's a number I recognize, one I'm not so sure I want to answer, but I do anyway.

"Nix Wilson?"

"Yeah?"

"It's Special Agent Adams from the TBI."

"I still have you in my contacts. So, why the call?"

"Angela Kersee. Consider this a courtesy call. You nor the Kings are a suspect. This isn't something I should be telling you, but you know it, anyway——"

"Reed Alverez and his thugs killed her," I finish for him.

"DNA is still undergoing processing, but I have no doubt we'll find something on them."

"I appreciate the courtesy call."

"That's not all."

Of course, it isn't. Lowering my phone, I press the speaker button and set it on my desk for Jake to hear.

"I didn't think it was. What's the real reason for the call?"

Jake pulls his cell phone out and taps the record button. I give him an approving nod.

"Hacker's Automotive, you know anything about it?"

"I can probably fill you in on some missing holes in your case, but I'm gonna need a favor in return."

"Yeah. What kind of favor?"

"One I'll save for later."

"Don't tell me your club is getting involved in illegal activities." His tone lowers, vocalizing his disapproval.

"No illegal activities, but we have the same problem —the Wild Royals."

"Isn't that the truth," he sneers. "I've got a growing gut and thinning hair to prove it. So, what information do you have to make my life easier?"

"Hacker's Automotive was a front for the Royals. It was their central location for drug containment and distribution. They loaded drugs into the vehicles that were supposedly there for repairs, then sent the drugs out to clients and dealers."

"How'd you get this information?"

"We have our ways."

There's a grunt on the other end of the phone. "Yeah. I heard about Rex Alverez. Hell, if I could put you on the payroll, I would."

"From what I heard, Rex got what he deserved."

There's another grunt and no argument after. "The explosion at Hacker's Automotive is being reported as a chemical accident that resulted in a fire. I can't help suspecting otherwise. The Royals have gathered themselves several enemies over the years."

"They sure as hell have."

"This is going to put them in deep shit with the drug cartel. They're going to owe them some serious cash."

"Maybe this is the beginning of the end for them."

"From the reports flying across my desk, I'd say the Royals have finally pissed off the wrong people or *person*. And I don't think this is the end of it either."

"It won't be any heartache to us to see them fall."

"Well, Wilson, I hope I don't see your name or the name of any of the Kings' members come across my desk if what this is, is a war."

"No worries, Adams. We're just a bunch of free-spirited bikers, selling custom bikes and beers."

Agent Adams chuckles through the receiver. "One more thing, Wilson."

"What is it?"

"Local PD reached out to Angela Kersee's family. They're coming to sign off on her cremation in a few days. Would you like the opportunity to say goodbye before they arrive?"

My throat tightens, my words lodged as memories of Angela flood my mind. The last time we were together, I gathered her leopard print shirt off the end of my bed and handed it to her as she finished dressing. With a salacious grin, she tossed the shirt, grabbed the waist of my jeans, and pulled me back on top of her. There was a time, I truly loved her. A time she made me happy. A time I considered a future with her before she decided I wasn't enough.

"No, I don't want to be reminded of what they did to her. I want to remember who she was before the Royals destroyed her." My tone is harsher than I intended, but I can't hide the anger that surfaces every time I think of her body lying in the dirt.

"I understand. Thanks for your time."

He disconnects, and I tap end call on my cell as I release a breath and fall back in my chair. My thumbnail is ground between my teeth as my thoughts drift off to Angela's death, Jenna's, Pat's, Bear's, and my grandfather's best friend, Ray Alverez—the man whose death began the blood feud and animosity between our clubs all those years ago.

"Adams believes the cartel will punish the Royals for the loss of their drugs; that's a benefit for us." Jake's voice snaps me back, my gaze darting to him. "When everything goes down, that's the first thing they'll suspect."

"Let's make sure they have no reason to believe otherwise." Standing, I shift out of my vest and leave it on the desk with Jake's. "It's time to get ready."

CHAPTER TWENTY-SIX

NIX

MY CREW IS ALL HERE on the first floor of the tobacco factory, our getaway trucks parked outside in the darkened parking lot, facing out for a quick exit. Five of us stand behind a six-foot metal folding table with a black duffel bag sitting on top. We've set up camping lanterns and thrown a few objects around to make it look like teenagers or homeless have been using the space. The extra two metal tables, a broken dresser, and busted bookshelf are all items we picked up from second-hand donation stores. They look worn, useful, and disguise their real use—coverage.

I've sent the text to Reed. Dominic and Jake are by the entrance, waiting for the Royals to show. Axel and Trevor are set up in their locations, awaiting the signal. Max, Wesley, Ink, and William are at the table with me. Wesley, Ink, and William are several steps back, giving coverage to my back while Max and I give the appearance the President and VP are ready to do business.

The roar of Harleys in the distance cause every muscle in my neck and back to tense. Max pats my shoulder.

"We're in this together, brother."

Nodding, I pat his shoulder, and hip check my Glock.

My chin rises as Reed's VP, Duncan, steps through the doorway first, surveying the scene as he slows his steps. Two more of Reed's thugs stomp in behind Duncan, followed by Reed and five more Royals. The only one missing is Rex, who's either still in the hospital or at home nursing his wounds.

Where we're standing, the door is to our right. The Royals continue forward, coming to a stop across the table from us with their left sides to the door. Dom and Jake are the last to enter. Leaving the door unlocked, they remain next to it. Reed's crew is tightly wrapped around him, giving him protection, but that won't matter.

"What a shithole you picked to meet in." Reed's gaze sweeps around the large space, taking it all in with a grimace.

"I wasn't gonna pick a place the cops would find. The last thing I need is for them to think we're making drug deals with the Royals."

"Right," Reed snickers. "Can't tarnish your squeaky-clean record, can we?" The other Royals snigger, but it doesn't faze us. Our minds are focused only on the plan.

"You know it wasn't always like this," I say to Reed.

My statement pinches his dark brows. "What do ya mean?"

"This place is where my grandfather, James Wilson, worked and met your grandfather, Ray Alverez. It was their mutual love for motorcycles that bonded them and started the Kings. It was meant to be a brotherhood. A club for riders who loved the road, the wild, and the wind, my grandfather would tell me. It was never meant to be a security team. James told me the story of how they were approached to provide security for a cargo truck. James said no, but Ray insisted it would pay well. They didn't need to buy guns as most of the men owned one, anyway. With his insistence, Ray convinced James, and they took the job." Shaking my head, I chuckle aloud.

"And that's where it all went south. At the last minute, James and several other Kings members decided the money wasn't worth the risk and tried to convince the others, but Ray, his son, Dante, and the remaining Kings did the job anyway. Someone wanted what was in that cargo truck, and they were willing to take risks to get it. Ray was driven off the road, his bike and body beyond recovery."

"Why the walk down memory lane, Wilson?" Reed growls. "I know how my grandfather died."

"Because it was your uncle's anger toward my

grandfather that influenced his decision to separate from the Kings and start the Wild Royals. It was your *uncle* who drew first blood, killing *my* uncle and raping *my* aunt! And it was *your grandfather's* greed that got him killed! My family has had to suffer for your grandfather's decision ever since, you piece of shit!"

Several of the Royals fidget uncomfortably, their gazes darting between me and Reed.

"It's been three generations of this bullshit, and it ends *now!*"

Axel and Trevor make their moves. Two flashbangs roll across the floor behind the Royals, their fuses igniting, bursting blinding light and an intense disorienting bang into the space. With our earplugs in, it's less severe, but still more than I anticipated. With my adrenaline pumping, I draw my Glock and aim for Reed's body. Pulling the trigger, a bullet explodes out of the barrel, clipping Reed in the shoulder. A gun fires back, hitting me in the chest, knocking me back as the vest under my shirt takes the majority of the impact. Among the chaos of guns firing and voices shouting, I make out Reed's body darting for the door, his hand over his open wound. Dom and Jake are at the exit, one of their guns taking out Duncan, his body collapsing on the ground with a gruesome thud as his head smacks stone.

Pulling my trigger, I shoot Reed in the side, his feet stumbling to reach the door. A gunshot whizzes past me, and I catch sight of the bullet hole Max put into the blond greasy-haired Royal who had his gun aimed at me. Returning my attention to Reed, I stare back at the barrel of his gun. I don't blink or hesitate, pulling the trigger of my Glock and unleash another bullet into his body. It hits him in the chest as another bullet strikes him in the neck from Dom's gun. Reed's arm drops, his gun clunking on the floor as he falls to his knees, blood spilling out of his mouth, chest, and side. I have no time to watch him die.

Max pulls another flashbang from his side pocket, pulls the clip, and throws it into the remaining group of Royals we have surrounded. Shielding my face from the light, I knock over the nearest table, duck behind it and bring my head up to aim at the Royals. Max and William drop down next to me. A trail of blood rolls down Max's arm, but he pays no attention to it as he unloads his clip into the group. Another body drops to the floor; the massive Royal who held William to the chair stares out with blank eyes, blood pooling out around his chest.

With a glance to the left, I find Wesley and Ink behind another table. My heart skips a beat, my eyelids expanding, my chest tightening so hard my breath stops. Next to Ink, Wesley is holding his neck as blood pours out of it. Ink shoves his shirt into Wesley's neck as Axel steps out from the bookshelf behind them and fires at the Royals.

Diving across the floor, I slide behind Wesley and

Ink's table, blood staining my hands as I apply pressure to Wesley's wound.

"Stay with me, old man!"

Color has drained from his face. Glassy eyes stare back at me with an expression of acceptance.

"It's over... for me, son. I'm not... making it... out of this," he sputters.

The scent of blood fills my nostrils as Wesley's breathing becomes weaker. Another gunshot explodes from the direction of the door as Dom puts down another Royal, then drops to his knees to help Jake. Blood is leaking from Jake's left leg, and the two work to create a tourniquet with Jake's belt.

"Yes, you are." I know deep down the statement is more to convince myself. I've lost so many I love, I can't bear to lose more.

"Stay with me, I'm gonna get you out of here." Putting his arm around my shoulder, I try to lift him. Ink does his best to lift Wesley from the other side.

A gurgling cough spatters blood across the floor. Wesley's knees give out, and we collapse. Lying across my thighs, he gurgles as he tries to speak. Tears gather in my eyes as the last man of my father and uncle's crew dies in my arms. Gripping his shirt, I roar into the air, sucking in the sulfur as I struggle to breathe.

Around me, the gunshots have stopped, but the yelling hasn't. Blood and bullet wounds cover half of my crew, but there's not a single Royal left alive. Max lands on his knees in front of me, gripping my arm with force.

"We need to go. We need to finish this."

"I can't leave him!"

Dom and Trevor lift Jake to his feet. Trevor's hand is wrapped, blood seeping from the fabric he tore off his shirt and tied around it. Axel limps toward the exit with Ink holding him up on one side. Max is holding his arm to his chest, grimacing through the pain. I don't want to leave Wesley's body in this disgusting mess, to be burned among the ashes of the Royals, but Max is right, if we don't finish this now, we endanger all of us. Max tugs at my arm again, and I release Wesley's body. Gathering his necklace, wallet, and keys I tuck them into my pocket and go to Axel's other side, helping him and Ink.

Everyone but Dom and I pile into Axel's truck. With William in the driver seat, he takes off to my house, where Liz is waiting to give medical aid or send them to hospitals, whichever she decides. The night before, the crew chose to include her in our plans, knowing there was a good chance of bullet wounds, and now, I'm thankful we did.

Standing at the tailgate of my truck, my adrenaline is crashing, the pain in my chest worsening from the bullet my vest took. Dom drags the gasoline tank from the truck bed, and I notice blood dripping down his boot. My gaze moves up his leg and finds the tear in his jeans and the blood in its place.

"You're shot."

Dom shrugs it off.

"It's a flesh wound. I'm fine."

Shaking my head, I begin to chuckle but am forced to cough instead. Sharp pain claws across my chest, nearly buckling me over. As he carries the gas tank inside, I continue taking deep breaths and walk around, checking our surroundings, ensuring the shooting didn't attract attention. With nothing but darkness that matches my broken soul, I inhale another breath and join Dom inside with the second gas tank. The two of us cover the space and bodies in the flammable liquid, but I can't bring myself to cover Wesley's. Seeing the old man's body lying at my feet digs a hollow hole in my gut. My nostrils flare as I fight back tears. Dom puts a hand on my shoulder as I stare back at the empathetic expression on his hardened features.

"I'll take care of it."

Nodding, I swallow the lump in my throat and walk away. Going over to Reed's body, I let my rage and anger fill me. The thought of Jenna's beautiful face is a memory as vivid as a photo. Squatting down, I wipe at a fallen tear, flick open the lighter, ignite a flame, and lower it.

"This is for all of them."

The flame touches fuel, and within seconds, the orange glow is spreading across his clothing. Dom and I waste no time running out of the building. Jumping into my truck, I put it into drive and speed out of the parking lot as flames rise behind the dingy windows in my rearview mirror.

CHAPTER TWENTY-SEVEN

NIX

STEPPING through my front door is a reminder of the horror we escaped. Jake's passed out on my couch in nothing but boxer briefs with his stitched-up leg raised and sitting on a pillow. Max is stitched, bandaged, and shirtless while he gathers blood-covered evidence in a black garbage bag. William is chugging a bottle of whiskey between filling a second garbage bag. Ink is sitting at the table with Liz and Axel, his hand against his forehead in angst as he watches Liz stitch up Axel. Looking around, I notice one of us is missing.

"Where's Trevor?"

Ink turns his attention to me with wild eyes and a beer in hand. "Hospital."

Liz lifts her head from Axel's shin. Seeing my condition—blood-covered clothes and stained hands— her lips thin below her wrinkled forehead. There's an uneasy tension she's holding back. "His hand wound needs to be looked at by a surgeon if he ever wants to ride again. Audrey took him."

Lifting my shirt off, I pull at the Velcro on the bulletproof vest. "You called Audrey?"

Liz's eyes widen as she stares at my chest.

"You need an x-ray."

"I need alcohol, a shower, and sleep."

Glancing down, I look at the damage. There's red and purple bruising all around the impact wound a few inches wide. The wound itself is dark purple, the skin torn and dried blood caked around it.

"I'm going to need to clean that and wrap it. You might have a cracked rib."

"I'll survive," I assure her.

Dom sheds his shirt and bulletproof vest. As he passes the table to the kitchen sink, Liz inspects him to ensure there are no wounds. Her gaze lowers down his leg and catches the dried blood on his boot.

"I'll need to look at your leg."

Dom gives an acknowledging grunt as he washes his hands. Coming into the kitchen, I wash my arms and hands, then gather my ruined shirt off the floor and toss it in the closest garbage bag. Reaching into my pocket, I pull out Wesley's necklace, wallet, and keys, my finger smoothing over the silver engraved Kings MC charm. Sorrow forms a lump in my throat as I stare down at his belongings. The pressure of tears prickles my eyes, causing me to pinch them closed. Opening them, I set the items in a drawer, avoiding the pain for now.

The garage door that connects to the kitchen opens, and Synne walks through it, carrying additional supplies. Shock hits me to the point of standing there like a deer frozen in headlights.

"Better yet, she can clean and wrap it," Liz says, nodding to Synne.

"Liz?" I admonish.

"I needed the help, and she needed to know you're okay."

Synne sets the additional hydrogen peroxide, gauze, and tape on the table and is quick to approach me. She eases into my open arms with tears in her eyes. Wrapping her hands around my back, she caresses me as she hugs me carefully.

"I love you, Nix, so damn much."

The scent of cinnamon and vanilla rises to my nose as my cheek rests against hers. A sensation of comfort eases into my tired muscles, diminishing some of the pain and guilt. Swallowing the lump in my throat, I whisper, "Even after knowing what I've done?"

She pulls back and stares up at me with nothing but love in her eyes.

"Yes. I'm not going anywhere. Not now, not ever."

Gently, she pulls me toward her, her warm, soft lips evaporating all thoughts from my mind as her kiss fills me with the warmth of her love. As I tighten my grip on her ass, she pushes into me, and I grimace from the pressure on my chest. Pulling back from our kiss, her gaze goes straight to my chest.

"Let me take care of you."

"All right, baby."

Taking my hand, she leads me to the sink, gathering the peroxide and gauze. Dabbing my wound carefully, she watches me with sad eyes every time I grit my teeth. When she's finished, she takes Liz's instruction and wraps my chest. William hands me the whiskey bottle, and I take several drinks. Liz finishes Axel's stitches and convinces Dom to have a seat. After I change, the rest of my brothers take turns showering and putting on the fresh clothes they stored at my house.

With all the bloody clothes, bandages, earplugs, and evidence gathered in bags, William and Ink tie them and load them into my truck along with a gas can. Driving over to my shop, they dump the bags in the steel commercial dumpster we've emptied and light them. From my porch, I watch the flames flicker above the top of the dumpster. Synne steps out onto my porch and takes my hand, her warm fingers sliding between mine.

"Whatever happens next, I won't abandon you."

Turning to look at her gorgeous face, I gather it in my hands and kiss the lips of the woman who's given me love I never dreamed was possible.

"I love you with everything I have to give. You're one of the best things that's ever happened to me, but if what happened tonight lands me in prison, don't wait for me, live your life. Ride hard, live free, and never look back."

Caressing my hand, she brings it to her lips and kisses it as tears well in her eyes.

"I meant it. I'm not going anywhere. I'll help Liz run the businesses and wait for the man who would sacrifice everything to protect the ones he loves, so I can love him the way he deserves to be loved."

Putting my head to hers, I breathe her in, cherishing this moment, freezing this memory in my mind, so I never forget how incredible it feels to be in her presence, touching her, tasting her, feeling her love. My mouth lowers, taking her lips, and with my kiss, I show her the passion she ignites within me.

"Come to bed with me."

The two of us pass by sleeping bodies and quietly ascend the stairs to my room. Behind the closed door, I slip her out of her clothes, get rid of mine, and lay her beneath me. My stretched cock slides between her pussy lips as she welcomes me with a pleasured moan.

THE AROMA of coffee wafts upstairs into my bedroom. With a groan, I drop my feet to the side of the bed, every movement reminding me of the ache in my chest and exhaustion of my body and muscles. Synne wakes and a moment later, rubs her hands on my shoulders, relieving some of the tension.

"Stay here, babe. I'll get you a pain reliever and coffee."

"Thank you. I'm gonna try to take a shower."

Stepping off my bed, I look over my shoulder and watch her round, tight ass, my cock lengthening in response. If my future is a jail cell, I'm going to spend the next several days fucking her as often as I can because it's going to be misery without her. Putting on a T-shirt and boxers of mine, she disappears out my bedroom door.

Forcing myself to stand, I palm my sore chest and amble to the bathroom connected to my room. Turning on the shower, I set it to the temperature I prefer and do my best to unwrap the bandage around my chest. Synne comes in just as I'm finishing, setting the coffee and Tylenol on the counter. She gathers the wad from my hand and tosses it in the trash as I swallow the pills and wash it down with warm coffee.

Taking off my shirt and boxers, she steps into the shower behind me. With her soft hands, she washes every part of me, everywhere she touches a mix of soothing and arousing. When she places her fist on my cock and strokes, it lengthens in her hand. She rinses me off, then turns her ass toward me and puts her palms on the wall. Taking her hip in one hand, I gather my cock in the other. Sliding into her wet, eager pussy, I fuck her as hard as I can and bring us to orgasm before my chest aches and my energy wanes. With a satisfied grin, she turns back to me, rubbing my chest with gentle fingers.

"I think we should move in together."

Pulling her closer, I kiss her soft, damp lips.

"I do too, baby. But not here or your place. Let's get a new place... together." My hand strokes the scarlet strands down her back, my hand falling to my favorite part of her. She giggles when I squeeze both ass cheeks.

"I'd love that."

Resting my head against hers, I lower my lips to her sweet mouth as fear tightens in my stomach.

"I don't want to lose you. Not now that I can finally be happy."

Caressing my cheek, her words falter as she swallows back her tears.

"I don't want to lose you either. I love you so much."

For several minutes, we stand in the spray of warm water, holding each other, afraid to let go. Even as we leave the shower and dry off, we're drawn back into each other's arms, unable to keep from touching one another. Pulling a comb out of a drawer, I do my best to comb her hair as she watches me with watery eyes in the mirror. Setting down the comb, I pull her back to my chest and kiss her head and neck.

"Don't cry, baby. It hurts me to see you cry."

"I'm worried about you."

"I know." Putting my arms around her, I caress her stomach, ignoring the sharp prickling of pins in my chest. "Come back to bed with me."

Lowering my hand, I massage between her legs. Her breathing heightens, turning into quiet moans. She turns her face toward me, and I smother those moans with my kiss. Leading her into my room, I pull the towel off her, and she does the same to me. Applying pressure to my waist, she encourages me to sit on the bed and straddles my lap, riding her pussy over my lengthening cock. As it grows thick, she reaches down, raises her hips and slides her pussy onto it. Her warm walls surround me, clearing my head and emotions. Holding her ass in my hands, I rock her forward and back as she slides up and down. My own pleasured groan fills my ears between the slick sound of her pussy riding my cock. Tightening my grip on her ass, I rock her harder as my orgasm builds, her hands grasping my shoulders as her head falls back. Another thrust and I reach the peak of our pleasure, coming inside my sinfully beautiful woman.

Lying back on the bed, I admire her as she sits atop me, her full breasts bare for me to see. Gathering them in my palms, I massage them, enjoying the feel of them and how her eyes light up with renewed desire.

"All I want to do is touch you and fuck you all day long, but I need to check on my crew."

Putting her hands over mine, she takes control, moving my hands over her breasts, encouraging me to squeeze them.

"I understand. Take care of them, then we'll get back to touching and fucking."

The corner of my mouth curls. "That's a deal, baby. When we're back in this room, I'm fucking you the way we both like it."

Dropping onto her side, her mouth curves into a lascivious grin. "That's a deal, babe."

As I sit up, the pins prickle across my chest, and she watches me with worry in her eyes.

"Are you sure you're okay? Maybe you should see a doctor."

Taking her hand, I caress it.

"I'm okay. It's a sore kind of pain, not an *I need a hospital* kind of pain. I promise. If it was worse, I'd drive a couple towns over and see a doctor."

"You swear you're not underplaying it?"

My hand slides between her legs, massaging her thigh, easing some of the tension I see in her wrinkled brow.

"I'm not underplaying it."

"All right. Stay put. I'll get your clothes."

Leaning my weight on one arm, I watch her go around my room, finding my things, and gathering clothes for me to wear. The way she cares for me is growing my love for her. It's the little things like this that mean a great deal to me. Swallowing the knot forming in my throat, I blink back the thoughts creeping into my mind again. The thought of losing her is so overwhelming, I have to look away to control the emotions flooding me. She brings me clothes and kisses me, worry filling her eyes as she studies me.

"Go on down. Get yourself breakfast. I'll be down in a minute."

Gathering her clothes, she goes into the bathroom. A couple of minutes later, I hear the outside door of the bathroom open and close, then her footsteps go down the hall. Dropping my head into my hands, I rub my face, an exasperated sigh escaping me. I need to get it together—for my crew, for her, and for my own sanity.

Thoughts of last night trickle into my mind, the image of Wesley's dead body in my arms. Tears threaten to spill, so I stand from the bed and get dressed. Going downstairs, I find most of the crew up and moving around. Ink and William have worked together to make breakfast. Dom is in the living room chair, checking the news. Jake is still asleep on the couch, but thankfully, his color is better, and he's in fresh clothes.

"Did he wake up last night?" I ask Liz as she sits on the edge of the couch, caressing Jake's face with the kind of affection she only has for him. Beneath her eyes are dark rings from a sleepless night, and in her soft gaze is worry.

"Yeah, he was in and out of sleep all night, had a fever, but it broke this morning. He's going to be okay. The bullet went straight through without any major damage, but he won't be riding for a while." She looks up at me with concern. "He needs to see a doctor though. He needs antibiotics."

"Take him to the same hospital as Trevor. Stick with the same story of a multi-motorcycle accident."

Liz stands and quickly gathers her things. "Can y'all help me get him into the car?"

Ink and William come into the living room and help lift Jake. His eyes flicker open, and he grumbles.

"We're taking you to the hospital," William tells him.

"I'm... fine," he mumbles.

Liz opens the door for them.

"Don't argue, baby. You need antibiotics."

Thankfully, he doesn't argue and lets William and Ink take him to the car without a fight. Following them out, I make sure they get him in the car all right.

"William, Ink, you mind going with them?"

"Not at all." William climbs into the passenger seat of Liz's Camaro, and Ink gets in the back with Jake. I watch them pull out as my anxiety begins to build.

Back inside, Synne hands me a fresh cup of coffee and a cinnamon roll. Dropping onto the couch, I try to eat it despite my lack of appetite. Synne serves Dom, Max, and Axel cinnamon rolls, then joins me on the couch.

"Anything in the news?" I ask Dom.

"Not a thing."

"Might mean the fire hasn't been reported yet," Max adds, coming up to the couch. He stuffs the remaining cinnamon roll from his hand into his mouth and shrugs.

"Synne," Dom calls, "you mind giving us a minute?"

"Yeah, of course." Leaning over, she kisses me, then picks up her coffee cup off the end table and goes outside to the porch. When the door closes behind her, Dom's gaze passes over each of us, then remains on me.

"It isn't over yet. There's still one Royal remaining."

"That's been on my mind this morning. If he's still in the hospital, we can't get to him. If he's out, we need to decide whether or not to take him out now or later."

"We need to take a drive by his house and see if he's there," Max adds. "If he is, we need to have a plan in place."

"It needs to be quick," I tell them. "In and out within minutes. No trace."

"I can take care of it," Dom assures me.

"No." I shake my head at him. "It should be me."

"Then we'll go together," he insists, sitting forward in the chair. "You're weak because of the impact to your chest. You'll need the backup."

I don't like admitting it, but he's right. The slightest pressure and I'm ready to buckle over.

"All right. We take one vehicle, park it half a mile away, walk to his house, in through the back door."

"I'm going," Max asserts. "Just in case we run into any trouble."

"Axel."

At the end of the couch, he looks over his coffee cup with tired eyes. Between the trauma of last night and the pain in his leg, he probably didn't get much sleep. We're all going to need serious time to rest and recover.

"Yeah?"

"You mind checking on Trevor and Jake and being our point of contact here?"

"Whatever you need," he says with dedication.

"Thank you, brother." Looking at the other two, I stand. "Let's gather what we need."

Max and Dom go into the garage to gather supplies. As they do, I walk onto the porch. Synne is sitting on the white, wooden, two-seat bench with her legs pulled up to her chest, looking in the direction of the shop dumpster. The sound of the door opening brings her attention to me, and her smile lifts, brightening her whole face.

"Hey, babe."

She lowers her legs, and I fill the empty space next to her.

"I have to leave. There's one more thing that needs taken care of."

"Can you tell me what it is?"

Staring back at her expectant gaze, my own gets lost in the flecks of gold-brown mixed in with the pretty olive green in her eyes.

"There's still one Royal left."

"Oh." Her hand slides over my leg and caresses as the light in her eyes dim. "Be careful, please."

Leaning toward her, I place my arm around her shoulders and bring her to me. "I will, baby." Kissing her head, I caress along her arm and side. "Will you be here when I get home?"

"Yes. I'm going over to the shop to reply to

voicemails and catch up on business. I need to stay busy, and I don't want you losing clients."

This woman, so caring and loyal—she's everything to me and the reminder of why I've taken the risks I have. Jenna and Angela didn't deserve to die, and Synne doesn't deserve to live a life of fear that she could be raped and murdered at any unexpected moment. Neither does my sister or any of the Kings' women. To me, the risk is worth it. I'd rather watch Synne and Liz live a life of freedom from a jail cell than bury another woman I love.

Locking my lips with hers, I feed every ounce of passion into the kiss. Her hand slides up my thigh and rubs over my dick, hardening it.

"Save those thoughts, baby. When I get home, we're satisfying them."

"I love you, Nix Wilson."

"I love you, Synne Jacobs, more than words can express."

Putting her hands on my face, she kisses me, then holds me there as she stares into my eyes, her loving gaze piercing my heart and spreading that warm tingly sensation all over my body.

"I've never loved anyone this deep. You're the man I want to be with and make a life with. I'm all in with you."

Taking her hands, I lower them and hold them in mine as I press my lips to hers, savoring the sweet taste of her kiss.

"I'm all in with you too. You're my woman, my gorgeous Synne." I kiss her cheek, then neck, pleased to see goosebumps rising on her skin. "I'll always protect you."

"I know in my heart you will."

The garage door opens behind me to Dom and Max, backing my truck out. Synne swallows, her head lowering. Putting my fingers under her chin, I raise it. It kills me to see tears pooling in her eyes.

"What is it?"

"Five years, I was with my ex, and he never came close to making me feel the love and security you do. I'm terrified of losing you."

Pulling her to my chest, I kiss her head. I want to tell her it'll all be okay, but I can't. I don't know what the consequences of our actions will be. All I can do is enjoy the time I do have with her, starting tonight.

"When I'm home, I promise to help you forget your fear."

I give her one final kiss and leave her on the porch as Axel limps out my door to join her. Climbing into my truck, Max hands me my bulletproof vest and a handgun as Dom backs us out of the driveway. I can't bring myself to look at Synne as we drive off. It'll only strengthen the gut-wrenching sensation in my stomach.

CHAPTER TWENTY-EIGHT

SYNNE

THANKFULLY, everyone who left messages this week was happy to hear from me. I got every one of them booked on the calendar for a repair or custom job. Wanting to stay busy, Axel joined me in the shop. For the last three hours, he's been working on repairs in the garage while I paid the utility bills, filed completed invoices, booked clients, and called two clients to pick up motorcycles that were ready for them. The second customer is just leaving when Axel limps into the office, wiping grease off his hands with a rag. He drops it on the counter, and by the red puffiness in his eyes, I can see he's tired and sore. I step off the stool and pat my hand on the seat.

"Here. You need it more than I do."

It hasn't slipped past me that Nix isn't the only one who's made sacrifices. Every Kings member has. Whatever their personal reasons, they chose to confront the Royals together and take whatever consequences there are, together.

"I'm done in the office. I'm going back to the house to cook all of you dinner. You ready to head back?"

Axel rakes a hand through his lengthy russet locks and blows out an exhausted breath.

"I am. Dinner sounds good. What are you making us?"

"Chicken, mashed potatoes, beans, and rolls. That sound good?"

"My mouth started salivating at chicken and mashed potatoes," he quips, his mouth curved on one side.

"Good. You okay to walk back to the house?"

"I'll make it, but I should probably put my leg up once we get back."

"Yes, you should," I order.

Looking through the door to the garage, I see he's already closed the garage doors. I lock the door in front of me, then gather my phone off the counter and the office keys from the drawer. Using the small one, I lock the cash drawer, then wave my hand for Axel to follow me out the front.

"Have you received any texts or calls from the guys?"

Axel grimaces with each step but doesn't stop.

"Yeah, Trevor and Audrey are coming back to the house. Trevor made it through surgery. He's going to have full function of his hand it sounds like. The stab wound didn't destroy his nerves or tendons."

"Oh, thank God."

Crossing the grassy yard, I see Nix's house in the distance and look for his truck, but it's not back yet. My heart sinks, worry dampening my palms and drying my mouth. I try not to think the worst and instead keep talking.

"What about Jake?"

"He's doing better. Liz got his antibiotics picked up, and they're headed back."

"Can you text the group and let them know I'm cooking for everyone?"

"Yeah. They'll like that. We could use a good meal together as a family."

Axel stops and blows out a breath. I can see the pain etched in his wrinkled brow and scrunched nose.

"Here. Use me for support."

I come close, and Axel waves me off.

"You're Nix's ol' lady. It's not right for me to be touching you."

"It's my shoulder, Axel. He's not going to get angry that you put your weight on me to help you walk."

Axel stands straight and shakes his head.

"Nah. It just doesn't feel right. I'll manage."

Rolling my eyes, I grab his arm and put it over my shoulder.

"Get over it. I'm helping you."

Axel recoils, but I keep hold of his arm and move us forward. With the ease of my help, he gives in and puts his weight on me.

"Thanks," he grumbles.

"You're welcome."

With the warm sun beating down on us, we amble across the yard toward Nix's house. Liz's Camaro pulls into the driveway, and my spirit lifts. Getting out of the car, William runs over to us, putting Axel's other arm around him. Axel's weight lightens, and we're able to walk much quicker. Ink and Liz help Jake into the house. From where we are, I can see Jake looks a lot better, his usual color back, and he's lucid. Coming into the house, Axel removes his arm from around me and uses William's help to the couch. Axel and Jake bump fists as they prop their legs up on the coffee table.

"Good to see you, brother," Axel says to him.

Liz smirks at them and puts a pillow under each of their legs. "I'll get you both something to drink. Axel, you need some pain meds?"

"Yeah, my leg is killing me."

She moves over to him and lifts his pant leg. He tries to wave her off, and she slaps his hand. With his pant leg pulled up, the pink, puffy swelling is visible. She looks at him with a frown and lowers his pant leg.

"You need to stay off it for the night and ice it for the next twenty minutes."

"All right, boss."

In the kitchen, I grab the bag of potatoes sitting on the corner of the counter and take them out to peel them. To my surprise, William joins me. Gathering a knife from the drawer, he collects a potato from the pile and starts peeling. When we meet eyes, the side of his mouth twists upward.

"I need to keep busy."

"I get it. I think we're all feeling that way."

"I kind of miss Maci, but I'm also glad she's not around. She wouldn't be taking things as well as you are."

"Don't let my calm exterior fool you. I'm freaking out on the inside. I don't want anything to happen to any of you."

William blows out a breath and swallows, his Adam's apple bobbing as his nostrils flare. "I don't either."

Dicing the potatoes, I drop them into a pot of boiling water. I've begun seasoning the chicken when the front door opens. My gaze whips to the sound, hoping for Nix to walk through. It's Nix's Aunt May, carrying Liam in her arms with Erika following behind. The three of them come into the living room, and Erika sets down Liam's playset. Liz rushes to Aunt May, who's outstretching her arms for Liz to take Liam.

"He was really good for Aunt May."

Liz wraps her arms around him, hugging and kissing him as she whispers private words in his ear. Jake puts an arm on the couch and looks over it at Liz and Liam.

"Bring him over here, babe. I want to hold him."

Liz brings him over and places him in Jake's arms. Jake tosses Liam in the air, and he immediately giggles, a huge smile puffing out his tiny cheeks. The spirit of the room feels lighter with Liam there. Everyone is watching him, entertained by his slobbery smile and excited laughter.

Erika leaves the living room, coming toward me and William in the kitchen.

"Get a beer and relax. I'll take it from here," she tells him.

Without argument, he pulls a beer out of the fridge and joins the rest of the guys. Dinner is nearly ready, and I'm putting the rolls in to bake when the door to the garage opens and Nix, Dom, and Max enter, completely unscathed. Quickly closing the oven door, I set the timer and rush to Nix. Opening his arms, he pulls me in and kisses me.

"I'm so glad you're home."

"Me too, baby." With a kiss, he releases his hold around me. "What are you cookin'? It smells good."

"Chicken, mashed potatoes, beans, and rolls."

"Thank you." Lifting my chin, he kisses me again. "We need a family dinner."

With a caress to my arm, he kisses me for the third time, and I can tell he's eager for us to have time alone together or at least be able to sit and be affectionate.

"Have a beer and relax. It'll be ready soon."

Dom is behind us, his mouth glued to Erika's as Max is reaching into the fridge for three beers. The guys take them from his hands and go into the living room to join the others.

"Where y'all been?" Jake asks.

Nix leans against the wall, his gaze roaming the room, lingering over the women.

"We had to finish the job we started."

Jake dips his chin in understanding. "Did ya get it finished?"

Dom taps Jake on the shoulder from behind the couch.

"Yeah, brother, we did. It's done."

"Any problems?" Axel asks, a touch of concern in his voice.

"None," Max replies. "It was a clean job."

William drops his head into his hands, running his fingers through his hair. "That's a relief to hear."

"That it is, brother," Axel agrees.

As I enter the living room, Nix extends his arm for me to be curled under it. With his arm around my shoulder, he nods toward the kitchen.

"Dinner ready?"

"Yeah. You mind getting the folding table out of the garage?"

"No problem."

Nix drops his arm and moves toward the garage as William and Ink stand from the chair and floor.

"We got it, Pres," William tells him.

With an appreciative nod, Nix pulls me back into his arm, bringing me close, so he can speak just to me.

"I'm glad you're here. Later tonight, all I want is to be with you."

My eyes meet his and see the need and desire

brimming in his irises. My fingers graze the scruff on his jaw, bringing his lips to mine.

"I want the same."

The warmth of his kiss spreads throughout my body. For those moments—our lips pressed together, our tongues tasting and teasing—there's nothing to fear, no emotion stronger than the love we possess.

As he pulls back, the corner of his mouth rises, and he stares at me with loving adoration as he pulls my hair through his hands and tugs, keeping my gaze matched with his.

"I love you."

"I love you too."

William and Ink return from the garage with the folding table. As they set it up against the dining table, the front door opens to Trevor and Audrey. The guys cheer, welcoming him with pats on the back.

"Good to see you back home," Nix says to him, extending an arm to cup hands with Trevor's good hand.

Trevor raises his bandaged hand and grins. "I can still ride, brothers. It's a good day."

"Yes, it is," Nix agrees.

Moving into the dining room, Liz, Erika, and I serve the dishes while Audrey sets out the plates. Around the two tables, we gather as a family. Before we eat, everyone looks to Nix. Retrieving a silver necklace with a Kings MC charm out of a drawer, he holds it up, moisture filling his eyes. What he's about to say is clearly hard for him.

"We lost a good man yesterday, a loyal brother who stood with us through the best and worst times. He won't be forgotten. His sacrifice will not be wasted. His memory, his name, his love for the brotherhood will go on." Nix reaches over to Liz holding Liam in her arms and places the necklace around his neck. "We will honor him by teaching the next generation what it means to be a King and what it means to be a great man like Wesley Holmes."

Holding back their tears, the men give Nix approving nods. Touching my leg, Nix gives it a gentle squeeze, an act to calm himself as he looks out at his emotional brothers. Liz and Aunt May both wipe at their damp cheeks. Putting an arm around Liz, Jake kisses her, then Liam.

"Brothers." Nix glances at me and swipes a finger under my chin. "Ladies. We're a family. And there are no lengths I won't go to, to protect this family. Not now, not ever."

William raises his beer in the air, and the rest of the guys follow.

"To Nix. To Wesley. To the future of the Kings."

Whatever stress these men have been carrying, they let it go for the next hour, the room filling with chatter, laughter, and praise for my cooking. As the meal is finished, Nix grips the bottom of my chair and slides me closer.

"Thank you for this." He kisses my cheek and leaves an arm around my shoulder as he talks with the guys.

It's well into the night before the last of the Kings head home. On tired feet, I head back to the kitchen to clean up. Taking my hand, Nix stops me.

"Leave it. The only thing that matters right now is us."

Leading me upstairs, he takes me into his room. The moment the door closes behind us, our lips are sealed to the other's. Only when our shirts come off, do we separate. Without clothing in the way, my thighs make contact with his bed, then they're lifted in the air. My back is laid on the unmade bed we left this morning, his warmth soothing my body as he lies above me. Slipping a hand between my legs, he strengthens the desire longing for satisfaction. Lowering my hand, I stroke his erection as he groans with relief into my mouth.

"Need you," he murmurs, "so much right now."

"Have me."

Returning his lips to mine, he slides into me, thrusting so decadently slow, I plunge into thoughtless oblivion. With each passionate thrust, he kisses along my body, his fingers entangled with mine, curling tighter as he pushes deeper.

"I love you." In a whisper pressed to my ear, he unravels me, exposes the most protected part of my heart, and claims it as his.

CHAPTER TWENTY-NINE

NIX

TWO WEEKS LATER...

PUTTING an initial on the last invoice in my stack, I gather the pile and file them in my desk for the associated month. Jeff enters my office, his peppered hair freshly washed and parted to the side, his mustache thick and combed. He looks well-rested and ready for his shift this evening. Thankfully, the clubhouse bar has made a quick rebound, especially with the Royals' bar getting shut down. With new tables, chairs, and liquor restocked, we've been happy to accommodate the new customers. This weekend will be our first clubhouse party in two weeks. My crew is healing, and our lives are moving forward, despite the cloud of uncertainty that looms over us.

"You got a visitor, boss."

Jeff's comment takes me by surprise.

"Who is it?"

"Agent Adams from the TBI."

My throat constricts, the lunch I ate not long ago becoming rapid heartburn.

"You want me to send him in?"

"Yeah."

Jeff disappears out my door, and I rake a hand down my face as my gut twists in agony. Moments later, Agent Adams enters, his law enforcement badge shining on the chest of his polo shirt. Motioning my hand toward the chair opposite me, I offer it to him.

"Good to see you, Wilson."

Putting on my game face, I smile back.

"Same, Agent Adams. What brings you in?"

Adams lean back in the chair, resting his elbows on the arms and his hands on the loaded belt around his waist.

"I have some information I thought I'd share with you." With a brow raised, he shrugs his shoulder. "Who knows, maybe you already know."

"Won't know until I hear it."

"That's true. Well, first things first. I'm retiring."

"Congratulations," I praise, wondering where this is leading.

"Thanks. I'm looking forward to it. My wife is even happier. She wants to do some traveling now that I'll have the free time."

"I recommend Yellowstone. We've done some riding in those parts. It's magnificent scenery."

Adams's bottom lip juts out and in, a reflex of his thought. "I'll look into it. Thanks for the recommendation. I'm not here for travel suggestions though." He taps the arm of the chair with his palm.

"I made a promise to myself that once I closed the case on the Wild Royals, I'd retire, and that's what I'm going to do. I've been working on this case, trying to bring them down for six years." He leans forward as the passion in his voice grows. "It's exhausted local resources, taken countless tax dollars, and been a strain on my health and marriage. That all changed about two weeks ago when I got a report an old tobacco factory had burned down, and there were human remains found inside."

Sweat dampens my palms and the back of my neck, but I remain stoic.

"That right?"

"Those remains were of the Wild Royals. Their motorcycles were parked outside, and among the ashes, jewelry and belt buckles were found with the Royals emblem."

"So, what happened?"

A smile curls the corner of his mouth, revealing his coffee-stained teeth.

"I thought you might ask. My report concludes the Wild Royals were assassinated by the drug cartel. Further evidence provides a clear story. Rex Alverez was also murdered in his home. The same execution-style as the tobacco factory. It appears the Wild Royals' drug-running and murdering ways caught up to them. Whatever happened to their distribution system at the repair shop was the beginning of their end. Losing nearly a million dollars of the cartel's drugs wasn't going to go unpunished."

Adams pushes off the chair and stands.

"You and I have something in common, Wilson."

"What's that?"

"The Wild Royals are no longer either of our problem." Adams dips his chin at me. "I'll be sure to talk to my wife about visiting Yellowstone."

My shoulders lower, and my breath gradually escapes. Leaning back in my chair, I watch Adams walk toward my door. With his hand on the knob, he stops and turns to me, a smile curves his mouth in a mischievous way, raising my brow.

"During my investigation, I saw two of your Kings members checked into a hospital about two weeks ago. One had an injury to his hand and another to his leg. You oughta tell them to be more careful on those motorcycles." The man's brow rises slightly as his smirk widens. "Take care, Wilson."

Blowing out a breath, a flood of emotions washes over me. With my adrenaline crashing, I remain frozen as the shock and relief sink in.

It's over. It's finally over.

Pulling my cell phone from my pocket, I leave the

chair and walk out to the clubhouse to ensure Agent Adams is gone. With no one but Jeff in the room, I dial Max.

"Get everyone in here. I have news."

IF THERE WAS EVER a night to celebrate, it's tonight. Jeff sets out eight shot glasses and adds one for himself. While the other bartender, Andrew, serves the customers, the Kings are lined up along the bar, lifting our shot glasses in the air.

"Together we live, together we ride, together we die," I toast.

All eight glasses are tilted and drained, the smack of glass bottoms making music across the wood surface. Jeff moves the whiskey bottle across the top of the glasses and refills, his smile reaching toward his ears.

"To the brotherhood of the Kings!" Max shouts.

We all drain the glasses. Hugs and pats on the back make their rounds. The Kings' women, at a nearby table, leave it to join us. Dom picks up Erika and spins her around, lowering her to kiss her. Jake puts his arms around Liz and kisses her. Trevor and Audrey hug tight, tears filling her eyes as she lays her head on his shoulder. Synne steps into my open arms, and I squeeze her ass, lifting her legs around my waist.

"The best way I know to celebrate is to be inside my gorgeous woman."

Beneath her thick lashes is a smile so bright, it lights up my heart. Carrying her out of the clubhouse, I lead her toward the private rooms. Behind us, whistles fade in the distance. Upstairs, I pick the largest room and lay her under me on the bed.

Unfastening her jeans, I peel them off her hips, taking her black underwear with them. Her red shirt, formfitting and lowcut, shows off her luscious tits. Lowering my face, I bury my mouth in them, licking and nipping at her firm skin. With her hand around my neck, she holds me there, encouraging my movements while lowering her top, letting her breasts spill out. Palming both, I fill my mouth with her nipple, letting it slip between my teeth with a pop. Her breath heightens, her need for me rising.

Putting her hand on my lengthening cock, I work her fist over it, the feel of her palm increasing my desire to have her pussy wrapped around it. Toying with her clit, I thumb over it, watching her head fall back with pleasure. Putting two fingers inside her, I stroke her G-spot, her eager moans crying for more. My movements are rapid, touching and teasing her everywhere that elicits moans from her sweet mouth.

With her desire in a frenzy, she pulls back from me, setting herself on her knees and swallows my cock, sucking it like it's her favorite fucking lollipop, making me one grateful son of a bitch.

With her warm, wet mouth thickening my erection and steering me toward a too-soon orgasm, I press against her shoulders, lowering her to her back. Gripping her knees, I flip her over, and she looks over her shoulder at me with a wicked grin that begs for me to be inside her.

Slapping her ass, I take pleasure in the mark it leaves—my mark, my ass, my woman. Pulling her hips to me, I guide my cockhead to her pussy lips and slide in, pull out, and thrust in harder, deeper, fucking her into blissful cries of pleasure.

With one hand wrapping around her hair, I pull her head back and quicken my pace. Her fists clench the bedspread, her moans so loud it matches the tempo of the music from downstairs. She comes hard, soaking my cock, purring with a satisfied moan as she loosens her grip on the blanket. Another thrust and I let my head fall back, the euphoric sensation taking over as I cum inside her.

Moments later, I pull out. Keeping her beneath me, I massage along her back. Lying over her, I intertwine my fingers with hers, kissing and sucking the tender crook of her neck and shoulder.

"I want to claim you in every way that a man can claim a woman. Marry me, Synne. Be my wife."

She turns beneath me, and I lie atop her, my fingers caressing her cheek and hair as she stares up at me with loving eyes.

"Yes. There's no doubt in my mind you're the man I want to spend my life with. I love you."

"I love you, baby. You stepped into my life and

brought with you the kind of happiness I never thought I'd experience again. You're everything I needed and more than I probably deserve."

"You do deserve me, just as much as I deserve you. We're what each other needed."

"You're right." Grazing my thumb along her jaw and lips, I take pleasure in the way she closes her eyes and releases a sensual breath. "And I'm going to spend my life showing you how grateful I am to have you."

Her eyes open and stare up at me with sincere passion in her gaze.

"You already show it in the way you love me. You're an incredible man, and I love with you with all of my heart."

CHAPTER THIRTY

NIX

THREE MONTHS LATER...

PULLING into our clubhouse parking lot, I cut the engine and glance over at my brothers. Jake sits atop his bike in pure bliss, finally able to get back on his Harley and take a long ride. All our wounds are healed, emotionally and physically. There's a new sense of freedom I carry with me now, no longer looking over my shoulder, expecting pain and misery to greet me. The last three months of my life have been the best I've experienced. My fiancée and I purchased a new house and are moving into it this weekend. It'll be an adjustment living more than walking distance from my shop and clubhouse, but a mile drive for us is worth beginning this new chapter in our lives. I'm letting go, letting the past remain where it belongs. Synne and I deserve a place that is ours, where we can build a life for the two of us and hopefully, our children. She's the fuel that drives me forward, the force that keeps me balanced. Without her, I would be lost.

"What do you think they have planned?"

Jake's voice snaps me out of my thoughts; I shrug my shoulders and take the steps up to the entrance.

"With our women, anything is possible."

My crew follows me into the clubhouse bar, our boots coming to a stop as we read the green signs taped to the floor that direct us to our private courtroom. Following the cut-out arrows, we open the door and step in. Audrey, Liz, Erika, and Synne are sitting around one end of the table with a cake in the center. To the left of the cake and paper plates are eight shot glasses sitting in a row with an unopened whiskey bottle at the end. There're balloons floating around the room, every single one of them is wearing a white T-shirt that reads, *blue or pink?*

My gaze looks at each of them, trying to figure out who's hiding the secret, but they're playing this game well. They all have mischievous smirks.

"Who's pregnant?" Max blurts.

The women laugh.

"Trevor," Audrey calls. "Would you like to do the honors?"

Trevor looks at Audrey, his eyes expanding to

bulbous globes. He glances at us, then back to Audrey with a smile beaming below red, flushed cheeks.

"Are you telling me you're pregnant, babe?"

Audrey stands from the wooden chair, tears filling her eyes as she smiles like a shining ray of sun.

"I am."

Trevor clears the space around the room in seconds, scoops her up, and kisses her, their love filling the room. "I'm going to be a father." His voice is muffled against her neck, but you can still hear the enthusiasm. "I love you."

Releasing her, he looks at the table and finds the cake knife. Gathering it in his hand, he waits for Audrey to place her hand over his. Together, they cut open the cake. Inside, the filling is a solid pink. The guys hoot and holler, cheering for them both.

"If she looks anything like her mama, you're screwed," Ink says to Trevor.

Trevor raises his scarred hand and flicks him off. The guys laugh, then move in to pour the shot glasses. My gaze finds Synne. She leaves her chair, meeting me halfway around the table. Tugging her ass tight against me, I kiss her dark pink lips.

"Mmm, is that cinnamon I taste?"

She giggles. "We had shots of fireball before you guys arrived, except Audrey, of course."

"This was some good planning, babe. Y'all definitely surprised us."

"Thank you. Speaking of planning, I found a place I think would be perfect for our wedding."

"Yeah, where at?"

Her arms rest around my neck as I caress her back, loving the way her eyes light up when she talks about our wedding. I'd marry her in our backyard if it was my choice, but I know weddings are a woman's opportunity to plan the perfect party, so whatever she wants, she can have it. I just need to know when to show up and a private room for after the wedding, so I can fuck my wife into wedded bliss.

"There's a lodge in the Smokies, so there're great roads for riding and a shit ton of breweries for you guys to check out. I looked online. The suite has a hot tub attached, and the views are beautiful."

"It sounds perfect. After we're unpacked in the new house, why don't we take a ride over there and check it out?"

A grin splits those full pink lips and swells her cheeks.

"I'd love that."

"Me too, baby." As I kiss her, I gather her loose hair in my hands and tug. Her lips slip from mine, and her chin rises, her gaze meeting mine as I stare down at her gorgeous face.

"After we leave here, you want to go home and break in our new bed? It's getting delivered this afternoon."

"What do you think?"

331

I lower to her ear, licking the shell before sucking it into my mouth, listening for her breathy moan.

"I think I'm going to fuck you so hard, you won't be able to sit at work tomorrow."

"Promise?"

"You know I only make promises I can keep." Biting her neck, I follow it with a light breath blown over her skin to tease her. "I promise."

I HOPE you enjoyed reading Nix and Synne's story as much as I did writing it. Their story was a challenging and emotional journey. One that leaves you cheering when they finally receive the happy ending they deserve. These two characters were explosive, their passion undeniable, and it was when they completely gave into it, they found their strength in each other. Nix stole my heart from the very beginning, but by the end, he became my favorite male character I've written so far. Just as Synne said, Nix is a man with a heart that'll love with everything he has and fight until he has nothing left to give. He's a book boyfriend who will stay with you long after the pages are read.

IF YOU'RE WONDERING if there will be more Kings MC Romances, the answer is... I hope so! The other Kings members have been chatting in my head, encouraging a story of their own. I'm hoping they don't stop chatting and give me the inspiration to write a book for each of them. Until then, I have other sexy and suspenseful stories to keep your Kindle steaming and your heart racing. ...

Fall in love with a swoonworthy cowboy in Fire on the Farm, a charming and perfectly sculpted kickboxing instructor in Unbreak This Heart, or prepare to have your heart stolen by a dominant, kinky, and undeniably sexy boss in My Hot Boss.

If you like a steamy and page-turning royal romance with a spice of ménage, then begin the Crowned and Claimed Series with Claimed Royalty for free!

YOU'RE welcome to join my Facebook readers' group, Betty's Book Beauties and Bad Boys, to connect with me personally, enjoy the fun, exclusive giveaways, and sneak peeks of future books! I'm in there once a week hanging out with my readers. :)

Keep turning the pages if you want to check out my other sexy and suspenseful stories, where to stay connected with me, and what signings I'll be at next!

If you enjoyed King of Kings, will you consider leaving a review? It's reviews from fans like you that help spread the word about my books, giving me the opportunity to keep writing them.

To book lovers everywhere;
you are my tribe
you make my dream possible
and for that
I thank you.

ALSO BY BETTY SHREFFLER

Kings MC Series

CASTLE OF KINGS

CLIPPED WINGS

Standalone Contemporary Romances

FIRE ON THE FARM

MY HOT BOSS

UNBREAK THIS HEART

Crowned and Claimed Series

CLAIMED ROYALTY

TWICE CLAIMED

FOREVER CLAIMED

Novellas

COUNTDOWN TO CHRISTMAS

https://bettyshreffler.com/

ABOUT THE AUTHOR

Betty Shreffler is a USA Today and International bestselling author of romance. She writes sexy and suspenseful stories with hot alphas and kickass heroines with twists you don't expect. She also writes beautiful and sexy romances with tough women and their journeys at finding love. Betty is a mix of country, nerdy, sassy, sweet and a whole lot of sense of humor. If she's not writing or doing book events, you can find her snuggling with her fur babies watching a movie, enjoying wildlife behind the lens of a camera, hiking in the woods, or sipping wine behind a deliciously steamy book.

Sign up for Betty's newsletter

Join Betty's Facebook readers' group:
Betty's Book Beauties and Bad Boys

Visit Betty's website for signed paperbacks,
or see where she'll be for her next signing:
https://bettyshreffler.com/

Made in the USA
Columbia, SC
19 April 2023